AMONG THE RED STARS

AMONG THE RED STARS

GWEN C. KATZ

HARPER TEEN

An Imprint of HarperCollinsPublishers

HarperTeen is an imprint of HarperCollins Publishers.

Among the Red Stars
Copyright © 2017 by Gwen C. Katz
All rights reserved. Printed in the United States of America.
No part of this book may be used or reproduced in any manner whatsoever without written permission except in the case of brief quotations embodied in critical articles and reviews. For information address HarperCollins Children's Books, a division of HarperCollins Publishers, 195 Broadway, New York, NY 10007.
www.epicreads.com

ISBN 978-0-06-264274-5

Typography by Torborg Davern
17 18 19 20 21   PC/LSCH   10 9 8 7 6 5 4 3 2 1

First Edition

For JR, who might have mentioned the war

★ONE★

THE VOICE ON THE RADIO SPAT OUT A FEW INTELLIGIBLE words before melting back into static. "... large crowd here in the City of Youth, despite the gloomy weather. They are all hoping to catch the first glimpse of ..."

"You're messing it up," I told Pasha, who knelt by his radio, fiddling with its wire innards. "We'll miss it!"

"It'll be in the papers tomorrow."

I gave Pasha a derisive snort. "I want to be able to say 'I was listening when the *Rodina* landed.' What good is it if I see it in the paper like everyone else?"

"When do I find out what we're listening to?" asked my cousin Iskra, leaning over from the chair next to me. Everyone thought slight, dark-eyed Pasha and I were related, even though we weren't. No one thought dainty, blond Iskra and I were related, even though we were.

I handed Iskra the newspaper clipping. It featured a photo of three smiling women in leather aviator caps and goggles, standing in front of a white bomber with long, graceful wings.

"Yesterday," I said in my most dramatic radio-announcer voice, "my namesake, the remarkable pilot Valentina Grizodubova—"

"You were named after our grandmother," Iskra interrupted.

"Do you mind? The remarkable pilot Valentina Grizodubova, the fearless copilot Polina Osipenko, and the beautiful and brilliant navigator Marina Raskova departed from Moscow in the sensational new experimental bomber *Rodina*."

"That's a good name: 'Motherland.' Who did they bomb?"

"No one, and you know it. They're setting a distance record. Six thousand kilometers nonstop, over mountains and swamps and frozen wastelands and every kind of danger."

"I heard Marina Raskova give a speech once," said Pasha. "About how more girls should learn to fly. Her voice sounded like the color indigo."

I said, "We'll be able to hear her for ourselves if you ever get that radio working."

"I've just about got it. . . . There."

A fuzzy but intelligible male voice came through the radio's homemade speaker.

". . . still a heavy layer of cloud cover here. We won't be able to see the *Rodina* until she comes in for her final descent. The

2

crew won't be able to see any landmarks, either. Raskova will have to navigate with a compass and sextant, like the explorers of old. Night must have been awfully lonely for her, by herself in the nose, knowing that the slightest error could leave them dozens of kilometers off course."

"See? You didn't miss it," whispered Pasha.

"Shh!" I held a finger in front of my mouth.

"For those just tuning in, we lost radio contact with the *Rodina* about eighteen hours ago. We believe their radio stopped functioning due to the cold. It is a mark of the crew's exceptional tenacity that they persevered in these conditions: thirty-five degrees below zero, cold enough to cause frostbite in fifteen minutes. Our ladies are, of course, bundled up in fur-lined flight suits, but I'm sure it's still feeling nippy up there.

"Their estimated time of arrival was one hour ago. However, the weather may have caused them to alter course and delayed their landing. We expect to see these history-making heroines at any moment."

I swallowed hard as I strained my ears for any hint about the *Rodina*'s fate. I felt as cold and isolated as Marina Raskova in the nose of her plane. I whispered, "They're in trouble."

"You're being impatient. They're only late," said Iskra.

"They can't be late!"

"Anyone can be late, even if they're beautiful and brilliant and—"

"It isn't them. It's the *Rodina*. They already retrofitted it to hold enough fuel to make it that far. If they're late, then . . ."

Iskra gave my shoulders a squeeze. "Baby cousin, you were just telling me what incredible pilots they are. Even if they've gone off course, I'm sure they can land safely."

I shook my head hopelessly. "Grizodubova and Osipenka, maybe. But Raskova, in the nose? If they crash, she'll be killed!"

The voice on the radio droned on with meaningless bluster. I waited all night, gnawing my fingers, for an update that never came.

In the morning, the state-owned newspaper *Pravda* reported nothing.

The *Rodina* was lost.

★ TWO ★

Three Years Later

LEANING AGAINST MY AIRPLANE'S WING IN THE MIDDLE of our dusty airfield, I flipped lovingly through the thin, black-covered paperback. The pages were falling out and the cheap print was almost too smudged to read. A broad-winged airplane in white embossing decorated the cover. *Notes of a Navigator*, Marina Raskova's autobiography. Proof of what an airwoman could do. Proof of what *I* could do. The flight of the *Rodina* had set the course of my life for the past three years.

The book's broken binding automatically fell open to the illustration of Raskova standing in the middle of the endless snow-bound forests of the Siberian taiga. One hand held a walking stick, the other shielded her eyes as she watched the broad-winged silhouette of her plane vanish over the treetops.

When a search-and-rescue plane spotted the *Rodina* in a frozen swamp, my joy was short-lived. The rescue team found the pilot and copilot unharmed but grave. Grizodubova had feared for Raskova's safety in the plane's vulnerable glass nose, knowing that they had to belly-land, so she ordered her to bail out. The *Rodina* ended up kilometers away. Grizodubova and Osipenko fired their revolvers but feared that Raskova had followed the echoes instead of the shots and walked the wrong way. Worse, Osipenko had found the navigator's emergency kit still in her cockpit. Wherever Raskova was, she had no food, no clean water, nothing but the contents of her pockets.

One long day and night passed. Planes circled low over the forest and search parties struck out in every direction, looking for any sign of the missing airwoman. But, in the end, she came to them. She stumbled into the clearing exhausted, muddy, half starved, and missing a shoe. She had survived alone in the taiga for ten days.

When the radio announced that all three airwomen were safe and sound, I screamed out loud. I grabbed Pasha and swung him in a giddy dance between the table and the overloaded bookshelf. The *Rodina* had flown 5,947 kilometers, shattering the previous record by more than 1,500 kilometers.

My aeroclub's beat-up bushplane was definitely no *Rodina*. Not a sleek, graceful aluminum bird, but a stubby, angular machine of steel, wood, and chipped paint. But what mattered was that, for the next two hours, it was mine. And I was no Marina Raskova, just a skinny, trousered eighteen-year-old with braids tumbling down her back. But I was a real airwoman, no matter how little I looked the part. Someday I'd have a chance to prove it.

I stuffed the book into my pocket and waved when I spotted Pasha crossing the rusted steel bridge. He trotted over, a scrap of something cupped in his hands.

"Hi, Pasha," I said, bouncing up onto the balls of my feet. "What have you got there?"

"Some foil I fished out of the canal. I'm going to make a semiconductor. It'll improve the sound quality."

Many Young Pioneers built radio sets, but few succeeded like Pasha. What had started out as a pencil stub, an old razor blade, and some wire had grown increasingly elaborate. A scavenged capacitor here, a speaker made from telephone parts there. To me, his ability bordered on wizardry. "Neat! We can put on some music after the flight. You ready?"

He brightened up.

I touched the propeller and spat on the ground for luck, then gave it a spin. The engine rattled to life. As I strapped myself into the pilot's seat, Pasha started to clamber into the back. I laughed and grabbed his arm. "What, are you a Party boss and I'm your chauffeur? Sit up front."

Pebbles pinged off the bottom of the fuselage as I taxied the little plane down the cracked earthen runway. Our aerodrome was a stretch of dirt distinguished only by a sun-bleached orange windsock fluttering from a pole. The town of Stakhanovo spread out on the other side of the canal, with its blocky soot-gray concrete buildings and its endless battery of coking ovens, each six meters tall but so narrow that a person could barely have squeezed in sideways. The ovens were kept hot twenty-four hours a day baking the impurities out of coal to make hard, spongy coke, the only fuel that burned clean enough and hot enough to turn molten pig iron into steel. Our fledgling nation had an insatiable appetite for steel. When I was younger, I had entertained an irrational fear that I would be trapped in one of those ovens.

As the aircraft lifted off, my breath stuck in my throat. This moment always caught me by surprise. No matter how many times I took off, one part of my mind was still overwhelmed by the sheer impossibility of flight. Iskra thought I was silly. She would write out the equations proving how flight worked. But Pasha gazed out the window with quiet awe. He understood.

I made a smooth circle around the little valley before rising above the foothills and into the open sky.

In the air, the plane felt more animal than machine. Through the trapezoidal window, I spotted a herd of shaggy dun-colored ponies grazing on the steppe below. The airplane reminded me of them: nearly tame, but not entirely. If I ever got too confident, the plane would remind me that it had its own ideas.

We were as high as the mountaintops now, the weathered ridge of the Urals running north and south like the bleached spine of a large and ancient monster before vanishing into clouds. The town of Stakhanovo crouched in one of the mountain crevices, its location betrayed by a plume of greasy smoke and the dark thread of the canal.

"*Kalinka, kalinka, kalinka of mine, in the garden is a berry, malinka of mine,*" sang Pasha absently. He often sang when he was happy. His smooth baritone was so incongruous with his timorous speaking voice.

Pasha was my favorite person to fly with. I took him up whenever I could. He didn't nitpick my flying like my flight instructor or make sarcastic comments like Iskra, who'd grown extra snide since she got her own pilot's license. All my life he'd been there, a quiet boy with an awkwardly proportioned face that looked like it had been assembled out of the wrong pieces. We'd each spent as much time in the other's next-door apartment as we had at home.

I peeled away to the east, swooping in and out among towering white clouds that dwarfed the monoplane and relishing the freedom.

"Sometimes I think this is the only way I'll ever get out of Stakhanovo," I said. "Straight up."

"What about Aeroflot? I thought you applied for a job with them."

I threw back my head and groaned, but I kept one eye on the instruments, because stalling the plane while flying with Pasha would be really embarrassing. "They sent me a letter telling me that they already have one female airline pilot and they don't need another. Can you believe it?"

"I'm sorry. I know how much that meant to you."

"I've been flying for three years! How much more qualified can I get?"

"It's just because they don't know you. If they saw you fly, they'd change their minds. It's too bad. I was already looking forward to seeing you in the cockpit of one of those big planes. I thought maybe you could take me somewhere." He looked at me with his guileless blue eyes.

I smiled back but quickly looked away, not sure why I felt suddenly awkward. Pasha was my best friend, that was all. He was allowed to say something nice to me.

Glancing out the window as I fumbled for a reply, I glimpsed a speck of someone in the aerodrome. I dived for a closer look. It was a young girl, waving frantically up at us.

"Is that your sister?" I asked Pasha. "What's she doing out here?"

Pasha's face turned serious. "Something must be wrong. Bring us down."

I brought the plane to a halt on the makeshift runway. Pasha's sister ran up to the door as we got out, her pigtails disheveled, one stocking sagging down to her ankle.

"You'd better come quick," she said. "It's happened."

"This war has been forced upon us, not by the German people, not by the German workers, peasants, or intellectuals whose sufferings we well understand, but by the clique of bloodthirsty fascist rulers of Germany who have enslaved the French, Czechs, Poles, and other nations.

"The Government of the Soviet Union expresses its unshakable conviction that our valiant army and navy and the daring hawks of the Soviet Air Force will deal a crushing blow to the aggressor and bring honor to the Motherland and the Soviet people."

Pasha's parents occupied the two comfortable chairs. His father was smoking and holding that morning's *Pravda* without reading it, and his mother was twisting the dress she had been mending, her knuckles pale. My parents were there too, my mother's brow knitted pensively, my father wearing his usual look of resignation. Iskra was sitting on Pasha's sagging bed. Pasha and I huddled beside her. Pasha's sister sat down at our feet and picked up an unidentifiable eyeless stuffed animal.

If I could have ignored the apprehension on everyone's face, there was a strange feeling of normalcy to the scene. We might have been listening to a concert instead of the announcement that our world had been shattered.

"The Germans broke the nonaggression pact," said Iskra.

"Of course they did," said my father. "Two-timing fascists. It's their nature."

"This is not the first time that our nation has had to deal with an attack from an arrogant foe," crackled the voice on the radio. "At the time of Napoleon's invasion of Russia, our people's reply was war for the Motherland, and Napoleon suffered defeat and met his doom. It will be the same with Hitler, who in his arrogance has proclaimed a new crusade against our country. The Red Army and our entire nation will once again wage victorious war for the Motherland, for our country, for honor, for liberty."

"Will we be okay?" asked Pasha's sister, clutching her shapeless toy.

"Shh. You heard the man on the radio," said her mother, reaching down to stroke her hair. "We'll win. It'll be a great victory. And in the meantime, we'll be safe here. They're twenty-five hundred kilometers away. When Napoleon invaded, half his army froze to death before they got to Moscow."

"They didn't have tanks and airplanes," said my father. "And Hitler is not Napoleon. He doesn't want to rule us. He wants to exterminate us. I've heard—"

"Stop. You'll frighten the children."

"We can't hide this from them," he said, then quieted down, because none of us wanted to miss a word from the radio.

"The whole country must now be joined and united as never before. Each one of us must demand from himself or herself and from each other the discipline, the organization, and the selflessness worthy of a real Soviet patriot in order to supply the Red Army, Navy, and Air Force with the means necessary to assure victory over the enemy."

"The air force," I whispered. "They'll need pilots. Lots of pilots!" I grinned. "The daring hawks of the VVS . . ."

"I'm afraid this won't be your big chance to join the VVS," said my father.

I looked at him uncomprehendingly.

"There's barely anything anything left of it," he said. "The airplanes, thousands of all kinds, were just lined up on their airfields for the German bombers."

"They can build more planes," I said. "They can't build more pilots."

"I don't think they're looking for teenage girls," said Iskra.

I raised my chin defiantly.

"The government calls upon you, citizens of the Soviet Union, to rally still more closely around our glorious Bolshevist party, around our Soviet government, around our great leader and comrade, Stalin.

"Our cause is just. The enemy shall be defeated. Victory will be ours."

★ THREE ★

AT THE POST OFFICE, THERE WAS A LETTER FOR ME FROM the VVS.

I hesitated before sliding my thumb under the flap of the envelope to rip it open, suppressing my own eagerness. As long as it remained sealed, the letter might not be a rejection.

"'Dear Valentina Sergeevna,'" I read aloud. The letter addressed me formally by my first name and my patronymic middle name, which seemed promising because the writer was talking to me like an adult, but my hope quickly withered when I read the body of the letter. "'Thank you for your repeated interest in serving in the Red Army Air Force. While the VVS appreciates your extensive aeronautical experience, we are pleased to inform you that the state of the war effort is not, at this time, so dire that we need to put young girls at risk in dangerous front-line positions. We encourage you to put your admirable patriotism to use aiding the war effort in another way. The women of the Soviet Union are urgently needed in the work force to keep our brave fighting men supplied. This role may be less glamorous, but it is every bit as important. Additionally, we urge you not to neglect your most vital contribution to the USSR, that of a future mother. You will someday be responsible for raising the next generation, and that alone is reason enough to keep you away from the dangers of combat. . . .'"

"At least it's a polite letter," said Iskra as we left the post office and entered a gloomy summer drizzle. "Very personal."

"I'm about to get personal," I grumbled. I pulled a pack of cigarettes out of my shirt pocket, but before I could take one, Iskra grabbed the pack and tossed it into the canal.

"Hey!" I said, resisting the impulse to jump into the scummy water after it. "I waited in three lines for those!"

"And that makes you a bad Soviet," said my cousin loftily. "I won't let you pick up that filthy habit. We need to set an example, you know. For the adults."

"You mean the adults who won't let me join the VVS?" I asked. "'Future mother.' Ugh."

"Mother Russia you are not," said Iskra. She snapped her fingers. "I know who you should write to: that airwoman from the *Rodina*, the one who's always talking about getting more girls into aviation. Marina Raskova."

"Raskova?" I scratched my neck nervously. "She's really

important, Iskra. She has better things to do than talk to a kid from Stakhanovo."

"As opposed to the commander of the VVS, who has nothing better to do."

I *had* written to Raskova. Over the month since the war had broken out, I'd spent hours sitting cross-legged on the mattress that Iskra and I shared, using *Notes of a Navigator* as a writing surface. I wrote and rewrote, rubbing out mistakes with a dirty eraser stub until I wore holes in the paper. I just never mailed it.

We found Pasha sitting on our building's concrete steps, heedless of the rain. His forehead was cradled in one hand, his hair sticking up at angles where he'd raked his fingers through it. I stopped abruptly, the importance of my letter shrinking away as I realized that something was wrong, really wrong.

"What's the matter?" I asked softly.

He didn't reply.

A slip of yellow paper was crumpled in his other hand. I reached down and unfolded his unresisting fingers, one at a time. I didn't need to read the paper to know what it said. "Did you just find out?"

He nodded.

"When are you leaving?"

"Monday."

Three days.

Iskra and I sat on the step on either side of him. Unsure what else to do, I took his hand in mine. It was soft and delicate. Not the hand of a coker. Not the hand of a soldier. Pasha had beautiful hands and I had never noticed them before.

Pasha's quiet presence had been a constant in my life since we were toddlers stacking blocks at the state-run day care. After Iskra's arrival, he became the tagalong kid, although he was less than a year my junior. I had taken it for granted that when I made it big as a pilot, I would leave him. It had never occurred to me that he might leave me first.

A flat-nosed towboat chugged sullenly down the canal, pushing a line of rusty rectangular barges lashed together. Pasha sat on the deck of the middle one, leaning against the side of the hopper with his arms wrapped around his knees and a battered rucksack resting beside him. The pale mountain of coke that rose above the rim of the coaming made him look very small. It was a humble way to leave for war.

I waited at the corner where the lead barge passed close to the edge of the canal, and when it appeared, I jumped onto its low, flat deck, holding my arms out for balance. I walked along the outside edge of the tow until I reached Pasha.

He said, "You weren't at the dock. I thought you weren't going to say good-bye."

"Not with all those people around," I said. I couldn't put my finger on why that made me so uncomfortable. I didn't have anything to say to Pasha that I couldn't say in front of everyone, did I? "I passed your sister in the hall. She was crying."

"She thinks I'm not coming back. It's as good as a law of the universe for her: People who leave never come back."

"You'll come back," I said with more conviction than I felt. "You'll go. You'll fight. We'll repel the invasion. And then you'll come home."

"That's what Iskra said too. But not everyone will."

I wanted to point out some trait of Pasha's that would help him survive the war, but I couldn't think of any. Instead I sat down on the edge of the deck. The barge rode so low that I could trail the tips of my toes in the murky water. There was no one else on the line of barges except the sailors in the towboat far behind. I wondered how much of our lives Pasha and I had spent sitting side by side while the world passed us by.

Pasha told me, "You can listen to my radio while I'm gone."

"I don't know how it works."

"My dad can show you."

Uneasy silence enveloped us again, the knowledge of what lay ahead hanging over us like a storm cloud. A half-submerged tire floated by, trailing weeds and trash like an industrial-age jellyfish.

I said, "They won't let me enlist, but they draft you. Soviet efficiency, huh?"

"Soviet efficiency," Pasha echoed.

"I saw a story in the paper this morning. Two girls wanted to fight so badly that they stole a fighter and flew it to the front. Didn't end well, but I'm a little jealous anyway. Maybe we could just take the old plane and fly away."

"Where to?"

I shrugged. "Who cares?"

Ahead, the canal curved away around a ridge and out of sight.

I nodded in the direction of the bend. "This is where I get off."

Pasha looked up at me out of the corner of his eye. "Do you have to?"

There was no Iskra around to tease me, none of the aeroclub guys who accused me of joining to meet boys. So I turned toward him. His face was suddenly close to mine. I reached out to touch his cheek, then hesitated. It was long enough that we both blushed and dropped our gaze. I gave him an awkward hug.

"Valka?"

"Yeah?"

Pasha fumbled with his hands. "Is it okay if I write to you?"

Of course I said yes.

★FOUR★

4 September 1941

Dear Valyushka,

I guess basic training is a luxury from an earlier time, because I only spent a couple of days doing drills with a wooden dummy rifle before I was dispatched to the outskirts of Moscow to dig ditches.

You'll be glad to hear that we have yet to see so much as an unfriendly plane in the sky. Those spiky steel tank traps feel almost lonely standing there in the road. They remind me of giant spiders waiting for a fly.

My NCO—the noncommissioned officer I report to—is a

sergeant named Pashkevich. I'm afraid of him. He has a sharp vermilion voice speckled with a brown Belorussian accent and he always sounds like he's yelling even when he isn't. He usually is. Yelling at me for being too small and skinny, or too slow and lazy, or for not knowing how to do things that I was never taught.

Pashkevich is very zealous about the war effort. Partly it's patriotism but mostly he really, really wants to kill some Fritzes. He wishes he'd stayed through the invasion of Belorussia so he could have become a partisan, sabotaging the Germans from behind their own lines instead of supervising a bunch of teenagers with shovels. I'm not sure if he's as tough as he talks or if it's all bravado, but it sure makes me feel spineless.

After that reception, I wasn't keen to meet the rest of my squad. They all seem to know what they're doing, and I was sure they were judging me. But while we dug, the big, burly soldier next to me said, "You get used to Pashkevich."

I asked why he was so angry.

The big soldier said, "He fled ahead of the invasion. He saw Minsk burn. Can you blame him?"

He assured me that the rest of the squad were draftees like me, confused and frightened. We all want to help the Motherland, but we're afraid we'll throw our lives away without accomplishing anything.

The big soldier took me under his wing. His name is Vakhromov and he has a wife and son and another child on the way. He wonders what his baby will be like and when he'll get to see him (or her) and whether he (or she) will think he's a bad father for not being around. That's something a kid like me can be grateful for. No one depends on me. I told him about my sister and my parents and about you and Iskra, since it doesn't feel right to talk about my family without mentioning the two of you.

When I'm not digging ditches I'm training to become a radio operator. It's the first time I've used a real radio, the kind with vacuum tubes. Do you remember the colors, Valka? The ones that match up with different sounds? When I tune my radio, it chirps and squeals pink and yellow like a robot from a science fiction movie. It has two settings: AM and CW. AM, which sounds just like my radio at home, lets us use it as a telephone. CW is continuous wave, which only transmits long and short beeps. It's for sending and receiving encrypted messages by Morse code. I can't tell you how the encryption works, but it's interesting, like a crossword puzzle.

The radio hooks up to a battery pack with a thick black cord. It has a pair of long coils of antenna that I can string out wherever we make camp and a shorter stand-up antenna for sending and receiving messages on the march. The battery pack is so heavy that Pashkevich assigned another soldier, Rudenko, to carry it. "He's almost as useless as you," said Pashkevich. "Keep an eye on him; everyone knows the Ukrainians welcomed the fascists with open arms."

They say the same thing about the Belorussians, but I didn't say so.

Rudenko is a nervous guy who winces at every loud noise, not my first choice to be tethered to by a radio cord. Pashkevich says the Katyushas made him funny in the head.

"Who's Katyusha?" I asked.

Pashkevich laughed an unkind laugh and said that I would meet the Katyushas soon enough.

Rudenko doesn't talk much. In the evening, he wanders off by himself and reads. He has an old book that he hides whenever he sees our commissar.

There's a poster on our barracks of a soldier holding up a sheepskin, inside of which is a wolf with a swastika on it. The caption says: THE ENEMY IS CRAFTY—BE ON THE LOOKOUT! I've never met a fifth columnist, those sneaky Russian traitors they say are hiding in our midst, but if movies are anything to go by, they act like Rudenko.

Then again, maybe he just wants to be left alone.

Give my love to everyone at home. And write soon. I miss you.

Yours,

Pasha

★

17 September 1941

Dear Pasha,

I've never written a letter to a boy before, much less a soldier, and I'm not entirely sure what such a letter should contain.

Feelings, I suppose. No doubt that's what Iskra hopes; she's sitting across the table pretending to read a book, but I know she's actually peeking at what I'm writing. I'm trying to think of what people write to each other about in war movies, because this feels like a movie—you the brave soldier and me the damsel waiting helplessly back at home. It's a shame neither of us fits the roles we've been forced to step into.

How could I forget the colors after all the rainy days we spent amusing ourselves with that game? I'd make a noise and you'd tell me its color. It made me feel close to you, as though I were getting a glimpse into your own secret world. Will you remind me what color my voice is?

So you are a radio operator now. All that tinkering has paid off. I will always remember the day I climbed the fire escape to throw that scrap-wire antenna over the roof. I was sure it wouldn't work. But there you were on the floor of your apartment, holding a paper cup wound with wire to your ear, and you said, "I can hear it!" And I took the homemade speaker and, sure enough, there were voices, fuzzy and indistinct like listening to the sea in a shell. It was magical. I felt as if that radio program had been recorded especially for the two of us.

Not much has been going on here, and it makes me miss you even more. Now I realize how often I'd say "Pasha, let's kick a football" or "Pasha, come wait for ration coupons with me." And all those flights together. It isn't as much fun flying without a passenger. Isn't that vain of me?

Since every combat-fit male pilot has been drafted, it's up to *those of us left behind—the female pilots—to train the rookies. Meanwhile, I'll stay behind and watch as, one by one, everyone goes off to fight except for me. It's not fair.*

I know I shouldn't be jealous of you, that you'd do anything to be here with me. But I feel so helpless stuck here half a country away from everything. I just wish I could do something.

Yours,

Valka

P.S. Don't call me Valyushka. You know I hate pet names.

★

1 October 1941

Dear Valyushka,

We were mobilized today. How the fascists keep advancing closer to Moscow in the muddy rasputitsa season is beyond me. The rain has turned the dirt roads into impassable quagmires.

My transceiver has a steel case with straps and it's heavy even without the battery pack. I have so much to keep track of: the radio, a canvas bag of spare parts, a logbook, a code book, and all my regular gear. And, most important, your letter. It makes me feel I have a place in the universe. I'm not just a nameless soldier among thousands of other nameless soldiers, I'm someone with an identity. Someone you can write to.

When I was packing up my things, I found an odd little object that I'd been issued without explanation. It's a smooth, hollow ebony cylinder the size of a rifle cartridge, stopped with a bit of cork.

"That's an identity capsule," Vakhromov explained. "You fill out the paper inside so they can identify your body."

I pried out the cork with the tip of my combat knife and extracted a rolled-up slip of paper. Name, rank, service number, address, next of kin . . . I took out my pen, but Vakhromov pulled it out of my grasp and shook his head. "You don't want to do that. It's like signing your own death warrant."

Rudenko nodded grimly. "Remember Vasilyev? He stepped on a mine not ten minutes after he filled his out."

I nervously looked around for unexploded ordnance, then tucked the capsule into my pocket. I can't say I feel safer for having followed their advice.

Vakhromov got a letter in the same batch as yours. He has a new baby girl. As we marched, he kept asking us questions about her as though we would somehow know the answers. What color do we think her eyes will be? Do we think she's fussy or calm? Do we think her brother likes her? I told him we'd do our best to end the war so he could find out for himself.

When we stopped for lunch, Rudenko was again off on his own with his book. It's a pretty book, with a green tooled-leather cover decorated with gold leaf, only a little of which has rubbed off. I sneaked a glance inside and saw a page full of curious black hooked symbols. I thought I recognized them, but couldn't recall what they meant or where I'd seen them before.

Each symbol was preceded by a small letter in red ink with a syllable of two or three letters printed underneath. The letters

*were old-fashioned Russian peppered with hard signs, but they
spelled gibberish. A cipher?*

*He wears a black cord around his neck that he keeps tucked
under his tunic. A picture of his girl, maybe? I suppose even fifth
columnists have loved ones.*

Yours,

Pasha

P.S. *Your voice is cinnabar red.*

"Cinnabar red," I mused as we crossed the bridge. "What color is
cinnabar anyway?"

"Red," said Iskra. We were headed to the airfield to teach the
rookies.

I rolled my eyes. "No, I mean, what does it mean that my voice
is cinnabar red? Is that a good thing?"

Iskra gave me an indulgent look. "Baby cousin, if Pasha said
it about you, it's a good thing. He's been sweet on you for ages,
despite your mannish jaw and sartorial ineptitude."

I felt a blush rise on my cheeks. It was usually easy to ignore
Iskra's teasing, but I found it harder to brush off comments about
Pasha. Truth be told, I was a little terrified—on the barge, something
had stirred inside me that now refused to be still. Tucking
my hands into the pockets of my overalls and shifting from foot to
foot, I said, "I'm a serious pilot. I'll become famous and fly all over
the world. I'll be too busy for boys."

My troubled thoughts about Pasha were swept aside when
we reached the airfield and found Iosif Grigorevich, our flight

instructor, holding a telegram. His face wore its customary scowl. He cleared his throat and said, "An old war buddy in Moscow sent me a telegram that I really shouldn't let you girls see."

"From Moscow?" I said. It had to be something exciting. I grabbed for the telegram, but he snatched it away and held it out of my reach before finally relenting with a chuckle. Iskra and I read the brief typewritten lines together.

```
KOMSOMOL CENTRAL OFFICE SEEKS FEMALE PILOTS
NAVIGATORS AIRCRAFT MECHANICS TO SERVE IN ALL
FEMALE FIGHTER AND BOMBER REGIMENTS. QUALIFIED
PARTIES REPORT TO MAJ M M RASKOVA AT ZHUKOVSKY
AIR FORCE ACADEMY MOSCOW OCT 13.
```

I stared. My eyes were glued to one phrase of the uneven dark printing. "Maj M M Raskova. Major Marina Mikhailovna Raskova? *The* Marina Raskova?"

"There aren't two of her," said Iosif Grigorevich in a tone that implied he'd have been happy if there hadn't even been one of them. "I'm a fool to let you see that telegram. But clearly I'm an even bigger fool, because I've already forwarded your documents to the Komsomol Central Committee."

Marina Raskova! Fighter regiment! I could barely get my mind around it. My stomach did a confused flip-flop of combined excitement and just plain shock.

"Hang on," said Iskra, taking the telegram. "October thirteenth. That's Monday. We could take the barge to Magnitogorsk tomorrow, but the train to Moscow doesn't leave until Tuesday—if it's running at all."

I stung with indignation. "No! Something important finally happens and we're going to miss it?"

Iskra shrugged. "Life is life, and Moscow is half a country away. Unless . . ." She tapped a finger on her pink lips. "Unless we had a faster way to travel."

We looked at each other, then at Iosif Grigorevich.

"No!" he said, his face reddening. "No, no, no. Absolutely not."

I folded my hands in a very non-Soviet gesture and begged him. "Pleeeeeease?"

"It's the only way we'll ever get there in time," said Iskra.

Iosif Grigorevich replied, "It would be a waste of time and fuel. Besides, don't you read the papers? The Hitlerites are sixty kilometers from Moscow!"

"We all have to make sacrifices for the war effort," I said, suddenly developing a sense of patriotism.

Iskra told Iosif Grigorevich, "You're always saying you hate teaching girls. Now's your chance to be rid of us."

He narrowed his eyes. "Is that a promise?"

"If we enlist, we'll be gone," I interjected.

"Let's make it a wager. I'll fly you to Moscow tomorrow. If you get accepted to whatever harebrained program they're cooking up, fine. If not, you find your own way home, and you'll withdraw from the Stakhanovo Aeroclub. Permanently."

Iskra and I shared another glance. One telegram had spun

dangerously out of control. Swallowing my hesitation, I stepped forward and shook Iosif Grigorevich's hand.

"Deal," I said in a voice far cooler than I felt. And with that, we were on our way to meet Marina Raskova.

★FIVE★

WE MUST HAVE BEEN THE ONLY PEOPLE IN THE WORLD
flying *into* Moscow on that dreary autumn day. Unable to get
clearance to land amid the chaos at the main airport, we ended
up at an aerodrome on the opposite side of the city. Iskra and I
said our good-byes to Iosif Grigorevich and headed for the nearest
metro station.

When I'd last visited, the brand-new Moscow metro was a
gleaming underground world straight out of science fiction. Now
it was a bomb shelter crammed with hundreds of camp beds, row
upon row beneath the cavernous art-deco ceilings. A Party member was handing out bottles of milk to a cluster of hungry children.
The ticket booth was empty. So we walked, weaving our way past

cars, wagons, pedestrians, even herds of livestock, all fighting to get out of the city.

At first I thought it was snowing, but the flakes that fell on my hand were gray and did not melt. When I rubbed them between my thumb and forefinger, they crumbled into powder, staining my glove. Ash.

A creeping dread began to grip me. I looked around nervously for the source, but it seemed to come from everywhere. The people of Moscow were burning everything. We passed a bonfire in the alley between the Central Telegraph Office and a looted bakery: a smoldering heap of half-burned letters, union documents, Marxist literature, and pictures of Party leaders. Iskra picked up a Party card, its red cover curled at the corners. The photo had been ripped out.

"Cowards," she said through her teeth. "You can see how deep their loyalty runs."

The streets of Moscow were a maze of tank traps and checkpoints. We picked our way around the pale, bulbous form of a grounded barrage balloon. The balloons occupied nearly every open space, giving the impression of a city full of beached whales.

As we neared the city center, the chaos grew. A mob had formed outside a factory, demanding their wages. Workers were hitting the chained steel gates with sledgehammers and trying to scale the cinder block walls. Farther down the street, some shopkeepers threw their doors open and let people take what they wanted. They figured the fascists would have it all in a few days anyway.

It hit me like a punch in the gut that it was all real, the bombs and the artillery and the tanks poised to crush our capital city. It struck me how different the war had been for me and for Pasha, that I'd been sheltered while he faced everything.

Iskra stopped in front of a cordoned-off block of apartments reduced to rubble. Her eyes widened. "This was where we lived."

I stared at the bombed-out shell. I had always assumed that, since Iskra was from the city, she must have lived a more sophisticated life than we did out in the sticks. But the broken walls outlined a concrete cube just like the concrete cubes in Stakhanovo.

I fumbled for something to say, but all I could come up with was, "At least it was empty. So nobody got hurt."

"Yeah," she said vaguely. "It isn't as if I could return here anyway." She looked around. "I shouldn't even be here now."

Iskra was supposed to stay a hundred kilometers from Moscow. That was the rule. Iskra had been a model Soviet all her life, but she was still treated like a criminal because her parents had been arrested on a trumped-up charge of trying to undermine the Soviet Union in order to make Communism look like a failed experiment. Wrecking, it was called. I remembered that Uncle Vanya kept a pencil tucked behind his ear and Aunt Anya always did three things at once, like telling me where to look for my lost mittens and helping Iskra with her math homework while preheating her Primus stove in the collective kitchen. Neither seemed like a wrecker.

I told Iskra, "There's a war on. No one is looking for you." I hoped it was true.

Zhukovsky Air Force Academy was camouflaged. Crude black-and-white paint coated the arches and pillars and ornate scrollwork of the old palace that now served the people, disguising it as a cluster of smaller buildings. We stepped into a spacious hallway barely warmer than outside. Since the Germans had seized all the mines to the west, Moscow had almost no coal. The factories still chugged out smoke, but there was nothing to spare for civilians, and electricity was being rationed.

Inside, it was packed, but the atmosphere was completely different. Hundreds, maybe thousands, of girls and women, all bubbling over with excitement. I didn't know there were this many female pilots in all of Russia. One name was on everyone's lips. Would she really be here? Would we really meet her? And then there she was at the end of the hall. Not a picture, but the real thing!

I'd always taken for granted that being a soldier, and being a pilot for that matter, meant looking and acting like a boy. Sure, there was Iskra, who fussed about color coordination and curled the ends of her already-wavy hair; for all I knew, she joined the aeroclub to meet boys. But Marina Raskova wasn't like a man at all. I'd never realized how young she was. Not even thirty, and she already had a list of accomplishments that ordinary people only dreamed about. Her uniform had a knee-length skirt and she had her long hair in two braids pulled into a knot at the back of her neck, just like she always did in photos. She looked warm and friendly, not soldierly. She glanced around at the hopeful girls and occasionally paused to greet someone, saying, "So you made it after all!"

Another female officer about the same age was walking with her. I couldn't resist leaning forward to catch their conversation as they passed me. The other officer asked, "How many were you expecting?"

"Based on the letters? Around a thousand, I suppose. How many are there?"

"More," said the other officer drily.

"And I'll have to disappoint so many of them. I should have asked for more regiments!"

"Do you want to split the interviews?"

"Nonsense. These are my girls and I need to get to know them. I won't have an aviation group full of people I've never met."

By the time she reached her office door, the noise level had become a dull roar. She turned to face us and held up her hand until we quieted down.

She asked us, "What are all of you here for?"

"We want to fight!" we shouted.

"But don't you know that the fascists will be shooting at you?"

Suddenly emboldened, I called out, "Not if I shoot them first!"

She said, "If you go to war, you'll face all kinds of hardships, and many of you will not return. But for those of you who insist on staying, I am going to interview each and every one of you personally."

For every girl who came out of that office walking on air, three or four trudged out downcast. I wondered what would happen to those girls. Some were from the Ukraine or Belorussia and had no homes to return to. And then there were the ones from Moscow.

One glance outside convinced me that they had it the worst of all.

Iskra, cheerful and relaxed, amused herself by watching the other hopefuls.

I tried to pretend I wasn't nervous, even though my palms were sweating. "What if we don't get picked? We could be stuck in the city when it falls."

"*When* it falls? Aren't you a ray of sunshine!"

Another worry struck me. "What if they pick you and not me?" Iosif Grigorevich always said I should fly more like Iskra, who did everything with textbook precision. "Or . . . what if they pick me and not you?" That would be a rare chance to lord it over her; but faced with the possibility of flying without my cousin, I found the idea unthinkable, even for gloating purposes.

Iskra shrugged as if that was a trivial concern and directed her attention to a beret-wearing officer who was leaning against the wall with her hands in her pockets, avoiding eye contact with everyone. "Who's that over there?"

"I don't know. Doesn't look like she wants to chat."

Iskra, undeterred, made a beeline for her. The woman, who looked to be in her late twenties, had straight hair cut just above her shoulders and light green eyes that squinted even though there wasn't a glare. Her expression seemed stern and distant, but as soon as Iskra said hello, it melted into friendliness. She introduced herself with a modest, almost embarrassed smile as Yevdokiya Bershanskaya.

"Hang on—I've heard of you," I said. "What did it say? 'A woman can't be an airline pilot unless she's someone like Yevdokiya Bershanskaya—'"

"Oh, dear. I didn't keep you from getting a job, did I?" asked Bershanskaya.

"Not one I wanted very badly," I assured her.

"Valka," said Iskra, "has her heart set on being a fighter pilot."

"Don't get your hopes up," Bershanskaya warned me. "Every girl here wants to be a fighter pilot. I'm hoping to become one myself, but Raskova called me here to talk about command." She held out her arms helplessly. "Do I look like a commander?"

Just then two middle-aged officers with punctilious military bearing came striding down the hall. The crowd instinctively parted to let them through. Both women wore men's uniforms with cavalry pants, but otherwise they looked entirely different. One had large eyes, dark curls cut short, and a cigarette dangling from her hand. Her collar tabs marked her as a captain. The other, a major with a severe face and close-cropped hair, wore a gold-bordered medal with a portrait of Lenin in platinum.

The major was asking, "No attack regiment, then?"

"Fighters, day bombers, night bombers," replied the captain.

"I could handle the fighters."

"You'll get them. You're the only woman here with command experience. Even Raskova can't handle her own regiment, even though she thinks she can."

I bristled at that comment.

"You said she already had a position for you?"

"Chief of staff," the captain said grimly.

The major looked at her with pity. "You poor thing. You're in charge of . . ." She looked around.

"All this," the captain finished, gesturing broadly with her cigarette.

The major curled her lip at the crowd of girls. "Look at all of them. When we were their age, we fought to enlist. Every step of the way, we had to prove ourselves better than the men. And now they get an invitation!"

I was about ready to march over and set them straight about the work it took for me to get here, never mind the fact that they were high-ranking officers, but Iskra's hand on my elbow gently held me back.

"Most of them aren't even pilots," said the captain. "Students, workers, farm girls . . . It'll be a job making them into soldiers."

"How will you manage?"

"Discipline, discipline, discipline. I'll get them whipped into combat-ready shape, so long as I can keep Raskova from coddling them."

"You'd better. Don't send them into combat one second before they're ready, no matter what the major says. If they can't measure up to the male pilots, the difference will be blamed on their gender. *Our* gender. I won't jeopardize twelve years of work because some teenagers get themselves killed."

They stopped in front of Bershanskaya, their faces stony. The captain said, "Lieutenant. I hear you've been sworn in."

"That's right, yesterday morning," said Bershanskaya.

"That makes you an officer," the captain replied. "An officer would know not to wear her cover indoors."

Bershanskaya abashedly took off her beret.

The major said coldly, "You may be an officer on paper, Bershanskaya, but until you can act like one, you're still a civilian pilot, as far as I'm concerned. You're not ready to fly for the VVS, let alone command."

They swept on.

"Who are they?" I whispered.

Berskanshaya lowered her voice. "Those are the Kazarinova sisters. The major is Tamara and the captain is her younger sister, Militsa. They've both been in the VVS for dog's years. A bit of free advice: Watch your step when those two are around."

"You ought to get along with them, Valka; they're almost as masculine as you," teased Iskra.

"Girls. I'm not kidding," said Bershanskaya, her friendly look vanishing.

Before I could respond, a voice barked, "Koroleva, Valentina Sergeevna!"

As I entered Marina Raskova's office, I was so nervous that I almost couldn't tell I was nervous; I just felt dazed. Marina Raskova gave me an easy, unaffected smile.

"Well"—her soft gray eyes flicked down to the file in front of her—"Valentina Sergeevna, you look like you're on needles, but I promise there's no need to be nervous."

"It's just I can't believe I'm meeting you for real," I said haltingly. "The *Rodina* changed my life. I can't begin to explain how much it meant to me. Also, we didn't count on there being so many people here. . . . We sort of don't have a ride home."

"I'll do my best to see that you don't need one," Raskova

promised. "What can I do for you?"

"I wanted to be a fighter pilot, but that was before I saw how much competition there was. Now I have no idea if I've got what it takes."

Raskova told me, "This isn't a contest—it's a chance to serve the Motherland. And what you need is five hundred hours of flight experience."

"Five hundred hours." I whistled. "The boys in my aeroclub are getting drafted with sixty or seventy."

"And you think that's unfair?"

"Well, it is!"

To my surprise, Raskova said, "You're right, it is. But it's the last unfairness. From here on, you'll be treated exactly like the male regiments. You'll wear the same uniforms, fly the same aircraft, and go on the same missions. But first you need five hundred hours in a powered aircraft." She added, "If you don't have enough hours, we're training many pilots as navigators."

"Please don't make me a navigator," I begged.

She said gently, "I'm trying my very best to meet everyone's wishes, but everyone wants to be a pilot. We have a greater need for navigators. It might be more interesting than you think."

"I'm the world's worst navigator."

"Well, how many hours do you have?"

"Six hundred and eighty. All but fifty solo." I paused a moment before asking, "But, um, what do you mean by 'powered'?"

That was the first and last time I saw Raskova caught off guard. "An aircraft with an engine . . . ?"

"The plane physically had an engine in it. It just wasn't always *running*."

She furrowed her brow. "What sort of plane was this?"

"No idea," I admitted. "I mean, it's a closed-cockpit four-seater monoplane with a nine-cylinder radial engine, and it has a steel body but a wooden wing, but we don't have a clue what model it is or anything."

And then I was foolishly spilling the whole story of the Stakhanovo aeroclub. How a peasant in our oblast found it, with its paint peeling off, in a shed full of rusty parts. How we bought it for our aeroclub. How we fixed the broken variometer with a piece of tape. How the engine was temperamental and we couldn't find replacement parts. How we figured out that it only stalled when you went into a shallow dive at exactly the right angle. How I became an expert at deadstick landings.

Raskova was quiet for a moment. Then she said, "You put in almost seven hundred hours in a plane without a fully operational engine."

"Yes."

"Or instruments."

"Yes."

"That you found in a shed."

"*I* didn't find it. But yes."

Raskova covered her mouth with one hand and I realized with dismay that my future commanding officer was trying valiantly not to laugh at me. "You and your aeroclub sound equal parts resourceful and reckless."

"I'm completely flubbing this, aren't I?" I sighed in resignation. I would return home in shame. The wager hardly mattered; I'd never be able to face Iosif Grigorevich after this.

So I was completely blindsided when Marina Raskova said, "On the contrary! All day I've interviewed girls who can fly perfectly under perfect conditions, but if there's one thing I know for sure, it's that conditions at the front will never be perfect. I need airwomen who can handle themselves when everything starts going sideways. I have just the assignment for you. Congratulations, Officer Cadet Koroleva, you're going to be a pilot."

I stifled an involuntary squeal by biting my fingertips and managed to squeak out a thank-you. In the flood of elation, I failed to note that she hadn't specified that I would be a *fighter* pilot.

Bouncing in my seat, I felt a weight in one of my coat's big front pockets. I pulled out the battered, black-covered book with the image of the *Rodina* printed on it and asked timidly, "Will you sign your book for me? Please?"

Raskova took the tape-repaired paperback, holding it carefully to keep the loose pages from falling out. She said, "This has been well loved."

"I've read it over and over. I dreamed that someday I'd have adventures like yours."

Raskova flipped open the book and took a fountain pen off her desk, but as she signed the title page in flowing cursive, she told me, "You won't listen, but I'm going to tell you this anyway, because it's important. Being lost in the taiga was not fun. It was not our plan. Everything turned out all right in the end—that time. But then, six months later, Polina was flying and there was another accident. And I lost a dear friend." She closed the book and met my gaze as she handed it back to me. "Rise to adversity when it comes to you. Never seek it out. Don't go to the front looking for adventure."

As predicted, I didn't listen.

★ SIX ★

ONLY THE FAINTEST STRIPE OF BLUE GRAY ALONG THE western horizon broke up the darkness as we assembled on the platform the next morning. The train station was packed. Some people clung to evacuation orders, some to nothing but wild hope. People slept directly on the concrete, indistinguishable from the untidy bundles of luggage surrounding them. The luckiest evacuees secured seats in the few passenger cars, but most were cramming into freight trains. Fistfights broke out. When the boxcars couldn't hold any more, desperate refugees climbed on top of them or hung on to the ladders on the sides.

By contrast, we, the lucky three hundred and eighty newly minted members of Aviation Group 122, made our platform look almost empty. Infantrymen guarded the sides of the platform, throwing off anyone who tried to climb the black iron fence.

We had unconsciously begun to sort ourselves. The pilots led the way, attempting to march despite their feet slipping around in oversized black boots; they were followed by the navigators, then the mechanics and armorers.

Iskra turned on her heel one way and the other as she walked and announced, "Ladies and gentlemen, here's Iskra Ivanovna Koroleva modeling the newest fashion for autumn."

Her sleeves were long enough to cover her hands and her trousers bunched around her boot tops. She had the brown leather belt cinched as tight as it would go to give herself the semblance of a waist. Raskova had told the truth: we were wearing the same uniforms as the men, right down to the underwear. I laughed. "You look like a sack of potatoes. But, I mean, a fashionable sack of potatoes."

Iskra pouted. "You, on the other hand, have never cared how you looked, and your uniform fits. It's a gross injustice."

I said, "What I want to know is how you got out of Raskova's office so fast. You were in there for about two minutes. What did you say to her?"

"I told her I wanted to be a navigator," said Iskra smugly. "She practically kissed me."

Three girls stood by the door of one of the boxcars; they were surrounded by a tight knot of admirers.

"We aren't even at the base yet and we already have a popular set," said Iskra. "Who are they?"

I craned my neck to catch a glimpse of their faces and gasped. "You're kidding me—it's the pyaterka! The aerobatics team! I didn't know they'd enlisted!" I'd seen photos of them in the paper. They were famous for their flashy flying tricks. A feeling of inadequacy washed over me. "I'm not going to be the best pilot in this aviation group by a long shot."

"It'll be a good experience for you," said Iskra.

We teased each other until we reached the nearest boxcar. Its dim, close interior was covered with thin mattresses and filled with a low cacophony of voices. I looked around at the other girls.

I'd made it into Aviation Group 122, but the fight wasn't over yet. Later in our training, we'd be divided into three regiments. If I was lucky, I'd be assigned to the fighter regiment and become one of Stalin's falcons, screaming out of the sky onto the enemy aircraft that were laying waste to our Motherland. If I wasn't lucky, I'd be assigned to the less glamorous day bomber regiment, the workhorses of the VVS. And if I was woefully unlucky, I'd end up in the night bomber regiment. Pilots in that regiment didn't even get proper warplanes, just trainers retrofitted to hold a few bombs. There was no glory in store for them, even if their flimsy planes didn't all get shot down in the first week.

Every girl who made it into the fighter regiment meant one spot less for me. But right now we all shared the same electric anticipation, and it was hard to think of them as competition.

Two spots in the back had been claimed by a couple of blond girls who were already talking and laughing as if they'd known each other for ages.

"Do you know where we're going?" one of the blondes, a petite girl with confident blue eyes, asked the other.

"South, to Engels," the other replied. "I got that from the chief of staff, along with an admonition about how to address a superior officer."

"It'll be a long trip, then."

Iskra claimed a mattress near them. I had just done the same when the train started, with a luggage-scattering jerk.

The first blonde, her face bright, announced, "If we're going to spend days in a boxcar together, we'd better get acquainted. This is Zhenya Zhigulenko. As there are sure to be a hundred Zhenyas in our aviation group, I'm calling her Zhigli. She's a navigator, but don't hold that against her. I'm Lidiya, but everyone calls me Lilya, as in, 'I wish I could fly as well as Lilya.'"

I decided on the spot that, competition be damned, I liked these girls. "We'll see about that. My name's Valka and this is my cousin Iskra."

"Iskra—'Spark.' That's a neat nickname. Very Soviet. How did you get it?" asked the girl called Zhigli. She was an athletic, long-legged Cossack with striking dark lashes rimming her eyes.

"My parents wrote it on my birth certificate," said Iskra.

Zhigli raised one neatly shaped eyebrow. "That isn't a real name."

Lilya furrowed her brow at Zhigli. "You told me that your father got *his* name by buying a passport off a disabled man."

"Well, yes, but that's different. He was avoiding the draft during the Civil War."

"Resourceful yet unpatriotic," said Iskra.

"No," Zhigli told her flatly. "He did what he needed to survive. Going to war to rebuff an invading fascist army is patriotic. There's nothing patriotic about Russians killing Russians, White or Red."

"What, someone can't be a threat because they were born here?" snapped Iskra. "Have you never heard of wreckers? Or fifth columnists? Our worst threats aren't from the outside. There are . . ."

Lilya's sunny expression had deserted her. Tension filled the air and I eyed Iskra uneasily. My cousin, who was just getting started, didn't notice.

"Girls!" I exclaimed. "I'm going to be stuck in this train with you for days. I won't listen to arguments the whole time. The next person who mentions politics is getting thrown out."

Lilya relaxed imperceptibly.

Brakes screeched and the train came to a halt again. A chorus of annoyed voices arose from all over the boxcar.

"What's the trouble?" asked Iskra.

"No idea," said Lilya. "Valka, you look tall. Can you see what's going on out there?"

I could just hook my fingers over the bottom edge of the boxcar's lone small window. Bracing a leg against the corner of the car, I got one forearm and then the other over the sill. The cold outside air met my face. I peered out across the maze of tracks. "We're letting another train by."

"Other troops?"

"No, evacuees."

"Those poor people," said Zhigli. "They'll never get them all out of Moscow in time."

"They'll be all right," said Iskra. "Moscow won't fall as long as Stalin is there to keep it together. You'll see."

"Yes, she's always like this," I informed my new friends as I released my grip and dropped lightly to the floor.

Zhigli said, "If it's fated to fall, it'll fall, and no one will be able to stop it."

Lilya unbuttoned her comically oversized tunic and held it up. "Well, if we're stuck on this train for days, we need to alter these uniforms. I don't want to show up at Engels looking frumpy."

"I'll help you if you'll do mine next," Zhigli offered.

"Deal." Lilya riffled through her kit bag, producing two emery boards, a wildflower identification book containing several pressed specimens ("Lilies for Lilya!" exclaimed Zhigli), and finally a sewing kit. She began snipping open the seams of her tunic with a small pair of gold sewing scissors shaped like a bird. Zhigli accepted a packet of pins.

"Who cares how your uniform fits?" I asked. "We're going to war, not to a beauty pageant."

The other three girls gaped at me as though I'd kicked a puppy. Zhigli explained with quiet gravity, "We might meet boys at Engels. Handsome boys in uniform."

"Zhigli. All. Women's. Aviation. Group."

"It isn't an all women's *city*. There will be boys *somewhere*."

"The odds have to be better than in Stakhanovo," said Iskra.

"Of course, given that boxcars don't have showers, we won't be presentable when we get there, no matter how well tailored our uniforms are."

"Disgusting. We'll never survive," mumbled Zhigli around a mouthful of pins.

Lilya patted her hair. "I'll need to touch up my roots soon, too. I wonder where to get peroxide on an air force base."

"From the hospital, if you can live with the knowledge that you stole it from wounded soldiers," said Iskra.

"All's fair in hair and war," said Zhigli.

"If you wanted to meet boys," I insisted, "you should have become nurses. As airwomen, we might never even see them."

"Nonsense." Zhigli took the pins out of her mouth and gestured evocatively with them. "Perhaps I'm forced to make an emergency landing at another airfield. All the male pilots rush up to my plane. I gracefully alight from the cockpit. I take off my flight helmet and shake out my long golden hair." She fluttered her black lashes and tossed her braid over her shoulder. "Then and there, every one of them falls in love with me."

"I take it back," I said. "You shouldn't be a nurse. You should be a writer."

The train still hadn't moved. Lilya complained, "The war will be over by the time we get to Engels."

I looked over at Iskra, who shifted uncomfortably. I squeezed her shoulder. "Don't worry. No one will be measuring the train to make sure it's a hundred kilometers from Moscow."

Only when I heard Zhigli quietly draw in her breath did I

realize what I'd said. Around Stakhanovo I didn't need to be careful about mentioning Iskra's secret because everyone already knew. I looked helplessly at my cousin, feeling the blood drain from my face. "Oh my god, I didn't mean to . . ."

Iskra threw up her hands, more in resignation than in anger. "Thus ends the world's shortest military career. It would have happened sooner or later."

Zhigli scooted to the far end of her mattress as though treason were contagious. She said to me, "You're . . ."

"No," said Iskra. "Not her."

Zhigli's uneasy gaze slid from me to my cousin.

Lilya said quietly, "Someone was taken from you."

"My parents," said Iskra in her matter-of-fact way.

"What happened?" asked Lilya. Not "What did they do?" but "What happened?"—as if it were an accident or a natural disaster.

Iskra shrugged. "They were wreckers. They got caught."

I explained, "You remember the 1937 census? They were part of it."

In 1937, Iskra's letters from Moscow burst with enthusiasm about our young nation's first-ever census. Her father was compiling maps for the census bureau, and her mother had been dispatched to the Ukraine as head statistician for an entire oblast. "It's a major responsibility," one letter crowed. "Life is better under Communism, and my family will help prove it!"

Then the results came in. According to the census, the USSR wasn't prosperous and growing. It was struggling to even keep the population level, and the Ukraine had it worst of all. The official response was that the data had been doctored to make the whole Soviet project appear a failure, but I remembered when Stakhanovo had been overrun with peasants fleeing their barren farms to escape starvation. Recalling their colorless faces, I couldn't believe that the country was thriving, as Stalin claimed.

Someone had to take the blame. The arrests began with the chief of the census bureau and worked their way down. The NKVD—the secret police—came for Iskra's mother a few months later, and because of her, they also came for Iskra's father, even though he had only drawn maps.

Zhigli's look softened into what might have been sympathy. "Wrong place, wrong time. That's rough."

"How long did they get?" asked Lilya.

"Ten years without right of correspondence." Iskra said it with the casual indifference of someone talking about missing a boat or failing an unimportant exam.

Lilya's eyes widened. She put her hand lightly on top of Iskra's. "I am so, so sorry."

Not being able to write to one's parents was harsh, but that seemed like an overreaction. Iskra apparently agreed. She drew back her hand. "Stop looking at me like I'm a lost baby animal. They were arrested, they got a fair trial, and they were punished. Justice was served."

"Is that why you're here? To redeem your family name?"

"No. I'm fighting to defend the Motherland, same as you."

"Same as me." Lilya sounded distant. "I suppose so."

Zhigli said, "We shouldn't be talking to you. You understand that, don't you? I know it sounds mean, but we could all get in trouble. *She* shouldn't even be with you." She nodded at me. "Her aunt and uncle are already a black mark on her record. Associating with you will only make it worse."

Anger rose in my chest and I leaped to my cousin's defense. "So, what, are you going to turn her in for a pat on the head? Because you're perfect and the rest of us are smudging your record?"

"I didn't say that! I just—"

"Before we all overreact, did anyone else hear?" asked Lilya.

I looked over my shoulder. The rest of the girls seemed happily absorbed in their own conversations. "I don't think so."

Lilya nodded, unquestioningly allying herself with us. "Let's keep it that way. Zhigli, can we trust you?"

Zhigli thought for a moment too long before replying. "Lilya. Valka. You're pilots. I could be your navigator. And Iskra. You could be my flight navigator or I could be yours. When we're on a mission and our lives depend on each other, we won't have the luxury of caring about whose relatives were arrested, or who knows whose secrets. Yes, you can trust me."

Although her speech sounded sincere, or maybe because it did, I wasn't entirely convinced. But Lilya said, "Good," and then the two of them went back to work altering Lilya's uniform.

As Zhigli held up a piece of Lilya's tunic, an envelope fell out of the front pocket. "What have we here?"

"It's none of your business," said Lilya, making a grab for it.

Zhigli snatched it away. "Is it a picture of your boyfriend? Your childhood sweetheart, left behind tearfully waving a handkerchief as his ladylove departed for the front?" That got all our attention. Iskra and I joined in, passing the envelope from hand to hand.

"Give that to me!" yelped Lilya. "I can take all of you!"

But she couldn't. There was a brief scuffle during which I received an unaimed but possibly deserved kick to the face, and then we overpowered the smaller girl while Zhigli took the photo out of the envelope. She unfolded it with great ceremony, announcing, "Ladies and . . . ladies, I am pleased to announce that Lilya's secret boyfriend is . . . Marina Raskova. I was not expecting that."

I released my glowering captive and looked over Zhigli's shoulder. Sure enough, it was the same photo as in my newly signed book.

"Lidiya Vladimirovna Litvyak, I hereby find you guilty of the extremely sentimental possession of your idol's photograph," Iskra announced, to the amusement of all the onlookers.

Lilya raised herself onto her elbows and retorted, "Well, I find you—"

Just then the inside of our car brightened as the rusty door slid open. "What are you girls up to?"

The four of us looked up and found ourselves looking at Raskova herself.

We froze for an instant and then dissolved into giggles. I collapsed onto the floor, snickering helplessly.

Zhigli recovered first and, pointing at Lilya, managed to choke out, "She keeps a picture of you in her pocket!" Remembering that she was in the military, she tardily added, "Ma'am."

"She does?" Raskova took the proffered photograph. I thought she blushed a little. "That's . . . actually very flattering."

She returned the photo to Lilya, turned to me, and asked, "Koroleva, you look like you've been in battle already. What happened?"

I gingerly touched the beginnings of a beautiful black eye. Lilya hastened to explain, "It was an accident."

"Yes, your boot accidentally met my face."

"I see," said Raskova mildly. "Seeing as it will be another six months before you girls are cleared for combat, let's keep boots away from faces for the remainder of the journey, shall we? Less horseplay and more rest. You'll need it; this is the last downtime you'll have for a long while. Now, if everyone can hear me all right, we'll go over some military regulations on our way to Engels."

Eyeing us, Lilya muttered, "You're all on my list."

Iskra, Zhigli, and I exchanged looks, biting our lips and trying not to laugh. And just like that, we were once again four new friends on a train.

★ SEVEN ★

26 October 1941

Dear Pasha,

It's funny how life can stand still for so long, then change so fast that your head spins. Four days ago I had no future beyond working at the coking ovens and maybe, if I was lucky, becoming a small-time flight instructor like Iosif Grigorevich. And then an unexpected telegram, a trip to Moscow, and my impossible dream came true: Iskra and I are joining the VVS! We found ourselves on a train to Engels, part of the brand-new, all-female Aviation Group 122.

We were in complete isolation from the outside world on the train, relying on an occasional newspaper bought at a station to even know whether Moscow was still standing. I scoured those papers trying to piece together where you are. I didn't expect how uneasy that made me. Aside from my trip to Moscow to visit Iskra, you and I have never been more than a few kilometers from each other the whole time we were growing up. Now letters will have to suffice. I've enclosed my new address. I expect you to write promptly.

We arrived on a freezing, rainy night. The city was blacked out in case of air raids. No one was there to meet us.

Captain Kazarinova, our new chief of staff, lined us up while Major Raskova went in search of the duty officer. The captain stalked down the platform, frowning as though she expected us to look like a military parade after being stuffed in boxcars for nine days and then marched through the rain. Iskra and I held hands like lost children.

Kazarinova stopped in front of us. Her dark eyes flicked over our tangled hair and rumpled uniforms. In a moment of panic, I thought she'd found out about Iskra's past. Maybe one of our new friends had spilled our secret, or Kazarinova had somehow looked up our family history while we were on the train, or else that piercing gaze just saw right through us and laid bare our secrets. Someone was about to get arrested.

After what seemed like eons, she shook her head and moved on. In the end, she didn't arrest anyone.

Worse. She ordered us to cut off our hair.

It was our first sacrifice to the war effort. I know that will sound silly to you, out there dealing with real hardships, but the feeling of braids falling down to my waist has followed me around my whole life. I remember thinking, "Last chance, Valka. If you want to back out, you'd better do it now."

Some girls cried. I held my tears, even though it was like cutting off one of my arms. I felt that weight leaving me and I knew that was it—I could never get it back, not for years and years. While she cut my hair, Iskra teased that there must be a real woman hiding inside me after all. It was her way of making me feel better.

I got my revenge by taking the scissors from her and informing her that her hair wasn't the regulation five centimeters long, either. She actually screamed in horror. I let her go and she got another girl to cut her hair. With its natural wave it still looks pretty.

Lilya, the movie-star-glamorous girl we met on the train, flat-out refused. There was begging, pleading, and wheedling, but Captain Kazarinova had to threaten to have her arrested before she relented. I think she's put herself on the list of troublemakers.

All three-hundred-odd of us are sleeping in what used to be a gymnasium. It has a wooden floor smooth with wax, marked up with black scuff marks and white lines setting off handball and tennis courts. There's a trace of the gymnasium smell of leather and sweat. The windows, high on the walls, are slathered with black paint.

Iskra, our new friends Lilya and Zhigli, and I ended up in

the northwest corner along with a military engineer who insists that we call her by either her last name (Ilyushina) or her rank (Captain) and a Ukrainian university student named Vera who's training to be a navigator. The Ukrainian girls have such funny accents: they pronounce g's like h's. Not like in Stakhanovo, where everyone sounded the same.

We're a proper flock of white crows. A hundred years ago, we would have had to disguise ourselves as men and run away to fight, like Nadezhda Durova, the cavalry maiden. Now we don't have to do that sort of thing, but nearly everyone had to move heaven and earth to get here. Lilya lied about her experience. Zhigli badgered an air force colonel until she wore him down. One of the other pilots said, "My father thought flying was not an appropriate career for a woman. He wanted me to be a steelworker like the rest of the family."

Zhigli asked, "What about you, Lilya? Did your father want to let you fly?"

The usually talkative Lilya went silent. Her mouth tightened. I came to her rescue with a story about accidentally killing the engine during my first flight.

There's a sleepover feel to our gymnasium dormitory. After lights-out we stay up late talking. Everyone except Captain Ilyushina, who warned us that morning would come early and went straight to sleep. She hasn't told us anything about herself except that she should have been sent to the front with the men and that we're too loud, too silly, and too undisciplined, and we'll probably all get ourselves killed.

Major Raskova has her own way of settling in. When we passed her room on our way to our gymnasium, she was upbraiding the officer on duty. He'd prepared her a nice comfortable room with a luxurious rug and a vase of fresh flowers, but she was making him take it all away. She said that if her girls didn't have such luxuries, then she didn't need them, either. I've never heard her sound so stern.

I must sleep now. Tomorrow the work begins. Write as soon as you can. I won't be able to focus on training while I'm wondering about you.

Yours,

Valka

★

31 October 1941

Dear Valyushka,

I hope this letter reaches you. Our ability to send letters has been limited during rasputitsa. Horse-drawn carts are the only reliable way of moving supplies down the swampy roads. Can you believe that Pashkevich is happy about the conditions? He says that the Hitlerites have it worse than us and that any time the weather is bothering us, we should imagine a tiger tank sunk a meter into the mud.

I'm all right so far. Scared. Vakhromov tells me that's normal. The soldiers we're reinforcing seem tired, mostly. Like they've spent so long in danger that they don't know how to be afraid anymore, even though it's only been four months. These guys are barely older than me. It's hard to believe.

They have a song that they sing while they work or march. A love song. A faint reminder that there's a whole other life waiting for us back home. It goes like this:

Apple and pear trees were blooming,
Mist creeping on the river,
As Katyusha stepped out on the bank,
On the steep and lofty bank.

Stepped out, began a song,
A song for the gray steppe eagle,
A song for her loved one,
A song for him whose letters she treasured.

Oh song, maiden's little song!
Fly toward the clear sun,
To that warrior on the distant border.
Bring Katyusha's greetings.

May he recall a simple maiden,
May he hear her song,
May he save our Motherland
As Katyusha saves their love.

I picked up the melody's pattern of colors and joined in. Pashkevich noticed that I could carry a tune and dubbed me Choir Boy. It is not an affectionate nickname.

After learning all the strict rules governing communications, I arrived at the front to discover that nobody actually follows them. I had scarcely staked the antennae of my radio in the fenced patch of mud we call a campsite before I was hailed over AM by a bored operator from another regiment in our division who had heard that I was the new guy. His voice was light orange. Speaking in the clear (that means unencrypted, which is never allowed), he asked me about my family and we got to chatting. He's a Muscovite and a big football fan. He complained that he had bet twenty rubles on Moscow Dynamo and would never get it back now that the Soviet Cup has been canceled. It's funny what people care about. We can't wrap our minds around the war. It's too big, too terrible. So we have to put it in terms of small things, things we can understand, like a bet on a football tournament.

It turns out that official communications constitute only a small part of radio use. The vast majority consists of chatting and griping. Griping about the war, about the food, about our commanders' obvious lack of strategy, and of course about rasputitsa. We've formed a long-distance friendship. It's fragile. One day you'll say good morning and a different person will answer. It seems foolish to befriend people who can be torn away from you so easily, yet I can't help caring about them.

I found out what Rudenko wears around his neck. It's a

small gold cross. He takes it out and kisses it when he hears bombs or gunshots. Sort of a good-luck charm, I guess.

And as for you, you've met your hero! I bet you never thought that would happen. You always adored your heroes so much. I remember when we went to the cinema to see Chapaev and you decided you wanted to be a machine gunner like Anka. For weeks you would pop up from behind cars or under tables and go, "Rat-a-tat-tat! You're dead!"

Tell me how your training is going. It will help me get my mind off everything. Finally one of us is someplace she wants to be.

Yours,
Pasha

★

9 November 1941

Dear Pasha,

Thank you for writing. Except for the part where you called me Valyushka again. I'm a VVS officer cadet now and I simply don't feel I'm being taken seriously when you're calling me by the name my parents used while they were toilet training me. If you call me that one more time, I'll be forced to stop replying. Do you know how sad that would make me?

Engels is an industrial city in the barren steppe, like a larger copy of Stakhanovo. A long rail bridge connects it to the much *prettier city of Saratov across the Volga River. The skyline is a succession of smokestacks, large and small. When the wind is right, oily brown smoke engulfs our aerodrome and reminds me of home. A corner of the city is fenced off to form our base. The brick buildings are slathered with fresh coats of off-white paint, but you can figure out that they used to be cafés or barbershops or, in our case, gymnasiums. Our wrought iron bedsteads make the place look like a girls' orphanage.*

The morning after we arrived, when the reveille music came on over those tinny speakers, I rolled over and tried to go back to sleep, but Iskra pounced on me and announced, "Good morning, Valka! You're in the VVS!"

By the time I'd thrown my legs over the side of my cot and rubbed my bleary eyes, Ilyushina was already showered and dressed and looking unimpressed with the rest of us. Vera was sitting on the edge of her bed puzzling over the rectangular pieces of cloth that we'd been issued instead of socks, as though they were a difficult math problem. Ilyushina shook her head and repeated the military saying "You don't know how hard life is until you tie your portyanki." I sat next to her and wrapped my own portyanki (I did learn a thing or two from Iosif Grigorevich) so that she could see how it was done. She gave me a serious sort of smile.

Some of the girls showed up late to breakfast because they'd heard that we were sharing the cafeteria with the male pilots and they wanted to powder their noses. Surprisingly, it was Lilya who couldn't stop rolling her eyes at this behavior. Zhigli says that someone as naturally pretty as Lilya can't understand the plight of the homely girl.

We are cramming three years of training into six months at the cost of our health and sanity. Ten classes a day plus two hours of drill. If our drill sergeant expected us to faint on our first march, he forgot that we're the sort of girls who do parachute jumps for fun.

Raskova is preparing us for conditions at the front by sounding the air raid siren in the middle of the night and making us form up outside. One time Zhigli thought she was being clever by throwing on her greatcoat over her nightgown, but that became its own punishment when she had to march around outside with the icy rain lashing her bare legs.

We're doing well for a pack of squirrely kids who didn't know which foot to put forward first. I've already been punished once for losing track of my own footing during a march. It was all your fault. You see, one of the other girls was leading us in a marching song, and I recognized it from your letter. I was so caught up thinking about it that I completely forgot that I was supposed to be marching.

Captain Kazarinova made me do push-ups and kept adding more because my form wasn't good enough. When she finally let me up, she informed me, "I'm not just tormenting you. We don't have the luxury of going easy on you kids. We're at war now. You need to be soldiers now."

We got our first test today. Still sleepy from the midnight wake-up call, we formed up to be inspected by a VVS marshal.

He's the commander of the whole front. As he was walking down the line, he stopped in front of one of the mechanics and pulled off her beret. Her glossy black hair came tumbling out. There was a faint but audible hiss across the parade ground as everyone simultaneously sucked in their breath. And Kazarinova . . . You've heard of looks that kill? But the marshal turned to the rest of us and said, "See, this is how a young lady ought to look. The rest of you look like boys!"

I am apparently indistinguishable from a boy, as I discovered when I sat among the men at the mess hall. They were discussing the new girls, particularly certain parts of them, in highly descriptive terms. Lilya was the favorite. One of them turned and asked me which of the girls from Aviation Group 122 I preferred. I asked whether I could pick myself. Breakfast was awkward after that.

But you haven't been eagerly anticipating this letter to hear me talk about hair, so I'll tell you more about training. We're back in ground school as if we were all fourteen again. It turns out that dogfighting involves math. I would be dominating if we were actually flying, but instead I'm getting schooled by Vera, who has never flown in her life but is studying physics. We have no textbooks and hardly any paper, so I hope you'll forgive me for taking notes in between the lines of your letters.

I am only just wrapping my head around Iskra's choice to become a navigator. In an odd way, it makes sense. We joined the aeroclub on the same day, but while I was a small-town kid who wanted to get away, she was a new arrival from Moscow who had just lost her parents and everything she believed in. I found freedom in the sky. She found order. And so she spends her time surrounded by rulers and compasses.

Lieutenant Bershanskaya, the woman we met at the academy, is studying dogfighting with us, but her hopes of becoming a fighter pilot are melting away. I overheard her talking to Raskova.

"No!" she was saying. "I couldn't command a flight of three planes, much less an entire regiment."

"You've captained an aircraft," said Raskova.

"An airliner. Crewed by civilians."

Raskova waved off her objections. "You'll pick up military regulations quick enough. I'd rather have a capable commander than an experienced one. Don't forget that this is my first command too."

"People listen to you. They don't listen to me."

"They will."

"You are not listening to me. Right now. I'm telling you that if you put me in command of the 588th, it will be a disaster. Your girls could die because of my lack of experience. Do you think that's acceptable?"

"I think you might wait until you actually fail before declaring yourself a failure" was Raskova's mild reply. "I'll give you my commissar. You'll do fine."

"I won't do it."

Raskova told her, "Lieutenant, you'll follow orders like everyone else."

You'd like Major Raskova. Do you know that she studied to be an opera singer when she was a girl? First a musician, then a chemist, then a navigator, thus becoming the ultimate retort for anyone whose mother has ever said, "You'll never amount to anything if you don't settle down and pick a career!"

And then there's Captain Kazarinova. She constantly punishes people for minor infractions, most involving boots. It's hard to do anything in boots five sizes too big. Sometimes when we're marching, someone will accidentally step right out of them. Raskova burst out laughing the first time that happened. Kazarinova did not. And if the mechanics have the temerity to slip out of their boots when they're climbing on a wing or squeezing into a tight space, they have to hope she doesn't spot them.

Ilyushina, who still hasn't told us her first name, says Kazarinova has spent her whole career among male airmen and is only strict because she expects us to be as good as them. I think she needs to get laid. Her sister, the major, didn't come to Engels with us, which I'm grateful for. I hear she's even tougher.

For Iskra, attracting the wrong attention could mean far worse than a five-kilometer run—and, thanks to my slip-up, two people already know. Lilya's all right. It's Zhigli I'm worried about. And believe me, I do worry. She's been nothing but friendly, but I'm still not sure about her. If it came came down to it, she'd put herself first.

Yours,

Valka

★ EIGHT ★

14 November 1941

Dear Pasha,

We received our winter uniforms yesterday just in time for it to dump half a meter of unseasonable snow. I hope they've got you properly supplied. I hate to think of you poor boys freezing out there.

When the weather cleared up, we pilots headed out to the airfield all roly-poly in our winter gear. After an invigorating couple of hours shoveling the runway, we finally got to fly some airplanes. Major Raskova watched from the ground, taking notes on our performance.

We're training on Polikarpov U-2s, but no one calls them that. They're always "crop dusters," "sky slugs," or "sewing machines." I wondered about the latter until I heard the ticking sound of the dinky five-cylinder engine. They're puny taildragger biplanes made of canvas stretched over a wooden frame, with two cockpits and two sets of controls so that a student can sit in front and an instructor in the back.

I couldn't help laughing as Lilya climbed into the cockpit, lost inside her oversized fur flight suit. This was the pilot who would have us saying "I wish I could fly as well as Lilya"?

Then she flew. She took off smoothly, executed a tidy chandelle over the aerodrome, and made a light touchdown. It wasn't a long flight or a flashy one, but it was carefully calculated to say that she knew what she was doing.

The pyaterka aerobatic pilots followed her, their flights full of flashy aerobatic maneuvers. Raskova had nothing but praise for all of them. Waiting my turn and talking to the others, I discovered that I was the only pilot in Aviation Group 122 who had never flown a U-2. I found myself wondering if I would dominate as thoroughly as I'd expected.

"Koroleva. My favorite bush pilot," Raskova called when my turn came. When I hesitated, she said, "Go on. You can handle it, I promise. After the plane you learned on, this will be child's play."

I approached the plane, trying to size it up. In the air, would it feel like our old beaten-up plane from the aeroclub? Would it respond to the controls the same way? I put a hand on its rough canvas surface. It lacked the cold bite of metal in the winter and it gave slightly under my touch. Not a wild pony, I decided, but a mule, slow and docile. I touched the propeller and spat. Then I noticed all the other pilots giving me funny looks. But Zhigli said, "Of course—for luck. I wish I'd thought of that."

I was relieved when I climbed in and found the same set of instruments I'm used to. I taxied slowly, sure I would bounce or make a mistake in front of everyone. So I looked away from the other pilots and pretended I was back home, flying for nobody but you.

I've never flown an open-cockpit plane before. You don't understand cold until the wind hits your bare face at 100 kilometers per hour (sky slugs are not exactly racing planes). My nose and lips went numb. If I fail at training and don't qualify for the fighter regiment, I could end up stuck in one of these for the entire war.

I told myself I wouldn't spend my VVS career in a "crop duster." I would fly brilliantly, better than Lilya, better than the aerobatic pilots, and I would end up in a sleek Yakovlev fighter.

When I landed, Raskova was beaming. But my pride was replaced with dismay when she said, "Beautiful! I knew you'd be a natural with the U-2." I don't want her to think I'm best suited for a trainer!

I couldn't help being a little jealous of the navigators when I returned from my flight. They got to stay inside where it was ~~warm~~ less cold, mucking about with Vetrochets. A Vetrochet is a wedge-shaped slide rule of black-and-white Bakelite. The *numbers are painted with radium so it can be used in the dark. It is a navigator's best friend.*

Iskra refuses to let me complain. She says that I could have chosen to be a navigator.

A forlorn thought just hit me. If I get the assignment I want, Iskra and I won't fly together. Fighter pilots don't have navigators. Four years of laughing at each other, arguing with each other, complaining to each other, and even occasionally encouraging each other will come to a sudden end. Who will take care of her? Who will keep her secret from getting out?

First you and I were separated, and soon she and I will be. I thought I was taking control by coming here, but I still can't prevent this war from separating me from all the people I care about.

Yours,

Valka

21 November 1941

Dear ~~Valyushka~~ Valentina Sergeevna Koroleva,

You worry so much about Iskra. I won't tell you not to worry, because I know how much you care about her—and so do I. But I don't think you need to be concerned about Lilya and Zhigli.

Your comrades in the Red Army, not the commanders but the people you actually live and die with, are their own kind of family. I've heard things on the radio that could get a man summarily shot, but I've never repeated a word of it. I know your friends would be the same way if you would only trust them.

Right now, half the talk on the radio is grumbling about the weather. It isn't just you who's noticed the cold. Pashkevich calls us wimps. Poor Rudenko is from Odessa, and he's freezing his toes off.

Amazingly, we're pretty well outfitted with clothes. Now that all the mud has frozen solid, supply vehicles can come crunching down the icy roads, their chains sounding pale violet and brown. We have quilted coats and gloves and felt boots and fur-lined ushankas to keep our ears warm.

Food is another matter. Have you noticed how much colder you feel when you're hungry? We've got black bread in sufficient, if unpalatable, quantities, a little lard to spread on it, some hard sausage, and whatever we can scavenge, which is precious little at this time of year. Tea, salt, sugar, tobacco? Ha!

Vakhromov taught me to make nettle tea. Growing up in the country during the food shortages, he learned all kinds of tricks we never learned in Stakhanovo, where coal dust chokes everything, even weeds.

Today we took shelter from the snow in a big domed building that was a church long ago before it was turned into a community health center by the local Komsomol branch and then stripped bare by the fascists. Underneath cheap paint and the remains of ripped posters warning people to abstain from alcohol were shadowy hints of the saints who had once decorated the walls.

As we entered the main room, Rudenko lagged behind the others and made a gesture from his forehead to his chest and then from his right shoulder to his left. A cross shape.

I suddenly knew where I'd seen the symbols in his book before: in music history class, when we were learning about old forms of musical notation. It wasn't a cipher. It was an Orthodox chant in Old Slavonic. And Rudenko wasn't a fifth columnist. He was a believer.

We put the radio in the onion-domed bell tower. The bells were missing, melted down for metals, probably. Icy light blue wind swept through the tower's open windows and dusted the floor with snow. As we set up, stopping now and then to blow on our numb fingers, I told Rudenko what I'd figured out. He gave me a distrustful look and said, "It's not against the law anymore."

I told him that I'd learned a bit about stolp notation in my music theory class and asked if I could see his book.

He hesitated.

I said, "We're at the top of a tower and it's freezing. No one will climb all the way up here to find out what we're doing."

He slipped the book out of his kit bag. We brushed the snow out of the tower's most sheltered corner and sat down side by side to look at the symbols.

I said, "I can work out a bit of the melody, but I can't read the words."

A trace of a smile played on Rudenko's face. "I understand the words, but I can't read the music! My grandmother knew

Church Slavonic, but only men sang the Znamenny Chant, and there was no one to teach me, since the seminaries closed. I prayed that when they reopened the churches, they'd reopen the seminaries, too. I wanted to become a priest."

"What does it say?" I asked, touching the page lightly, as though I might damage it.

"It's open to the Christmas section. Have you ever celebrated Christmas?"

I shook my head.

"You should. You ought to see a church the way it's meant to be, when the nave is bright with candles and incense is burning and the bells are ringing. You don't know how wonderful it will be to hear that music again!"

I warned him that I wouldn't sound brilliant. "I only studied it for a few days. They told us it was obsolete."

Rudenko sighed. "Close enough. You Soviets have done a good job stamping out that sort of thing."

I didn't like the way he said "you Soviets," as though it was my fault.

He read the words and I hummed the music and we figured out the tune together. The music is strange. Folk music, the kind we sang in choir, is humble and warm and familiar, like a hug and kiss from a friend. This . . . I don't know how to describe it. Not cold exactly, but distant. Powerful. Something to be respected and maybe frightened of.

Rudenko says the word I'm looking for is "reverent." Do you know that word, Valka? It's a church word. The book is full of *new words, strings of melodic syllables that feel unfamiliar on my tongue. "Octoechos." "Irmologion." "Triodion." They are sea blue and deep verdant and they sound like water running over rocks. This music has no place in our new world, but it's sad to lose something old and beautiful, even if I don't understand it.*

Yours,

Pavel Kirillovich Danilin

"Octoechos, irmologion, triodion," I murmured to myself, as though by repeating the words I could make myself feel what Pasha felt. But to me they were only words. His world of colors was a locked garden to which I didn't have the key.

I was leaning against the wall of the mailroom. The mail had just come through and half the girls were there, reading their letters. Major Raskova had one from her daughter. She mentions her in *Notes of a Navigator*, but I could never quite accept her existence because the idea of Marina Mikhailovna Raskova changing diapers, or whatever else you do with babies, was so unfathomable.

My friends were clustered around Zhigli and giggling. Iskra waved me over. "Come here, Valka. Zhigli's got a bunch of photos from when she was a kid and they're adorable."

I took a peek. There was one of her riding a black cavalry horse, and one of her as a little girl in a traditional Cossack dress with her hair done up with flowers and ribbons, and finally her, beaming, beside a glider.

"I had to go to glider school at night because I was attending university and taking music classes in the daytime," Zhigli explained. "But I did it—here I am!"

"You don't mind that you didn't end up a pilot?" asked Lilya.

Zhigli raised her chin. "Why would I mind? Navigators are an elite group. We've been to university, we're intelligent, we're well-read, and we have good manners." She leaned heavily on the last phrase and eyed me and the other pilots.

It had been a month and my initial fears about her were fading. If someone was going to rat out Iskra, there had been plenty of opportunities. Maybe Zhigli really was just another girl trying to follow her dreams and protect the Motherland. It was hard to consider someone a threat when I'd seen pictures of her playing dress-up.

Our giggles died down as I noticed a girl standing apart from the rest of us and crying silently. It was Zhenya Rudneva, who everyone affectionately called Zhenechka, a cute blue-eyed girl in an impeccably neat uniform. She shared a name and position with Zhigli, but otherwise they were as different as two people could be.

"What's wrong?" I asked softly, looking down at the letter in her trembling hand. The news I most feared to receive filled my mind.

"I-it's from my astronomy professor," she choked. "The observatory in Leningrad has been bombed. I was studying there." Fresh tears trickled down her cheeks. "What happened to the sixty-five-centimeter refractor? The new solar telescope? The library with all those beautiful old books and manuscripts?"

I looked away awkwardly, unable to think of anything to say

that didn't sound empty and forced. I had sought out the war, but the people of Leningrad had been thrust into it against their will. It tore me up, thinking about how many civilians died every day we spent in training. Hundreds? Thousands? We girls were in a bubble, shielded from the real war raging outside. The one Pasha was living in.

I clutched my own letter and the knowledge that, as of two weeks ago, Pasha was safe. It was horribly selfish of me, but my concern for him made the rest of the war feel like an afterthought. It ate at me more and more every day that passed without a letter, and when one did show up, I walked on air for the rest of the day.

Raskova came over to Zhenechka and put her hands on her shoulders. She had the words of comfort I couldn't find. "You must be brave. There will be many more losses before this war is over."

"I'll try," said Zhenechka, wiping her cheeks with the heel of her hand. She smiled through her tears. "And I'll dedicate my first bomb to avenging the observatory!"

NINE

Dear Pasha,

You win. You may call me Valyushka if you must, only please don't use my full name again. And don't expect any Pashenka nonsense out of me. I'm an air force cadet now, not some doe-eyed village girl.

Yesterday I went on my first night flight. I felt like a little kid being allowed to stay up late for the first time. Iosif Grigorevich didn't trust us to fly after dark; he barely trusted us to fly during the day.

Everything changes at night. In the daylight, the snow is

piled into slushy drifts stained with mud and engine oil. But under the dim blue moonlight, everything is new and mysterious and a little bit frightening. The planes are commonplace trainers during the day, but at night, they're black silhouettes in the aerodrome lights.

When I lifted off, I was terrified. It felt like I was hanging in the middle of a void with nothing to distinguish the sky from the ground except the areodrome's lights. Trees and buildings were just patches of missing stars. There was no horizon. How would I know if I went wrong?

Partly because of the temperamental instruments in our aeroclub's plane, like the leaky variometer that said you were holding steady even when you were plunging into the ground, my first instinct is to double-check. But last night I couldn't. I had to let go of sight and focus on everything else. The wind biting my face. The solid weight of the air under my wings.

And then a searchlight came on in my face.

You can't tell when you see them at a distance, but searchlights are bright. It felt like needles stabbing my eyes. I knew I had to get out of the beam, but I couldn't think clearly. The best I could do was fly straight and hope to get away from it, but whatever asshole was operating it kept tracking me. Eventually the operator had mercy on me and turned it off.

I came around to land, and who was standing there by the searchlight with her arms crossed but Lieutenant Bershanskaya. She was wearing her ushanka with the ear flaps down, which made her look like a spaniel, and she was giving *me her most unimpressed squint.*

She said, "I caught you in that beam and you just sat there. If I were a fascist with a flak gun, you'd be dead."

All the replies I thought of would have earned me more push-ups.

I hope to hear from you soon. I'm in no danger here in a city far behind the lines, but I never forget where you are and what you're going through. Please tell me you're keeping safe.

Yours,

Valka

"Hey Valka, I heard you had a dazzling experience out there." Iskra was lying on her cot with one arm behind her head and the other holding her Morse code cheat sheet.

I set down my letter. "It wasn't fair! I wasn't expecting it. Three other girls flew before me and she didn't shine a searchlight on any of them."

"Do you think the Germans will call you ahead of time and say, 'Pardon us for the interruption, but we were hoping to shine a spotlight on you, if it isn't too big an imposition?'" Iskra turned to Vera. "Nikolay."

"Dash dot," said Vera. She lay with her eyes closed, savoring a cigarette while they practiced their Morse code. With her round face, girlish rosy cheeks, and curly golden-brown hair, she reminded me of an oversized doll, which made her smoking an incongruous habit.

I said, "You wouldn't have flown any better."

"At least I wouldn't have acted so surprised," said Iskra. "Konstantin."

"Dash dot dash."

I insisted, "Even you would be distracted with a hundred million lux shooting directly into your eyeballs."

"You want to talk about pain? Stick your hand on an engine block in this weather," said Ilyushina. She held up a palm red and weeping where the skin had peeled off. We all grimaced with vicarious pain.

"The point," I said, "is that dealing with searchlights is more difficult than it looks from the ground."

"Sideslip. That's all," Iskra told me. "Yelena."

"Dot. Now you're making it too easy," Vera replied.

Sitting on the end of my bed, I unwrapped my sweat-sticky portyanki and wiggled my toes. "Sideslipping is a highly technical maneuver. It isn't easy to do blind and with a headache."

"If you can't fly with a headache, you'll be useless as a fighter pilot," said Iskra.

"Did you become a navigator so you could criticize my skills without having to fly yourself?"

Vera cracked one eye at us. "Do you two not like each other?"

I said, "What are you talking about? Of course we like each other."

"Yeah, I *looooove* my little cousin," Iskra cooed. She hopped over to my cot and squeezed me in a tight hug.

I rolled my eyes. "Little cousin? I'm eight centimeters taller than you."

Iskra ignored me and turned back to Vera. "As for you, smart girl, question mark."

"Dot dot dash dash dot dot."

"Now you're showing off," said Iskra.

Vera flicked her cigarette butt into the ashtray at the end of her bed. "Memorization is the easy part."

"Yesterday you told me flight calculations were the easy part," said Lilya.

"That's only geometry." Vera pronounced it "he-ometry." "Didn't you learn that in secondary school?"

"There is no difficult part for you, is there?" Lilya exclaimed.

"Well, I've never actually been in an airplane. . . ."

"Do you find yourself appreciating Kazarinova now?" Iskra teased me. "If it had been her, the spotlight would have been on the flight plan."

"No thanks!"

"What's been up with her lately anyway?" asked Lilya. "She made me run two kilometers just because I made one extra pass over the airfield before landing."

"Yeah, who pissed in her kasha?" I said.

Zhigli said, "Didn't you hear? Her sister got caught in an air raid. Broke her leg. Open fracture. She won't be fit to fly again for months, maybe never."

I winced sympathetically. I didn't, as a rule, harbor much sympathy for the Kazarinovas, but the major was a hopeful young pilot like me once, pursuing her dreams, only to see them shattered in one burst of heat and light.

★ TEN ★

Dear Valyushka,

Today we began an offensive. And I helped. I was the one who received the orders and decoded them and passed them along obediently. This is the turning point, they tell us, when we drive off the fascists and save Moscow. Pashkevich believes it, or seems to, but I think that as long as he's in the fray exacting his revenge, he'll be happy.

We weren't even in position yet when we got into a firefight. I saw the gunfire before I heard it. Not the muzzle flashes—it was daytime—but the yellow-green stripes they painted in the air as they whistled past. I stood there dumbly, trying to place the sound.

Rudenko grabbed me by the arm and dragged me into the ditch by the road. I landed hard at the bottom, the edges of my radio jabbing into my chest. I'd broken through the layer of ice in the ditch. Freezing muddy water soaked my quilted clothes.

There was one soldier slower than me. Emelianov, another new recruit. He wavered for an instant, just long enough for another light green streak to hiss toward him and find his neck.

He clutched his throat. It was a bubbling mass of blood. He couldn't talk. He couldn't even scream. And I realized with helpless certainty that I was watching someone die.

I was surprised how easily it happened. One moment he was struggling on the road, choking on his own blood, pleading with his eyes for us to help him. Then he wasn't.

Rudenko's face turned white and he stumbled away to vomit into the ditch water. I wordlessly handed him my handkerchief. He sheepishly wiped his mouth and chin without meeting my eyes.

There was a cornfield on the far side of the road, the stalks rotten black and frozen because no one had been there to harvest the corn. The Hitlerites were in there somewhere. We crouched in the ice and mud, weighed down by our radio equipment, while the others fired over the edge of the ditch. Rudenko kissed his cross. Eventually nobody shot back.

We cautiously emerged. I tried to pretend I was only shivering because I was wet. Emelianov lay in the road. Otherwise there was no one, no trace of the enemy.

I stupidly asked who won.

"Nobody," said Pashkevich. "Let's move."

I looked down at the body at my feet: Emelianov's face was frozen in a mask of shock. "What about Emelianov?"

"What about him?"

I hesitated. The thought of crossing Pashkevich gripped me with a fear as intense as the firefight, but Emelianov hadn't chosen to be drafted and he hadn't chosen this death and it wasn't fair to leave him there like garbage. So I worked up the courage to say, "We should bury him."

"There's no time. What if the fascists come back?" The sergeant was already turning away.

"All the same, we ought to bury him." Vakhromov had come up beside me, his big arms crossed over his chest.

Pashkevich curled his lip. "Fine. Make it quick."

While Vakhromov tried to break the frozen ground, his shovel scraping with a stone-gray sound, I went through the dead man's clothes. They were already stiffening with frost. I found his identity capsule. He had filled it out. Foolish man.

We put him in the ground and I fumbled for words while Pashkevich muttered about wasting time on some idiot who didn't know to duck when he was being shot at. Rudenko joined us. He made that sign with his hand and whispered something in Church Slavonic.

I look at him differently now that I know about him. At school, they taught us that there are two kinds of religious people:

the deceptive, conniving clergy who use fairy tales of hell to keep the common people subdued, and the common people themselves, foolish and deluded. Opiate of the masses, you know. I suppose Rudenko ought to be the first kind, since he wanted to be a priest, but there's nothing deceptive about him, unless it's his use of a beard to make himself appear older.

That makes him the second kind. But he doesn't seem very, well, opiated. He's scared and jittery. When he prays, he looks desperate, like he's begging for his life.

But there's also a hidden well of enthusiasm in him, carefully buried in the face of the state's disapproval. I discovered it that day in the tower. Since then, the Znamenny Chant has become our shared secret. Because he carries my battery, we have a perfect excuse to spend time together. I set up the radio in some secluded corner—a fringe benefit of being a radio operator is that if I say "the radio needs to go here," no one questions me—and then, as soon as we're alone, we set to work, quietly, on another piece of music.

Even translated, the words don't mean anything to me, but somehow they encapsulate Rudenko's whole life. He heard this music at everything from weddings to funerals. Today, after Emelianov, he flipped to a page near the front of his book and said, "I think we should do this one. It goes, 'Save thy servants from harm.'"

"Will it work?" I asked. It was an honest question.

Rudenko turned his face away from me and wrapped his arms around his shoulders. He said, "I . . . I think it would make *me feel better. I just have this sense that—"*

"No," I broke in with sudden urgency. I knew what he was about to say and I couldn't let him go down that road. "Don't say that. We'll learn the chant."

But working on it only reminded me of the danger we were facing.

Maybe we really will win. Or maybe this will become another disaster and we will end up encircled, then silenced. Our commanding officers would throw our lives away for the tiniest advantage, real or perceived. But if we refused to follow them, then we would have no one and no orders. Is a bad plan better than no plan?

If you were here, you would think of an option other than to fight and get shot, or to surrender and get shot, or to desert and face court-martial and then get shot. That's why you're the clever one.

Yours,

Pasha

★

10 December 1941

Dear Pasha,

I ask you to tell me you're safe and you tell me about a firefight! I didn't think a radio operator would end up in so much danger. But the shifting front lines don't make any distinction, not between infantrymen and radio operators, not even between soldiers and civilians.

I saw it in the paper today: You've done it. The Germans are retreating from Moscow, the line moving back west except for one stubborn salient, a snaky tongue of fascist-held territory surrounding the town of Rzhev. I read through the whole paper looking for any mention of the Fifth Rifle Division, but there was none. Why do newspapers never report what you actually want to know? Forget about how many tanks we captured—I want to know what happened to Pasha!

What worries me most is the way you talk. No, you don't have to stop. I want to know how you're doing, how you're honestly doing and not what you think I want to hear. But this war has hurt you, and I think that even if you make it through without a mark on your body, you won't be the same.

Yesterday Raskova assembled us to meet the commander of the fighter regiment. Rumors have been flying about who would get the coveted post, but the woman who came out to meet us wasn't on anyone's list: Tamara Kazarinova. The elder one. We thought her days in the air force were over, but there she was, on her feet, though she favored her left leg. She stood before us with her hands clasped behind her back, the Order of Lenin gleaming on her chest, and announced, "There are three kinds of people I do not tolerate. Traitors to the Motherland, sloppy fliers, and cadets who try to get familiar with their superiors. If you can avoid being any of those, we can work together. If you can't, your career with the VVS will become a cautionary example."

Iosif Grigorevich called me a sloppy flier all the time, but it's the first item on her list that has me worried. She didn't get that Order of Lenin for her flying. She got it by denouncing traitors. Iskra isn't out of danger yet, and I'm beginning to think she won't be until we're safely back in Stakhanovo.

The other girls weren't any happier. Raskova's office was immediately flooded with angry fighter-pilot hopefuls, Lilya and all three pyaterka among them. They refused to be commanded by an outsider who, thanks to her injury, can't pilot so much as a glider.

Raskova, in her firm, quiet way, said that she had made her decision and that the matter was not open to discussion. If anyone absolutely could not serve under Kazarinova, she would be happy to assign her to the night bombers. That shut everyone up.

With all the regimental commanders selected, they can begin deciding the regimental assignments. That means it's time to put our countless hours of dry theory to use. To prove what we can do.

Raskova insists that there will be no winners and losers. Everyone will get the assignment best suited to her skills and everyone will play an equally vital role in winning the war. As if anyone believes that. There are no world-famous bomber pilots. They don't become aces or get featured in newsreels or get decorated as Heroes of the Soviet Union. If I want to accomplish anything, I need to fly a fighter.

Today was my big chance: the mock dogfight. All the pilots had assembled to watch, the pyaterka in front following each duel with particular interest. The judge was Major Kazarinova. Armed with a clipboard and a scowl, she watched the planes carefully, noting even the tiniest mistakes.

I faced off against Lilya. She was as small and delicate as ever, but when we shook hands before getting into our cockpits, she met my gaze with the hard eyes of a soldier. She didn't have to speak to make herself clear: We might be friends on the ground, but in the air we were enemies. No quarter would be given.

I grinned. Just the way I wanted it.

The rules were simple: The first pilot to get on the other pilot's six (that means on her tail, six o'clock according to the clock-face system) was the winner. We took off in opposite directions in our little biplanes. It was a beautiful, clear winter day. Sunlight glinted off the wings of the planes on the airfield. With sharp air on my face and adrenaline coursing through my veins, I felt—there's no other way to put it—I felt like myself. Like I was doing what I was born to do.

Lilya did a barrel roll (show-off) and headed away from the aerodrome at full throttle, teasing me to follow her. I didn't take the bait. Since our planes are the same speed, the only way to catch her would be to dive, which would place her above me and give her the advantage.

Dogfighting, you see, is all about managing energy. As you climb, you gain altitude but lose speed. As you dive, you lose altitude but gain speed. If you perform each maneuver precisely right, you come out with as much energy as you began with. But if you're sloppy, you waste energy, a little at a time, until you're *too slow to fend off attacks.*

Proud that I'd seen through her trick, I climbed and did a slow circle over the aerodrome, waiting for Lilya to come to me. Sure enough, she turned and came back. And the dance began.

A good dogfight is like a dance. Each move is precise and carefully planned. We circled each other, now close, now far, now crossing each other's paths, each of us waiting for the slightest mistake to give her an opening. I was immediately on the attack—what you'd call the lead in dancing. I would try and get on her tail and she would execute a countermove to try to switch positions.

The whole thing only took a few minutes. At first I was excited. I had the advantage and I was sure that in a moment I'd close in on her and claim my victory. But after every maneuver, Lilya's position was slightly better and mine was slightly worse. Soon she was on the attack. Whenever I thought I'd shaken her, she appeared behind me again. My temper flared. I attacked the controls like they were my enemy. My maneuvers became less accurate and I lost speed. Lilya was all over me.

Out of airspeed and ideas, I put the little biplane's nose down and went into a steep, circling dive. The world spun around me. Lilya followed. She was trying to get on my tail and win the fight before I could finish the dive. The ground loomed. I belatedly realized that I could crash and die if this maneuver went wrong, but I don't recall being afraid. Blood pumping hard through my veins, my mind was dominated by a single desire: to win.

I pulled up out of the dive so low that the girls on the ground scattered. When I'd leveled out, I looked around for Lilya.

There was no sign of her. She'd pulled out early, while I was looking at the ground.

My pulse raced. Suddenly the dogfight felt very real. I went into a tight climb. I had to spot Lilya before she pulled off whatever attack she was planning—and, more importantly, before everyone on the ground realized that I had lost her like a stupid rookie. I looked left and right, trying to see if she was in the blind spots blocked by the big double wings. And then, too late, I spotted her, diving down on me out of the sun, nearly invisible against the glare. The falcon punch. A Russian fighter pilot's favorite maneuver. She was on my tail before I could do a thing. I could only land, burning with humiliation.

Lilya hopped out of the cockpit, her face red with cold and bright with pleasure. Unable to look her in the eye, I grudgingly held out my hand to concede the victory, but instead she pulled me into a hug and said, "You were great. I had such fun. We must do it again sometime!"

I was completely disarmed. It's impossible to resent Lilya, even if she just beat you at something. Besides, I had to admit it was a fair victory. She hadn't broken the rules or played any dirty tricks. She was just that good.

We excitedly talked over our favorite parts. I said, "That was quite a dive at the end. I wonder if you could make a U-2 do a loop."

"These crop dusters? Not a chance," said Lilya.

I told her it depended on how talented a pilot was at the controls. She laughed and shoved me.

My spirits recovering, we headed over to face the major's evaluation. A few of the younger pilots broke into spontaneous applause for us. I allowed myself a small daydream. Maybe someday I'd fly as Lilya's wingman. Given what she was like as an opponent, imagine having her as an ally.

Kazarinova frowned at us and then at her clipboard. She said, "That was an adequate performance given that you're both rookies. But it's nowhere near up to par for a pair of real fighter pilots."

My mouth dropped open.

It got worse. She turned to me. "Koroleva, you were sloppy from beginning to end. You lost energy on nearly every maneuver. And when you lost sight of Litvyak, why wasn't the sun the first place you looked?"

The humiliation settled back on me. I studied the ground, trying to avoid looking at the other pilots, who I'm sure were laughing into their hands.

"As for you, Litvyak, it's no great tribute to your skill that you bested Koroleva. You should have been able to get on her six much more quickly, and without relying on the overused falcon punch. Instead you wasted your time with barrel rolls and flashy maneuvers. They were tolerably effective, but fighter pilots are not so concerned with appearances." On the last word, her eyes drifted onto a stray curl of yellow hair poking out from under Lilya's flight helmet.

Prokhorova, the captain of the pyaterka, stepped forward. "Ma'am, with all due respect, this is not a fair evaluation. Litvyak's maneuvers were tight and well executed and they got the job done. And Koroleva—well, she wasn't perfect, but she did a nice—"

"Officer Cadet Prokhorova. You will not contravene your superior officer!" barked Kazarinova. "What gives you the authority to have an opinion about this?"

"I can fly," said Prokhorova.

For a moment I thought I was about to witness a murder. But the seething Kazarinova maintained her composure, made Prokhorova do twenty push-ups, and sent her to the guardhouse to await further punishment.

Then she dragged me and Lilya move by move over our every mistake, large and small. By the end, I didn't even care anymore. If I become a fighter pilot, will every day be like this?

Yours,

Valka

Lilya set her tray down hard on the dented mess table. "And do you know what she said next? She asked me if I was sure I could reach the pedals in a Yak-1."

"Unbelievable," I replied. We were both still rankled by Kazarinova's unjust criticism.

"I see Prokhorova is back among us," said Iskra, nodding in the direction of the pyaterka pilot, who had just entered the mess hall.

"Raskova let her out a few hours ago," I told her. "Luckily, Kazarinova isn't in command of Aviation Group 122. Only the fighters, however that happened."

"She's sleeping with someone at headquarters, isn't she?" Lilya wondered aloud.

"With that face?" I mumbled around a mouthful of noodles.

"Don't talk with your mouth full," said Zhigli.

Lilya amended her statement. "Her sister is sleeping with someone at headquarters, isn't she?"

I swallowed. "Still seems remote."

"There are enough rumors about illicit relationships going around without you girls starting another," said Iskra.

"Rumors? What sort of rumors?" asked Zhigli, looking up eagerly from her navigation assignment.

"The garrison chief called Raskova into his office to accuse us of homewrecking."

"Seriously? He is vastly overestimating how much fun we're having," said Zhigli. "What did she say?"

"She asked him why he was so interested in women's gossip."

"What do you have against Major Kazarinova anyway?" Iskra asked us.

"Nothing as a person," said Lilya. "I mean besides her haircut."

"And her heinous love of leather pants," Zhigli added, gesturing with her pencil.

"Lilya Litvyak and Zhigli Zhigulenko, airwomen by day, fashion critics by night," said Iskra.

Lilya said, "But seriously, how can she give orders to pilots in Yak-1s if she has no idea what the plane is capable of? She wasn't even a fighter pilot before she was injured. She flew ground-attack aircraft."

"Bershanskaya flew an airliner," Iskra pointed out.

"And she's going to command a regiment of trainers."

Iskra hazarded, "Maybe if you weren't all so dead set on being fighter pilots—"

"Speak not this blasphemy," Zhigli told her, with a look of mock gravity.

"You're always talking about being a serious airwoman," said Iskra in a tone of supercilious wisdom. "You know what serious pilots don't do? Constantly whine about their superior officers."

"Because their superior officers can do their jobs!" I snapped. She was getting on my nerves.

Iskra said, "You could at least try not to assume that Tamara Kazarinova is the worst thing that's ever happened to women's aviation. It isn't her fault about her leg. Do you think you get top-of-the-line medical care after an air raid? She's lucky she can still walk, and she's still in a great deal of pain, even though she doesn't show it."

"Is that why she acts like such an asshole?" I asked.

"Language, Valka," Zhigli chided.

I thought nothing of the conversation then. Iskra and I argued all the time. It didn't mean anything. But later that day, at drill, Iskra wasn't at her usual place by my side. I wanted to look around and see where she was, but I had to stand at attention.

She didn't show up for dinner, either. Then I was sure she was avoiding me. In confusion, I went over my words. I'd spent the past four years annoying my cousin and she'd still come all this way to enlist with me. What had I said this time that was over the line?

Then Vera told me that Iskra hadn't been in class. Confusion gave way to anxiety. Iskra would have had to be literally dying to miss one of her navigation classes. At lights-out, I was forced to abandon all fanciful notions of extremely important errands that might explain Iskra's absence and admit that she was missing. I spent a restless night biting my fingertips and telling myself that it wasn't what I thought, that something else had happened, anything else. The next morning, I got up early, dressed, checked that my uniform was as correct as humanly possible, and went to see the chief of staff.

Swallowing hard, I rapped on the door marked "Captain Militsa Alexandrovna Kazarinovna, Chief of Staff" and received a curt "Enter!" in reply. I opened the door and discovered with a start that both of the Kazarinova sisters were in the office. The younger was reassuring the elder, ". . . general hatred of authority, but no particular agenda, certainly none that she's clever enough to carry out. You know the type. She shouldn't be a problem. And if she is, you won't have to deal with her. She's already earmarked for the night bombers." She looked up as I saluted. "What is it, Koroleva?"

"That's the other one?" the elder sister quietly asked the younger. The younger gave her a short nod.

Under the severity of their combined gaze, I found myself losing my nerve. I had never spoken to either of them beyond the requirements of military courtesy.

"Well?" asked the younger Kazarinova.

I finally managed to say, "Ma'am, Officer Cadet Koroleva, reporting a missing person. It's my cousin. She hasn't been seen in eighteen hours."

She looked at me impassively. Smoke curled upward from her cigarette.

"Your cousin," said the elder Kazarinova. Her voice was deep and coarse, and for no conceivable reason I found myself wondering what color Pasha would say it was. "Officer Cadet Iskra Ivanovna Koroleva."

"Yes, ma'am."

"Daughter of Ivan Grigorevich Korolev and Anna Petrovna Koroleva."

My heart leaped into my throat. My aunt and uncle. Their names instantly brought back that old defensiveness, the armor I'd worn when I was questioned about them. We'd all worn it in those days. We had to.

The elder Kazarinova continued, her cold words stripping away my last shred of irrational hope. "While I was going over the regimental assignments, I noticed an irregularity in her autobiography. Both of her parents were convicted of wrecking, a fact which she conveniently forgets to mention. Your local Komsomol committees were supposed to screen for anomalies of this kind, but it seems that yours chose to overlook this one. The matter will be looked into."

Her keen black eyes flicked over me in quick movements, sizing me up. "Did you have any knowledge of your aunt and uncle's actions?"

I scrambled for the right response. "Only afterward, ma'am. I lived in a different city. I was ten the last time I saw them."

The elder Kazarinova said, "Her parents' activities cast suspicion onto her own motives for joining Aviation Group 122 and her acceptability as a navigator. She is being investigated."

"She's been arrested?" I cried. No. No. No. It couldn't have happened. I couldn't have let it happen.

"Yes."

"Permission to say something on her behalf?"

"Go ahead," said the younger Kazarinova.

I kept my voice as steady as I could. "Iskra has been an upstanding Komsomol member since she was fourteen. She's the youngest member of our village committee. She is the most ardent supporter of the Party that I've ever known."

"Her parents were also, to all appearances, upstanding Party members. Your cousin may be following in their footsteps," said the elder Kazarinova.

"Your opinion has been noted, Koroleva," said the younger Kazarinova briskly. "You are dismissed."

I started to open my mouth, but the Order of Lenin on the elder Kazarinova's uniform caught my eye and I realized in time what thin ice I was treading. I saluted and left the room.

Then I buried my face in my arms and cried.

★ELEVEN★

1 January 1942

Dear Pasha,

Three weeks and this is the first time I've pulled myself together enough to write. Iskra has been arrested. Every morning I look over at the next cot and I expect to see her doing up her portyanki and buttoning her tunic. She has to be there—she has to. And every morning she is still gone. Somewhere along the line, I ran out of energy to even feel sad. Now I'm just empty.

There are things that you know with a creeping dread will happen sooner or later but can't do anything to prevent. It was like that with the war, wasn't it? So many reassurances, but we heard what they said about lebensraum, about us Slavs being subhuman and fit only to be slaves, and even though no one said so, we all knew that no treaty in the world would protect us.

Iskra has been in danger ever since her parents were arrested. We managed to keep a lid on her past while she was in Stakhanovo; being Iskra, when she said, "I moved out here to help with the development of industry for the glory of my country and the Party," it was totally convincing. She might have been safe there, where the worst she had to deal with was Iosif Grigorevich. But she had to enlist and I had to let her.

I hate myself for that. Would she have enlisted if I hadn't? I don't know. If I'd asked, she would have said it was her own choice: that she wanted to do her part to defend the homeland she loves so much. She knew the risks better than I did.

But I still should have protected her.

I'm useless, aren't I? You were drafted and I couldn't do a thing about it. Iskra was arrested and I couldn't do a thing about that. I knew that saying good-bye to her when we got our regimental assignments would be hard, but she was ripped away from me without my ever having a chance.

After I stopped crying, the first thing I did was march off to find Zhigli. I'd been right about her from the start. I caught her crossing the empty shooting range on the way to class and shoved her against a plywood cutout. "You told on her!"

She claimed not to know what I was talking about.

I said, "Liar. You and Lilya were the only people who knew and you're the biggest gossip in Aviation Group 122."

"I am not. Don't be such a—" She clapped a hand over her mouth. "Oh no. Iskra."

It was a perfect imitation of sincerity. A few months ago I would have believed it, but now I know better. I said, "It had to be you! You told Kazarinova and now Iskra's gone and I'll never—"

I choked on my words as I almost started crying for the second time that day.

She said, "If there's anything I can do . . ."

I pulled away and told her she'd done enough.

If I wanted to help Iskra, I had to aim higher. Captain Kazarinova hadn't listened to me. Luckily, she's not the biggest fish in this pond.

Then a horrible thought struck me. What if Marina Raskova had ordered Iskra's arrest? My mind revolted against the idea. It can't be. Not her. We call Marina Raskova the grandmother of Soviet aviation. I figure that makes all of Aviation Group 122 her family. And, as you said, you don't turn in your own family. But I can't deny that she had the means and the opportunity.

There was one way to find out. Iskra had been branded a traitor. Speaking out in her defense would make me a traitor. If Major Raskova was purging anyone who might compromise her aviation group, I would give her a perfect opportunity. If I ended up in the camps alongside Iskra . . . well, at least I'd be the one suffering for my mistake this time.

Raskova's office was filled with classical music from a tinny radio on the shelf. She hummed along as she filled out forms.

I marched in and began to blurt out my request, but Raskova held up a hand, her eyes on the radio. "Shh. This is Rimsky-Korsakov."

Rimsky-who-cares-akov. This was important! My opinion must have shown on my face, because she told me with a mild look, "If we are to serve in the military, we must learn patience and self-control. The war won't end before the first movement of the symphony."

And so I stood there, my shoulders slumped, and waited. I have to admit it was nice music. When the radio went to a public service announcement, Raskova folded her hands and gave me her undivided attention. "Now, Koroleva, what is it?"

These could have been my last words as a free woman, but I don't recall being nervous, just resigned. Either I'd help Iskra or I'd share her fate. I said, "Ma'am, it's about my cousin. Iskra Koroleva. I need you to secure her release. Please."

"Why do you think I can do that?"

"Because you work for the NKVD." Even saying the name of the secret police makes me feel cold.

Marina Raskova is like any other Soviet. There are parts of her life she chooses to publicize. And there are parts she doesn't. You don't earn the luxury of doing whatever you set your mind on, the way she does, unless you have a way to grease the machine's wheels. I don't remember where I heard that fact about her, nor do I know exactly what she did for the NKVD. I'd rather not think about it. She couldn't have hauled people out of their homes, beaten them, and threatened to shoot their families until they confessed to crimes they never committed. Inside my heart I knew she couldn't be like the men who took my aunt and uncle. She couldn't be.

Raskova took a silver cigarette case out of her pocket and put a cigarette in her mouth. "It's not a becoming habit for a woman, I know," she said as she lit it. "I never smoked before the war. I'll quit when it's over."

She offered me one, but Iskra had put so much effort into preventing me from smoking that it felt like cheating to start while she was gone.

Raskova asked me what I expected her to do.

"I don't know. Call Stalin." It sounded pathetic even as I said it.

Raskova's voice was kind but firm. "Koroleva, you don't know one percent of what goes on in this aviation group. You don't have the slightest sense of the work and sacrifice I've put in to get you girls here or how easily it could all be undone. And you don't understand what your cousin is caught up in. Go focus on your work. I'll focus on mine."

She hadn't exactly said no, I tried to reassure myself, but it was futile. The whole thing was futile. As if anyone would risk her own neck for a tainted girl like Iskra. A fortnight later, there's still no sign of my cousin. Raskova's answer seems clear.

I should be worried about what will happen to me, I know. Iskra's arrest puts me under immediate suspicion. After spending as much time with her as I did, I'll be an obvious accomplice to whatever crime they pin on her. Iskra will never turn me in no

matter what they do to her, but that won't make a difference.
Yet I'm not afraid. Not for myself. I brought Iskra into danger.
It would only be fair to share her punishment.

Today is New Year's. You have a sister, so you know how
much girls love this holiday. Everyone here had a fortune-telling
tradition to share. We wrote fortunes on scraps of paper and hid
them under each other's pillows.

This morning, the girls were laughing and sharing the
fortunes they had found. It was easy to guess who mine was from.
It said: "I didn't tell. I promise." I caught Zhigli's eye across the
gymnasium and crumpled up the note. I don't believe in all that
superstitious stuff anyway.

And yet I wrote "You will come home" on a torn bit of
newspaper and hid it under Iskra's pillow. Now I'm looking over
at her perfectly neat, empty bed and desperately hoping it will
come true.

Yours,
Valka

On cold days in Engels, the smoke from the factory chimneys
didn't rise but hung in the air, forming a thick layer of acrid yellow
that Zhenechka said reminded her of the clouds of Venus. It made
open-cockpit flying a dirty business. In the white-tiled bathroom,
I took off my goggles and flight helmet, ran a hand through my
mussed hair, and attempted to transfer the greasy detritus from my
face onto a towel. I gave up, dropped the towel, and stared at my
own haggard face in the mirror.

The grief came in waves. Some days I was very nearly my old self. Then something would happen to remind me of Iskra's absence and it would wash over me again, just as strong as the first time. This time it was the holiday. They said that how you spent New Year's was how you would spend the rest of the year, and Iskra was spending it languishing in a cell somewhere. Or worse.

Hot tears stung my eyes. I'd long since realized there was no point in trying to hold them back.

The bathroom door banged as Lilya entered. "Hey, Valka—oh." Her voice dropped. "Are you all right?"

"Go away," I growled. "I don't want to talk to anyone."

"I'm getting that impression." She glanced in the mirror over my shoulder and patted her soft blond curls.

"You wouldn't understand."

"You're wrong." Lilya took me by the shoulders and spun me around so that we were facing each other. "Valka. Do you know why I enlisted?"

I shrugged. "Same as everyone else. Defend the Motherland. Kill fascists. Fly fighters."

"Some of that. But that wasn't the main reason." Her clear blue eyes flitted from mine to the floor. "I haven't told anyone else about this. So please don't . . ."

There were many ways to finish that sentence, but I said, "I won't."

Lilya wet her lips. "They took my father too."

It couldn't be true. Lilya was always so bright and cheerful. I'd never seen her worried or upset—except for that moment on the train to Engels, when Iskra went off about wreckers. Could it be that all the time she was laughing, doing her hair, and showing off over the aerodrome, she was as hurt and broken as the rest of us?

I tried to think of something to say and failed. Instead I threw my arms around her and pulled her small body into a tight hug.

Lilya spoke quietly into my ear. "It was 1937. He was a railway man. Not political. He hadn't done anything; we had no idea . . . They just came for him one day. We never even found out what the charges were. I was sixteen. When I heard about Aviation Group 122, I thought, 'I can't bring him back, but maybe, if I fight well enough, I can at least redeem my family name.'"

"Oh, Lilya." I slowly released her. "I didn't realize. I'm sorry I've been such an ass."

"It's all right. I would be too. I keep wondering why it was her and not me."

I thought it was obvious. "Because no one knew about you."

Lilya looked at me reproachfully. "Valka, you mustn't. You've lived with Zhigli and trained with her for months and she never said a word about Iskra. And she's devastated. How could you think such a thing?"

What else was I supposed to think? But I didn't want to argue with Lilya. I didn't want to argue with any of the girls ever again. So I said, "You take care, okay?"

"I will." Lilya paused. "Valka?"

"Yeah?"

"Do you know what I'm most afraid of?" She swallowed hard. "It isn't getting killed. I know that might happen. It probably will.

It's going missing in action. Maybe you're over the ocean. Maybe you survive the crash and are taken prisoner, or you walk away and get killed crossing the lines. But now we have Order 270."

"Order 270." I echoed Stalin's remorseless words: "There are no Soviet prisoners of war, only traitors."

Lilya explained, "Unless they have proof that you were killed in action, they'll treat you as a deserter. My mother and brother would be all alone and they wouldn't get any benefits from my death. Yuri's only thirteen. Can you imagine what life would be like for him with two traitors in his family? I need to succeed as a pilot."

I looked at my friend, 150 centimeters tall, girlish and delicate. She as wearing a scarf she had made out of dyed parachute fabric. Lilya Litvyak was an enigma.

I knew one thing: I didn't envy anyone who had to face her on the battlefield.

★ TWELVE ★

7 January 1942

Dearest Valyushka,

I can only imagine what you're going through right now. I know there are no words I can put in this letter to make the pain go away. I wish I were there. Then I wouldn't need to use words.

I'll admit I was jealous of Iskra when she first showed up in Stakhanovo. You were so taken with her. She was so smart and sophisticated, and somehow you two seemed to have more in common from your one visit to Moscow than we did from our entire childhood. How could a kid like me compete? But Iskra was always sweet to me and she doted on my little sister, and

whatever we were doing, she always made sure I was included.
Pretty soon it was like having an extra sister.

Now I know that I didn't need to worry about losing you as
a friend. There are friends who come and go, but then there are
friends who are your second family, and those friends you never
lose, no matter what happens.

I know it's no consolation, but it needn't have been Zhigli
or Lilya or anyone who turned Iskra in. It won't make you feel
better to take it out on your friends. There's a purge going on in
the Red Army. I keep hearing about it on the radio. The other
operators' voices are on edge as they report this comrade or that
suddenly hauled off by MPs.

Our commissar stalks around, his sharp eyes narrowed,
looking for any sign of dissent among the ranks. Rudenko and I
had to stop learning liturgical music for fear that he would catch
us. It's a tense time for everyone.

But it isn't over for Iskra. You must keep hoping for her.
You talk as though Iskra has already been sent to the camps.
But I believe in her. Iskra is smart and resilient. Four years ago,
she was in a tight spot. Her parents were gone. She was under
suspicion from the NKVD. And she lived in the biggest, most
heavily policed city in the Soviet Union during a time when
anyone could disappear without notice. She could have been
arrested and shot. She could have ended up in a state orphanage.
When she fled to your family, she could have dragged that
suspicion with her and brought all of you down.

Instead she graduated school with a gold medal, earned a

pilot's license, and got a seat on the Komsomol committee. And she made it look easy. I don't mean to downplay the seriousness of her arrest. I know how much danger she's in. But don't underestimate Iskra.

I'm not one to talk, though—I worry about you. You'll say I'm silly, but I do. You'll be in combat someday and I have no illusions about how VVS pilots fare.

Whatever happens, please, please don't do anything stupid. Asking for Iskra's release was a big risk, even with someone as kindhearted as Raskova. If you get arrested, you only strengthen the case against her and make her chances of release that much slimmer. Keep yourself safe. That's the best thing you can do for her right now.

Yours,
Pasha

13 January 1942

Dear Pasha,

The navigators began flight training a few days ago. Iskra and Zhigli know how to fly, but most of the others are students with no aviation experience at all. Some of them have never been in an aircraft before. It was a little bit satisfying seeing Vera wobbly and miserable with airsickness. She is undaunted. She says that she'll go up in that transport plane as many times as it *takes for her stomach to settle down.*

Major Raskova is rotating us so that every pilot gets a chance to fly with every navigator. Yesterday I did a night flight with Zhenechka. I didn't think I would like her at first. I lost my temper and yelled at her because she misread our altitude as 9200 meters instead of 2900 meters, a mistake only a silly college student who's never flown could make. I could just hear Iskra's voice in my head saying, "The big hand is the hundreds. . . ."

But as the flight went on, my misplaced anger faded and Zhenechka began to grow on me. She's a dreamer who tells fairy tales and jots down poems among her notes and is nearly impossible to dislike. She pointed at the sky and said, "Look, Valka, there's Sirius."

Still, it's hard not to think of the navigators, no matter how clever they are, as "not Iskra."

Everyone is trying to be nice to me because of what happened to Iskra. I admit I'm not taking it very well. It turns out the only thing I'm worse at than giving sympathy is receiving sympathy. Partly it's that I hate being coddled. And partly it's that nobody wants to be too nice. No one will say, "It isn't fair—she did nothing wrong and everyone knows it," because they're all too conscious that they might be next.

The worst part is the lack of news. If I knew she'd been sent to the camps, I could come to terms with it. I could get properly angry. But for now I'm just anxious. Don't worry, I haven't asked about her again. I'm acutely aware that I'm on shaky ground myself. I think I may have squeaked by because

I wasn't a Party member. Nobody gets the Order of Lenin for denouncing a teenager from the Urals.

Bershanskaya, bless her heart, kept Iskra in the rotation with the other navigators, rescheduling her when her turn came as if she was having an endless string of sick days. Captain Kazarinova upbraided Bershanskaya for that and informed her that Iskra Koroleva was no longer a member of Aviation Group 122. And then that trace of my cousin, too, was gone.

Yours,

Valka

★ THIRTEEN ★

28 January 1942

Dear Valyushka,

*   Someone got hold of today's* Pravda. *The article on the front page tied my stomach in knots. It honored the courage of a Russian partisan killed by the fascists. It was a girl, your age. There was a picture of her and she was tall, like you, and she had dark hair, like you, and it was cut short, like yours.*

*   Being in the infantry is harrowing, but it's playtime compared to becoming a partisan and fighting behind enemy lines. Here at the front, we have the support of artillery, aircraft, and our comrades in arms. But when partisans cross the lines to*

plant explosives or burn down buildings, they are alone, a small band of Russians darting in and out among the fascist forces. Is that bravery or suicide?

The higher-ups in Moscow assigned her to burn the village of Petrishchevo, where a fascist cavalry regiment was stationed, but the fascists caught her. The people in the village say she was brave. They say she didn't tell them anything through that long night of interrogation. In the morning the fascists marched her through the village and executed her. And she was still brave. She said, "There are two hundred million of us. You can't hang us all!"

But the things they did to her, Valyushka, I can't get them out of my mind. I keep thinking of you in your airplane, so quick and deadly in the sky, so vulnerable on the ground. What would become of you if you were hit and had to land behind enemy lines? Do you ever think about that, about what might happen to you in the field? Are you afraid?

They say our offensive was a victory. I guess that depends on your perspective. Moscow is safe. But four whole armies, a hundred thousand men, were trapped behind enemy lines at Rzhev. They're holding out for now, but for how long? And if any of them throws down his weapons and surrenders, he's a traitor.

We are encamped on the shores of the Ivankovo Reservoir. It's on the Volga. I'm glad you're on the same river as me. If it weren't frozen and I had a boat, I could float gently down the river, around its twists and bends, through cities and dockyards and collective farms, and eventually I would get to Engels and I'd be with you.

The snow is so thick that you can't tell where land ends and water begins; the reservoir is a smooth patch without any trees, its shores punctuated here and there with stands of dead black reeds. Boats rest frozen in place, rows of icicles hanging from their gunwales.

The Germans are on the west bank and we're on the east. We took a few potshots at each other before getting bored and running low on ammunition. We can hear them sometimes, their voices brown and gunmetal gray. It's dangerously cold. The Germans are suffering in their thin coats, posting shorter and shorter watches to keep from freezing at their posts.

We're not much better off. When the wind kicks up and the cold gets unbearable, I think of happier winters, like the year you returned from your trip to Moscow with a brand-new pair of ice skates and we spent every waking moment out on the canal. Your nose and cheeks were always red and you had that big smile. Those were good skates. My sister still has them.

Vakhromov and I went in search of farms to scavenge food. It's the only way we can avoid starving. It's touch and go. The farmers would be struggling through the harsh winter even if there weren't a war, and then the Germans came through— twice—and stripped everything and burned most of it. At this temperature, the snow is a fine powder that doesn't stick together. Underneath, everything is bone dry. Fields of stubble go up instantly when they're lit during a retreat or hit by a stray rocket, ours or theirs. We have no skis, so we had to trudge through thigh-deep snow, Vakhromov carrying a sledge on his back.

We came upon what had once been a wheat field but was now a battlefield pockmarked with icy craters. It put me in mind of one of the chants I'd learned, and so I began to sing to myself: "I was entrusted with a sinless and living land, but I sowed the ground with sin. . . ."

I trailed off awkwardly when I noticed Vakhromov looking at me. He said, "You don't have to stop. You're a good singer. What was that?"

I said it was something Rudenko had taught me.

Vakhromov said, "I don't understand that guy. Whenever I ask him about his family, he clams up. Maybe he doesn't like me." He shifted the sledge on his shoulders.

"It's not that," I said, and asked if I should take a turn carrying the sledge.

"I'm fine. It isn't heavy."

We came across a collective farm that hadn't been despoiled. The peasants came out and kissed us, calling us liberators for driving off those filthy Hitlerites. One of the women brewed us tea. She kept apologizing that they had no sugar or lemon. It didn't matter to us; we've had nothing but water since our vodka rations ran out two weeks ago. I felt guilty taking the beets and potatoes from their root cellars. But we were full for the first time in ages.

Now we're on sentry duty. There's a fox sniffing around nearby, a red flame against the snow. She's lucky. Yesterday, we would have eaten her and made her fur into gloves. But right now I feel that there's something inviolable about her, the intent way she paces around on top of the snow, never breaking through, nose to the ground. I can hear the soft lavender crunch of her footfalls.

Have you ever seen a fox hunt in winter? She sniffs, stops, pricks up her ears, and listens. And then she leaps into the air and dives straight down through the snow, leaving her hind legs sticking up in the air. When she comes up, she has a mouse. Vakhromov thinks this is the funniest thing he's seen in ages and he laughs every time. I think that's unfair. She's better at finding food than we are.

And here's the strange part: She always jumps while facing north. I took out my compass to check. How does she know? I can't guess. But somehow facing north helps her find her prey. I think foxes are as clever in real life as they are in stories. Anyone who can survive out here must be.

Yours,

Pasha

"Do you know that foxes can find north?" I asked whoever was awake. Vera and I were both staying up to read letters.

"Magnetoception," said Vera. "Birds use it to navigate by dead reckoning, just like we do. Charles Darwin figured that out."

"Do they also use Vetrochets?" I asked. I was getting annoyed at how Vera always knew more than anyone else, regardless of the topic.

"It has never been observed," said Vera, brushing off my sarcasm. "Zhenechka!"

She waved Zhenechka over and patted for her to sit down beside her on her bed. "I have news for you."

"What is it?" asked Zhenechka.

Vera folded her letter. "I just got a letter from a boy who was at MSPI with me. He was an absolute wreck at calculus back then. He kept begging me to help him. We spent many nights practicing antidifferentiation together. If that sounds like a euphemism, it isn't; we really were practicing antidifferentiation. On his final exam he got top marks. He wanted to kiss me but I didn't let him."

"I would have taken the kiss if he was nice." Zhenechka lowered her voice to a whisper. "I'll tell you a secret: I've never been kissed by a boy."

Vera nodded sagely. "Men are intimidated by intelligent women."

"We can't all be as lucky as Valka," said Zhenechka, looking across Lilya's sleeping form at me. I was chewing my pen cap as I worked on my reply.

"I've never kissed a boy, either," I said around the cap. "Pasha and I aren't really . . ." I trailed off, not ready to face the snarl of emotions pulsing within me, definitely not ready to explain it to my friends.

"Why not?" asked Zhenechka. "He sounds so sweet."

I thought back to the moment on the barge, before Pasha saw combat, before I got letters filled with pain and hopelessness. We'd sat beside each other like friends. Like children. Was that why I hadn't kissed him? Because if we stayed children, we wouldn't have to face the reality of what was happening around us? I'd wanted to kiss him, I now realized, wanted it badly even though I wouldn't have admitted it then. I'd let that chance slip away and I might never have another.

I shrugged, trying to pretend it didn't matter. "I guess we didn't have time to figure things out. He was just the kid next door, and then he was gone."

"At least you have someone to write to," said Zhenechka. She rested her cheek on her hand and cast me a wistful look.

"You'll have plenty of time for boys after the war," I promised her.

"They're overrated," said Vera.

I asked, "So what happened to your friend?"

"He became an army engineer. I heard from him a few months ago. He was helping construct an ice road across Lake Ladoga."

I perked up. The ice road had been all over the news, a tiny artery pumping life into starving Leningrad. "The Road of Life!"

"The very same. He sent me a letter full of equations about the weight ice can bear."

"How fascinating," said Zhenechka.

"Seriously?" I said, but Zhenechka's guileless face looked completely sincere. "Sometimes I think you navigators are a different species."

"It's not our fault you can't appreciate the beauty of mathematics," said Zhenechka loftily.

"They're going to get supplies into Leningrad and save thousands of lives," said Vera. "And he told me that it might never have happened if I hadn't been sitting next to him in math class that first semester. I told him that I knew someone who had studied in Leningrad, and if he wanted to repay me, he could ask the drivers to bring news."

Zhenechka dropped her eyes. She picked up Vera's Vetrochet, lying on the foot of the bed next to some half-finished calculations, and fiddled with its wheel. "I don't think I want news out of Leningrad."

I didn't blame her. Ever since the fascists laid siege to Leningrad, each rumor from the city had been more horrifying than the last.

Vera gave Zhenechka her serious smile and held up the letter. "You'll want to hear this. He sent someone to visit the observatory. The towers and pavilions were ruins, just as you heard. But do you know what the professors told him?"

Zhenechka shook her head.

Vera lowered her voice as if she was confiding a secret. "Almost everything was saved. They moved it all to the basement when the bombing started. The instruments. Those irreplaceable books."

"The refractor?" whispered Zhenechka. "The whole tower was destroyed."

"They saved the lens. They can rebuild it when the war is over."

"Saved" was all Zhenechka could say. Tears sparkled in her eyes.

"Everything will be waiting for you at the observatory. You can pick up your studies where you left off," Vera told her.

"This war can't be over soon enough. An occupied country is

no place to do science." Zhenechka gave Vera a sly sidelong look. "But I still would have taken the kiss."

They covered their mouths with their hands and snickered. Vera said, "He wasn't my type."

"Vera?" said Zhenechka after a moment.

"Yeah?"

"When this is all over and you're off in Kerch corrupting the youth, you'll send the brightest of them our way, won't you?"

"Naturally. But right now we should go to sleep."

"As if I could sleep the night before we find out our assignments!" Zhenechka bounced in place. "I've enjoyed flying with everyone. I can't begin to decide who I want as my pilot."

Vera pointed a warning finger at her. "You can't have Tatiana Makarova. She's mine."

Tanya Makarova slept on the opposite side of the gymnasium, but I could often hear her laugh from my side.

"Tanya?" said a puzzled Zhenechka. "But she's so rude! And reckless."

"She's a whole different person in the air. Besides, she likes me. She said I was way better than that silly girl she flew with yesterday."

Zhenechka gasped. "She flew with me yesterday!" She grabbed Vera's pillow and hit her with it.

"Don't take it out on me!" said Vera, covering her head with her arms.

I warned Vera, "You're in for a disappointment. She's far too good to end up in a bomber."

"That's what everyone says, but two-thirds of you will," Vera pointed out.

"Who do you want as your navigator, Valka?" asked Zhenechka. Then she clapped a hand over her mouth. "I'm so sorry. I didn't think about what I was saying."

A pang went through me at the reminder. Every time I thought I'd come to terms with Iskra's arrest, something else happened to bring it freshly back to my mind. It never hurt any less. I retreated into the assurance I kept giving myself. "It's all right. I won't be flying with any of you. I'll be in a fighter." And I returned to reading Pasha's letter.

8 February 1942

Dear Pasha,

Yes, I saw the article about the partisan girl. They've found out her name: Zoya Kosmodemyanskaya. She has a mother and a younger brother. They waited for months before they learned her fate. I understand how they must have felt all that time, sometimes despairing, sometimes daring to hope, only to find out that it had all been futile.

But I'm not afraid of facing Zoya Kosmodemyanskaya's fate. It's too remote, too abstract an idea. But there is another fear. Something real and physical. Fire. Being trapped up there in the cockpit and knowing I'm going to burn. That's what I'm afraid of.

Today was the day I've been counting down to since we arrived: the day we got our regimental assignments. Whenever I pictured this day over the past few months, I saw myself on top of the world, screaming with joy that I'd finally achieved my dream and become a fighter pilot. Instead I'm lying here on my cot, trying to figure out what I did wrong.

I feel Iskra's absence palpably, like a lost tooth. As long as the pilots and navigators were still being tested out together, I could convince myself that she would be there next time, and that she would fly with Lilya or Tanya or me. But now it's too late. The regiments have formed and Iskra is not a part of them.

This morning I was just about boiling over with anticipation. Is anything worse than standing at attention when you're worried? You can't fidget or pace, you can only stand stiffly with your eyes fixed straight ahead. Raskova informed us that she knew there would be many disappointed faces tomorrow and that, while she's sorry that she can't give every girl her ideal assignment, she doesn't want anyone bursting into her office in tears demanding an explanation. She may know us too well.

I made a decision as they began reading out the assignments for the 586th, the fighter regiment. Iskra would never see the front. She would never fight to defend the Motherland that she loved so unconditionally. But I still could. I would prove myself in combat. I would be the best damn fighter pilot the VVS had ever seen and every fascist I killed would be for Iskra.

The pyaterka aerobatic pilots all got assigned as squadron commanders or deputies. And Lilya is going to be a fighter pilot! I was sure my name would be next.

And then they called out the last name and mine wasn't

anywhere. They moved on to the 587th Day Bomber Regiment, Raskova's regiment. I hardly listened. The guilty side of me says: What did I expect? How could I look forward to finding out my assignment when my cousin gets no assignment at all? How could I be willing to abandon her to get into the regiment I wanted? I wanted to fly a fighter more than I'd wanted to fly with Iskra. Now I get to do neither. Which is exactly what I deserve.

My name wasn't listed in the 587th. Neither were any of my friends' names. As they finished reading out the assignments for the 587th, there was a murmur of disappointment as everyone whose name hadn't been called—me, Zhigli, Vera, even Tanya—realized that we had all ended up in the night bombers.

The 588th Night Bomber Regiment is my new home. Bershanskaya will be my commander. Her brow knotted pensively as her name was read out. I should care about the people who were listed, my future comrades in arms. Ilyushina will serve as the regimental engineer. Zhenechka, despite her constant claims of being bad at navigating, managed to become a deputy squadron navigator. And yet I can't make myself feel anything for this army of not-Iskras, neither excitement nor disappointment. And that's wrong of me, too, because they're my friends.

The commander of the squadron's second flight is Tanya, and Vera is the flight navigator. I caught Tanya surreptitiously mugging at her new navigator from the other side of the parade ground. Vera diligently ignored her but grinned to herself. Zhigli is also in the flight, just my luck. And then they got to me. I'd begun to think I would get no assignment at all, which would have been a fair reward for not taking care of Iskra. But when it came, I was completely blindsided. Pilot: Valentina Sergeevna Koroleva. Navigator: None assigned.

I stood there uncomprehending as we were dismissed. I checked the roster myself. There it was in indelible ink: my name and an empty space beside it where a navigator belonged. Now I'm back in the gymnasium, watching the other pairs of pilots and navigators find each other and trying to make sense of it all. Did Raskova make a mistake? Or was there not a single navigator in the regiment who was willing to fly with me? I can't—

ISKRA IS BACK! She's here, Pasha, and she isn't hurt or anything!

I was just lying here writing to you and feeling sorry for myself when a voice nearby said, "I haven't seen you mope like that since the day the Rodina disappeared." I glanced up and found myself looking into a familiar heart-shaped face framed by blond hair just long enough to show its wave.

Jumping to my feet, I dragged Iskra into a rib-cracking squeeze that lifted her clean off the floor. She kissed me on each cheek. Tears stinging my eyes, I attempted to talk but only managed to stammer, "You're . . . I was so . . . I can't . . . How?"

Iskra said simply, "I've been released. I just got back. Militsa Kazarinova gave me quite a scolding for missing the regimental assignments, but she had a position for me anyway. Apparently there's a pilot in the 588th who needs a navigator?"

"We're flying together!" I screamed.

"Aren't you disappointed that you won't be flying a fighter?"

I'm not anymore. Not even a little. I'm exactly where I belong.

When I finally put my new navigator down, Iskra took my hands and turned them over. "Baby cousin," she said softly, "look what you've done to your fingers."

The skin around my fingernails was bitten away in raw, ragged strips. I hadn't even noticed. "I guess I was worried."

Iskra shook her head. "It's good that I'm here. You need someone to look after you. I knew it back in Moscow all those months ago when I asked Raskova to make me a navigator so I could fly with you."

When she reclaimed the bed next to me, Iskra found the note under her pillow. She laughed when she read it. I said, "Don't laugh at me for caring about you."

She replied, "I wasn't. I was laughing because you called Engels 'home.'"

Iskra doesn't want to talk about her ordeal. It isn't that she's afraid to or that it's difficult for her; she just doesn't seem to think there's anything important to say. "They investigated me, they found I had done nothing wrong, I was released," as if that was a perfectly self-explanatory sequence of events, and she won't hear a word otherwise. She brushed off my attempt to intercede for her as sweet but unnecessary. When I asked if they'd hurt her, she said, "Of course not," like I was being silly.

I asked her if it didn't bother her that she had spent two

months in prison after being wrongly arrested. She said, "This is war and there are fifth columnists trying to undermine us. The NKVD has to follow every lead if they hope to catch them, and some of those leads will be dead ends. I can't be angry if one of them happens to be me."

So I asked, "What if it was me?"

She didn't answer.

And then I thought of you. Order 270 could tar you a traitor as easily as anyone else. Whenever I hear news from the front, my skin prickles with anticipation that the next words might be "The Fifth Rifle Division was encircled and destroyed." And I realize none of us are safe.

> Yours,
>
> Valka

★ FOURTEEN ★

19 February 1942

Dear Valyushka,

I'm so glad to hear that Iskra is back! I knew she would be. I don't think any force in the universe could keep you two apart for long. Then again, I might have said the same thing about us once, and, well, it doesn't look like either of us will be home soon.

My friend Rudenko will never return home. All this time I was worried he'd fall victim to the purges. But my fear was misplaced. It wasn't the purge that caught Rudenko. It was the war.

He wasn't even fighting. He was at the back of the lines

with me, carrying the battery pack, when a shell exploded in the road not ten meters from us. A fountain of dirt and snow erupted, and for a minute I was stunned by the intense whites and yellows ringing in my ears. As they died away, I heard my friend screaming. He was on the ground. Blood spilled onto the snow. A piece of shrapnel had hit him in the belly. My head still spinning, I crawled through the rubble to his side and made a futile attempt to stop the bleeding with my hands while I shouted for our medic.

The medic patched him up, but he was bleeding internally. There was an air ambulance, one of your U-2s but with pods on the wings to hold stretchers, hopping onto and off the battlefield and picking up a couple of men at a time. Its propeller made a drab orange thrum. "It'll come get you the next time," I told Rudenko each time it flew away, even though there were thousands wounded and only a single plane.

He grabbed my sleeve with one blood-crusted hand and said, wild-eyed, "The book. The Znamenny Chant. Take it."

"It's not mine to take," I protested. I didn't have the heart to tell him that it didn't mean to me what it meant to him, that I'd never really understand those words in dark blue and green.

"If I die, or even if I only get taken to the hospital, the commissar could go through my things and find it. You have to keep it safe for me."

So I took the book and tucked it inside my coat with your letters. Its weight against my heart feels like a responsibility. I couldn't help Rudenko when he was half a meter away from me;

at least I can protect his book.

He was clutching his little cross so hard that it left an impression on his palm. I asked him why God had allowed him to get shot. He said he didn't know. I told him I thought God was supposed to be all-powerful and control everything. He said that God could control everything if he wanted to and that he could make us all do the right thing all the time, but he doesn't want to. He wants us to choose to do the right thing of our own accord, and he loves us so much that he allows each of us to make our own choices, no matter how terrible those choices are.

"Even Hitler?" I asked.

"Even Hitler."

I said, "But you were shot because of him. He's caused so much death and destruction and horror. We're giving our lives to bring an end to it, but God could stop it all in an instant and he doesn't? What good is God at all if that's so?"

He said, "God doesn't stop it all now. But someday he will put it all right. He will make everything new." And then he told me what it was to be made new. How when people repair broken things, they are never the same, but how God will make the world new and wipe away all wrongs not only in the future, but in the past, too, for God is beyond time. And then none of this will have happened.

I wish I could see the world the way he did, I really do. But I can't. I can't make myself believe that I will be made new. If I am killed, there will no longer be a Pavel Kirillovich Danilin. That's all.

It got dark and the plane stopped coming. The temperature had been well below zero all day, and at night, it plummeted. Rudenko couldn't keep warm.

He was supposed to lie still but he kept getting agitated. He asked me if he would die, and I had to keep telling him no, he would be fine, because what else am I supposed to say? He kept saying that he didn't want to die, that he hadn't had a chance to lose his virginity or become a priest.

It was wrong of me to be frustrated with him when all he'd done was get wounded, I know, but he wouldn't stop talking and he distracted me so that I encrypted a message wrong and didn't notice until I was halfway through transmitting it. I had to start over. I got a grumpy reply telling me to pay attention to what I was doing. So finally I got angry and told Rudenko that I wished he would shut up.

He looked so hurt that I immediately felt terrible. I apologized and offered to sing him something. For an instant all the fear and anxiety melted from his face and he looked the way he must have looked to those who knew him in Odessa before the war, before everything. He said, "I'd like that."

So I sang him the first chant we had learned together, the one from the church tower. He closed his eyes. I felt that I ought to sing quietly in soft sage and lavender, like a lullaby. By the time I had finished, he was gone. And then there was a flood of things I wanted to say to him. I couldn't ask him to forgive me for snapping at him nor tell him how much it meant to me that he'd trusted me with the secret of his religion, nor even thank him for all those hours carrying the battery for me.

He was my closest friend in the whole squad and he'd died cold and scared and hurting. I don't know where he is now or what he's feeling, but I hope that he went to be with his God.

Yours,

Pasha

★

27 February 1942

Dear Pasha,

Poor Rudenko. Please don't blame yourself. You didn't order the offensive and you didn't fire the shell. And because of you, your friend had someone by his side who cared about him. I guess that's the most any of us can do.

Now that she's back, I never want to let Iskra out of my sight. She'll be heading to the toilet and I'll find myself yelling, "Hey, Iskra, where do you think you're going?" and she'll laugh and say, "We're cousins, not Siamese twins!"

The other navigators were nearly as delighted to see Iskra as I was. Now they're laughing and catching her up on gossip. Iskra's arms overflow with a week's worth of Pravdas that Vera used to make a second copy of all her notes.

I tried to warn her about Zhigli. Of course she didn't listen. She grabbed me by the shoulders and looked me dead in the eye and said, "Valka. It's over. I was never charged. I have nothing to fear from here on out—I never did. I intend to put this whole thing behind me as though it never happened. Can you? Or will you drag it out because you have a grudge?"

Well, I'm not like her. Everything doesn't just roll off my back. And no matter how long we spend in the same regiment, I will never forgive Zhigli.

Major Raskova took me aside and told me that Iskra had been through a difficult time and that I shouldn't expect her to immediately be her old self. She asked me, since I knew Iskra better than anyone, to keep an eye on her and to report on how she was managing in a month or so.

She added, "See? When you are patient, things have a way of working themselves out."

Iskra is different. She slept through reveille twice and was duly punished by Captain Kazarinova. She's nervous in crowds. She has trouble following conversations, especially when several people talk at once, and struggles to make up all the material she missed. Vera works with her evening after evening and never loses patience when she can't figure out a calculation that she did with ease in November.

But, day by day, her normal self returns. There's no outward sign of her ordeal, nothing except what she carries inside, which she refuses to share. I have to put her strange behavior from my mind as we focus on transitioning from being Koroleva and Koroleva, cousins, to Koroleva, pilot, and Koroleva, navigator.

No one but Iskra could ever have been my navigator. Your navigator is more than the girl who reads the map. She is your *friend, your sister, your comrade in arms, the person who shares your triumphs and failures. No matter how many people you fly with, no one can ever replace your navigator.*

We don't get to slack off now that we have our assignments. We deploy in two months and that's all the time each of the regiments has to learn their new aircraft. And I do mean new aircraft. The fighters have Yak-1s, delivered straight from the factory along with many bitter remarks about the shortage of aircraft and the foolishness of wasting the best new machines on a bunch of girls. The Yak-1s look gorgeous lined up on their skis, those red stars standing out on their snow-white wings. The girls of the 586th are taking full advantage of their new planes' capabilities, doing mock dogfights and aerobatics overhead while we in the night bombers try to sleep. How jealous they make us!

Meanwhile, we get . . . a different model of U-2, one with bomb racks and a peashooter machine gun. The planes arrived on flatbed trucks with their wings detached. Ilyushina supervised our mechanics on their first bit of real work, reassembling the aircraft. So far the wings have stayed on. I've enclosed a photo of our plane: Number 41. She's no fighter, but I like her. I think she's the scrappy type that doesn't know she's small.

Major Kazarinova works the fighter pilots like a slave driver. There is no such thing as acceptable performance for her, only "not good enough" and "not nearly good enough." She was serious about not fraternizing with her subordinates. Lilya says they still don't know anything about her outside of her military service. Then again, if I were thirty-seven and single for glaringly obvious reasons, I probably wouldn't talk about my personal life, either.

Ilyushina says Kazarinova is doing us a favor because we'll be deployed soon enough and we'll need to have our act together then. A few more months and I'll be a daring hawk of the VVS, delivering deadly strikes against our enemies. My heart races thinking about it. But another bit of me remembers the horrors you've described and wonders if my experience won't be so heroic after all.

Raskova somehow finds time to train the fighter and dive-bomber regiments during the day and still be on the flight line with us every night. I have no idea when she sleeps. On top of all that, she's still learning herself. She knows everything there is to know about navigation, but she can barely fly. She's determined to get her skills up to par by the time her regiment is deployed.

She got a visit a few days ago from Valentina Grizodubova, her old commander from the Rodina. Grizodubova curtly brushed off the admirers who gathered around her and settled down with Raskova in the officers' mess to catch up.

Grizodubova, who now commands an all-male bomber regiment, scoffed at Raskova for wasting her time with girls and told her that she ought to come fly with them. But Raskova smiled and said that her girls were doing quite well, actually, and that she had no intention of quitting after all the work she had put into us.

Grizodubova said, "With your connections, you could have any position in the VVS that you wanted."

Raskova replied, "I know. That's why I'm here."

Yours,

Valka

★FIFTEEN★

6 March 1942

Dear Valyushka,

    Thank you for the picture. I'm keeping it in the inside pocket of my coat along with your letters and Rudenko's book. Although it's a little awkward when the other guys show each other pictures of their girls and I only have a photo of an airplane.

    I'm never sure what to tell the other guys about you. I'm sure you'd beat me senseless if I called you my girlfriend. But I'm not sure what the truth is. The only thing I do know is how proud I am of you.

    The growing certainty that we won't see each other again for a very long time and the growing suspicion that we might not ever see each other again emboldens me to say things I would never tell you to your face. Like how beautiful you are. You're going to say I'm remembering wrong, but I can still picture your face perfectly. The brightness in your eyes and the color in your cheeks when you've just finished flying. That image kept me going in the days after I lost Rudenko, when everything seemed pointless.

It was hard for me to accept that, in the eyes of the Red Army, Rudenko was insignificant and his death meant nothing. But Pashkevich simply assigned Vakhromov to carry the battery pack and that was all.

Over here, our supply lines have finally caught up with us. At last we have enough to eat, and hot meals, too! We're getting mysterious British food in unmarked tins, but we couldn't care less what it is as long as it's edible. The food put us all in good spirits, even Pashkevich, who demonstrated how to drink tea the old-fashioned way with a sugar cube between his teeth.

With full stomachs and a new supply of ammunition, we pushed to the other side of the still-frozen reservoir. For once, we actually won a fight. We drove off the Germans and claimed their campsite with only a few casualties. One of them was our commissar. He was shot in the face. I won't miss him much, but it was an ugly way to die and I don't think he deserved it.

Around the rough log barracks we found rows of hastily dug graves, graves of men defeated by General Winter. "By the power of God," Rudenko would have said. It feels odd occupying their old barracks, even though they're warmer and cleaner than ours were. Vakhromov says he feels like the dead Germans' ghosts are watching us. But for me, being here brings back memories of the barracks in Stakhanovo. Do you remember? I was only three or four when they burned down. The way my parents tell it, the coking ovens were built first, but the construction crews never got around to building the rest of the town. A one-room apartment sharing a bathroom with the entire floor felt like luxury after that.

Along with our rations we got a special treat: good Russian apples, shriveled and wrinkly, but apples nonetheless. I ate mine immediately. Pashkevich hoarded his for later. But he soon regretted his choice. The next morning he threw his pack aside in a fury and yelled, "Which one of you stole my apple?"

Of course everyone denied it. That only made him angrier. He had everyone searched, which devolved into confusion as three people had apples that they claimed were their own and nobody could remember who else had eaten his and who hadn't.

Going through our supplies, we discovered that Pashkevich's apple wasn't the only thing missing. One man lost a tin of milk. Vakhromov lost the most: a piece of bread, two tins of unspecified British meat, and, worst of all, his entire packet of sugar cubes. Just what we needed, as if we weren't stressed enough already: a reason not to trust each other. We'd starved together, shared the last slimy beets salvaged from the despoiled fields, but now that we had all the food we needed, someone had gotten greedy.

When we had worn ourselves out with accusations and finger-pointing, cooler heads observed that, since we hadn't found the stolen items anywhere around the barracks, most likely the thief was an outsider. Pashkevich switched from berating us for stealing to berating us for keeping such a lax watch that some fascist deserter could sneak into the middle of our camp and rob us.

That evening, Vakhromov and I were at work patching cracks in the walls of the barracks. I'd left my half-full mug of tea on the windowsill along with my sugar cubes. A moment later Vakhromov was lunging through the open window and grabbing someone by the collar. There was a high-pitched scream and a light green hiss as hot tea hit the snow and then Vakhromov pulled the thief in through the window and it wasn't a fascist deserter at all.

It was a boy. A skinny, untidy child with a very dirty face. He was dressed in a ragged quilted coat fastened with twine because it had lost all its buttons. He had four permanent front teeth but was missing a couple of back teeth, which I noticed because he was howling like a wild animal. Vakhromov let go, sat down cross-legged on the floor, and said, "You can stop that. We're not having an air raid."

The boy shut his mouth and looked up at us, wide-eyed and trembling. He crawled backward into the corner of the barracks. When his back hit the wooden wall, his eyes darted to the left and right, looking for a way to escape.

Vakhromov said, "I won't hurt you, I promise. Look, I don't have any weapons." He held out his callused hands, palms up. "My name is Vakhromov. Why don't you tell me yours?"

"Petya," whispered the boy, his voice a faint trace of cyan.

"Petya, it makes me sad when a little boy doesn't know any better than to take things that are not his. Did you take some of our food?"

Petya adamantly shook his head.

Vakhromov asked if he wanted to be a Young Pioneer when he was older.

Petya nodded.

"Young Pioneers must be good boys and girls and they mustn't lie. If they do something wrong, they admit it and say they're sorry. Now, did you take those things?"

A pause. Finally Petya gave his head the slightest nod.

Vakhromov told him, "Admitting that is very brave of you."

About then Pashkevich arrived. He was unimpressed. "An eight-year-old managed to sneak past all of you?"

Vakhromov said, "Petya, this is Sergeant Pashkevich. It was his apple that you took and he's angry because he only had one. Why don't you apologize to him?"

Petya silently studied his rope-soled shoes.

"Later, then," said Vakhromov. "But you couldn't have eaten all that food at once. Do you still have some of it?" At Petya's nod, he said, "I'll tell you what. If you show me where you hid it, I'll scrounge you up a proper hot dinner."

Petya put away a bowl of our squad's signature watery cabbage soup with a speed that put even us half-starved soldiers to shame while Vakhromov tried to figure out where he had come from. When he offered to take Petya home to his parents, the boy's brow trembled and he clung to Vakhromov's waist.

Vakhromov asked his superior officer if they could have a word alone, so they stepped outside. I was expecting a loud exclamation of "No! Absolutely not!" from Pashkevich, but none came. They came back in and Vakhromov told the little boy, "You shouldn't be out here all by yourself. I think you ought to come with us."

Later I asked Pashkevich about it. I told him, "I thought you didn't like children."

He grunted. "You think there weren't any kids in Minsk?"

His expression did not invite any questions as to what that meant.

He added, "He needs someone to take care of him and Vakhromov needs someone to take care of. This'll keep them both out of trouble. But if there's ever another shipment of apples, that kid is not getting any of them."

Yours,

Pasha

12 March 1942

Dear Pasha,

Yes, I remember the barracks and the fire. Do not mention them again.

If your last letter was insinuating that I should send a picture, you're overestimating how attractive I look. I've got a terrible secret for you: I've kept my hair short. It's easier to manage. You wouldn't call me beautiful if you saw me in my shapeless uniform with my wind-chapped face and my eyes red from lack of sleep.

Engels is finally showing the first signs of spring. The airfield is no longer covered in slick black ice. Wherever there are patches of bare earth, opportunistic early wildflowers are popping up. Lilya keeps bouquets in the cockpit of her plane. Neither Kazarinova is amused by this!

Yesterday I remembered that I had promised to report to Major Raskova about Iskra, so I got up early, which is late for people on a normal schedule, and went to find her. She's usually the last person up, but this time there was no light on in her office. Captain Kazarinova, who was locking the door of her own office down the hall, told me briskly, "She isn't here, Koroleva. She told me she was going into the city, meeting with some Party officials about getting better planes for the day bombers. She won't be back for another few hours."

But then Zhenechka caught up with me. She told me quietly, "I know where Marina Raskova is."

"Captain Kazarinova says she's not here," I said.

"And Militsa Kazarinova knows everything that goes on in Engels?" replied Zhenechka. She led me off to a part of the base where I'd never gone.

As we were winding through the halls, I heard something I've never heard here before: Someone playing piano. I didn't even know there was a piano here. It was coming from a little side room. Zhenechka cautiously opened the door and we peered through, and there I found Raskova, still in uniform, playing something beautiful that I didn't recognize but you might have. We slipped into the room and sat down against the wall, hugging our knees. Iskra and some of the other girls were already there.

Raskova must have noticed us, but she kept playing, her tapered fingers moving smoothly across the keys. I realized for the first time how tired she looked. She's poured her blood, sweat, and tears into Aviation Group 122 and it's beginning to show. When she finished the piece, she looked at us sadly and said, "Such dear girls. How can I send you off to be killed?"

I ventured, "We'll do our best not to be."

Raskova smiled. She began playing again while we listened. Iskra slid close to me and put her head on my shoulder. I have never felt as close to anyone as I felt to those other girls at that moment.

Yours,

Valka

★ SIXTEEN ★

24 May 1942

Dear Pasha,

Guess where I'm writing from? That's right—the front! You are now speaking to Junior Lieutenant Valentina Sergeevna Koroleva, pilot of the 588th Night Bomber Squadron.

Leaving Engels was bittersweet. We're becoming real combat pilots at last. But we're also saying good-bye to our friends in the other regiments, which has been all the more difficult knowing that some of us won't return. Lilya says this isn't the last I'll see of her: she promises she'll be on the front page of the paper soon.

Major Raskova has left us too. It's funny how the hero I

once worshipped from afar became someone I can't imagine life without, but today, after escorting us to our new base in the village of Trud Gornyaka, she passed us off into the hands of Major Bershanskaya. The girls are not sure about this new commander. She's not the sort of person you immediately trust. She doesn't talk much and she has a way of squinting into the distance as though she's somewhere else. Plus she has no more combat experience than the rest of us. Captain Kazarinova was dead set against her, but I figure that's a plus.

While we were packing, I caught Iskra very carefully wrapping up an aeronavigation book I'd never seen before. I asked her where she got it, but she wouldn't tell. She didn't bring it from home—that much I know. I bet one of the instructors gave it to her. Teacher's pet. She's probably the only member of Aviation Group 122 who owns a textbook.

I touched Number 41's propeller and spat before takeoff. Old habits die hard. We flew in formation as a regiment for the first time. It was exhilarating to see those sets of double-decker wings to my left and right, above and below, and to be in the middle, among all those red stars. We felt like a swarm of bees off to sting the fascists. Twenty of those five-cylinder engines all going at once sounded like a swarm of bees, too. Engels and Saratov, clinging to a bend in the dark ribbon of the Volga, vanished behind us.

As we neared our new aerodrome, we heard a roar, and the black silhouettes of a squadron of fighters came cutting through the clouds. Iskra said, "That'll be our escort!" But they didn't act like an escort. They circled us, then dived straight through the middle of our formation. One passed so close that I could feel Number 41 buffeting from the wind. I couldn't hear any gunfire, but how could I hear anything over all the engine noise? We had been warned that there were enemy aircraft in the area.

"We're under attack!" I yelled in a surge of panic, pulling our plane into a sharp turn and breaking away from the group in the sky slug's best approximation of a hurry. The other bombers were also scattering. The fighters pulled back to a safe distance. And then we passed through a patch of sun and it picked out the bright and unmistakable red stars on the fighters' wingtips.

It was a test. And we had failed miserably.

Humbled, we managed to reassemble and come in for an untidy landing in the rutted potato field that serves as our new aerodrome. As we formed up, heads hanging with shame and humiliation, the male pilots who had gathered out of curiosity laughed and jeered, "Can't you tell a star from a swastika?"

Raskova and Bershanskaya were waiting for us. Bershanskaya sighed and shook her head. Raskova said, "That could have gone better."

Unfortunately, that was when we met our division commander.

At first he didn't say a word, just stalked around us with his face set in a deep-creased frown, his commissar in tow, examining our aircraft and not even glancing at us. Finally he approached Bershanskaya and said, "You're in command of these little princesses?"

She said that she was.

He asked, "Are they all terrified of their own escorts, or only some of them?"

She looked helplessly up at her new superior.

Raskova stepped in. "I had hoped that they would react better to that exercise. But they've never been in combat, and we can't expect perfection right away. They're good airwomen, though. I know they'll perform to your satisfaction."

He said, "I would be satisfied if I was given another regiment of real night bombers, not girls in U-2s. But I've been told that I'm stuck with you."

Unable to get rid of us, he punished us. He assigned us two more weeks of training before he would allow anyone, even our commander, to fly an operational mission. And even then, we're on probation. "I can't cross Raskova, but that doesn't mean I have to put up with you," he told Bershanskaya when Raskova had left. "Give me the slightest reason to disband you and I will."

I would have liked to give him a piece of my mind or to watch Iskra expound to him about Marxist gender theory until he wept with boredom and despair, but apparently I've learned self-control after all, because I resisted.

Bomber pilots are all about objectives. Destroy this bridge. Take out that ammunition dump. So I set myself this objective: We will prove that we can fly and fight as well as any male regiment. No. We'll prove that we're the best damn bomber regiment the Red Army has ever seen! And Colonel Dmitry

Dmitrievich Popov will admit it.

There are only two nice parts about our arrival at the front. One is that Iskra and I have put several hundred kilometers between us and the Kazarinovas, and the other is the village of Trud Gornyaka. It's a cluster of a few dozen log cottages surrounded by collective farms. It was bombed once before the division arrived, but the villagers have repaired their homes and replanted their fields as best they can. We were expecting dugouts, so it was a pleasant surprise to discover that we're being put up in the villagers' houses.

Iskra and I are staying in a split-log cottage with a widowed peasant named Anna Alexandrovna. Faded rugs cover the walls of its single room. There's no room for a bed, but the big brick oven has a platform on top with blankets piled on it. Anna Alexandrovna told us that we can sleep there during the day and she'll sleep there at night, and if we ever need to sleep during the night, why, we'll all pile on there together as cozy as anything and it will be almost like having her own daughters home.

Right now we're sitting on the oven with our slipper-clad feet dangling over the edge, and we're holding sweating glasses of cloudy bitter-sharp kvass made with raisins. It's difficult to believe that we could be fighting and killing in a matter of days.

Yours,
Valka

★

Dear Junior Lieutenant Valyushka,

I am so proud of you! You're an officer now—if we crossed paths, I'd have to salute you and stand at attention. So would Pashkevich. Wouldn't that grind his gears? Outranked by a woman.

Something is going around at our camp. Everyone is sick. Maybe it's the food, maybe the reservoir water, maybe the bird-sized mosquitoes that pester us now that it's warm. I'll spare you the details, but Pashkevich is even more grumpy than usual when he has to visit the trench behind the camp every ten minutes.

I met an old friend for the first time today. Isn't that a funny thing to say? The division chief of staff sent a message asking to borrow me, saying that the radio operator in one of the other regiments had requested my help. So I went, trying to ignore Pashkevich's remarks questioning what I could possibly be good for.

I'd never seen the other radio operator before in my life, but he threw open his arms and said, "If it isn't Pasha from the ass end of the Urals!"

At the sound of his light orange voice, I knew him. It was my radio friend, the football fan who never encrypts his messages. We hugged like we'd known each other our whole lives. He showed me his problem. His radio had gone on the fritz and he remembered that I knew how electronics worked.

"Why don't you get the radio technician?" I asked.

"He ate it last month. Funny story: He wasn't even shot or anything. He got diptheria."

I didn't think that was funny at all.

The problem turned out to be simple. The insulation had frayed off a wire and it shorted out. He sighed with relief as I replaced it. "At least it's only a wire! If it was a vacuum tube, I'd be flat out of luck. You'd have to sell your firstborn child to get a vacuum tube these days."

That got me thinking. Was it possible to fix one of these field radios if the vacuum tube broke? My radio at home doesn't have a vacuum tube, just a pencil and a razor blade. I'll have to experiment.

Petya was supposed to be our squad's little secret, but word got out to the other squads, then the other platoons, then the other companies, and soon the whole regiment knew. A child! A reminder that once we had hoped to start families of our own, ages ago when everyone wasn't trying to kill each other. I was sure we'd catch hell from our new commissar when he arrived. But he's fond of children. He adopted his little niece after his brother was killed in combat.

It's hard to tell what Petya thinks of all the attention. At first he wouldn't say a word beyond his name. Mostly he clung to Vakhromov. Vakhromov kept trying to draw him out of his shell, giving him piggyback rides and teaching him children's games, but Petya just watched quietly, with round, solemn eyes.

My sister is only a few years older than him. When I left, she was a wild girl who could count to a thousand while skipping *rope without tripping once. What will the war do to her?*

The only time Petya makes a sound is at night. He has night terrors. He sits bolt upright with a look of panic and screams at the top of his lungs. Pashkevich grumbles, "Will someone shut that kid up!" He's worried that someday the noise will put us in danger. Vakhromov picks Petya up and talks softly to him until he falls back asleep, mindless of how the boy thrashes and hits him.

I don't know what horrors Petya relives in his dreams, but when I hear his cyan screams, I see bullets hissing past me through the cornfield, Emelianov's throat gushing blood, Rudenko freezing in a ditch and pleading with God not to let him die. I cover my ears and try not to listen and hope Pashkevich won't notice how frightened a child's nightmare makes me.

Pashkevich ruled that Petya must be able to take care of himself if he's going to stay. The boy struggled with a regular Mosin-Nagant, so the sergeant found an M38 carbine and is teaching him to handle it. It's going poorly. Teaching is not one of Pashkevich's strengths.

I was on guard duty this morning during one of these sessions, sitting on an overturned bucket and practicing harmonica to get my mind off my leaky boots. I've never learned harmonica properly. I covered different combinations of holes with my tongue and wrote down the resulting colors until I figured out the scales. I don't know how people learn music if they can't see the colors.

Petya ran up. His eyes were puffy, his face wet with tears and snot. I asked if Pashkevich was yelling at him again. He nodded.

I said, "I should say that he's doing it for your own good. But he isn't. He's just mean."

I played a quick scale on the harmonica. The boy's large eyes fixed on it. I offered him the little brass instrument, but when he blew on it, he only succeeded in covering it with spit and making a muddy-brown noise. Gravely he handed it back.

"There's a trick to it," I told him, and broke into a folk tune. Petya watched, mesmerized. It was the first time he'd shown real interest in anything, and I was determined not to waste the moment. I said, "I need help. You see, I know the tune of this song, but I've forgotten the words. I remember it was about a berry bush, with red berries with white flowers. Can you remind me how it goes?"

Petya's lips parted ever so slightly and he said in a tiny voice, "Kalinka of mine."

The grin that splashed my face was completely involuntary. "That's right—I remember now. How does the rest of it go? Kalinka, kalinka, kalinka of mine . . ."

"In the garden is a berry, malinka of mine!"

We sang the chorus several times, faster and faster. Then I jumped to my feet and danced in a circle, playing the tune on the harmonica. Petya laughed and clapped.

Petya is still quiet and serious, but I broke his silence. And I think that, even if I never accomplish another thing in the Red Army, at least I helped him.

Later, when he'd wandered off, I began singing "Katyusha" to myself. I don't know why that song makes me think of you, because it's all wrong: you're not at home treasuring my letters and I'm no brave steppe eagle. And yet it does. I wish I could see you, not how you looked back in Stakhanovo, but how you look now that you've become what you always wanted to be.

Yours,

Pasha

★ SEVENTEEN ★

OVER THE CHATTER OF BIRDS IN THE TREES I COULD JUST hear the drone of the German bombers that had been hammering a rail line near the front all morning. It was a mild, sunny June afternoon, so when I came off my shift guarding the aircraft, I was unsurprised to find my friends shunning the mess tables and sitting directly on the grass around a slightly squashed cardboard box, looking gleefully through the contents.

"Come join us," said Iskra, waving me over. She sat at the edge of the group, the tiniest distance away from everyone else. Before her arrest, she would have been in the middle. Nobody else noticed these things, but I did, and I worried about what they might be a symptom of. "Zhigli's parents sent her a massive package full of

American magazines. We haven't a clue what they say, but we're having fun looking at the pictures."

"I don't want to look at magazines. We should be flying," I grumbled. By now, the division commander's plan was clear: If he couldn't find an excuse to disband us, he'd simply ground us indefinitely.

"The magazines won't change when we get into combat," said Zhigli.

I regarded her suspiciously. Iskra rolled her eyes. "Come on, Valka. Don't be a brat."

I sat down on the opposite edge of the group from Zhigli, next to Galya, our squadron's aide-de-camp. Galya would have been rather plain-looking if she weren't constantly beaming with enthusiasm. She had accessorized her straight brown hair with a polka-dot headband with a bow on it, which made her hard to take seriously.

I peered skeptically into the box as though my grudge against Zhigli might have tainted the magazines. "Nothing interesting, looks like."

"Maybe not to you," Iskra retorted.

They were mostly fashion magazines, their glossy covers bearing photos of cherry-lipped women posing in square-shouldered jackets and patent leather pumps or frolicking on the beach wearing cat's-eye sunglasses. The pilots and navigators delightedly passed them around.

Galya looked at a photo of a socialite in a long cream-colored gown and kitten heels and then, sorrowfully, down at her hand-altered cavalry pants and artificial-leather boots. She said dreamily, "Raskova says that when the war is over, we'll wear beautiful dresses and white shoes and she'll throw a big party for us."

Riffling through the box, I found a red-bordered magazine depicting a large four-engine bomber in flight. "I found a news magazine."

"Can you read English?" asked Zhigli.

"No, but there are pictures. Look at the size of that bomber, the V-24!"

Iskra looked over my shoulder and whistled. "Our Peshkas would look like tiny insects next to that."

I licked my thumb and leafed through the magazine. There were more pictures of aircraft inside. "Look—the Americans paint pictures on the noses of their planes."

"We would have an even harder time passing ourselves off as serious airwomen if we did that," said Iskra.

Galya leaned over to see what we were looking at. She blushed and started giggling. "Most of them seem to be, um . . ."

"Half-naked babes," I said. "There does seem to be a lot of that."

"Boys will be boys," said Zhigli.

"Hang on, here's a dragon. Oh, wait, it's holding a naked babe."

"Pretty dragon, though," said Galya.

Iskra wondered, "How can she twist like that without breaking her back?"

"American women must be flexible," I said. "*Really* flexible."

"If that's what they're into over there, that dashes my hopes of eloping with a handsome American pilot," said Zhigli with a sigh.

I slapped the magazine shut and stood up. "To the airfield, Iskra! These photos have inspired me."

"To do what?" asked Iskra.

"We shall paint a naked man on our plane."

"Have you ever *seen* a naked man?"

"I . . ." I felt my face color. "There's no correct way to answer that question, is there?"

Galya's giggling redoubled.

"Pasha doesn't count," said Iskra. "Seventeen-year-olds aren't men."

"Iskra, please tell me the quickest way to make you stop talking." Baseless as her teasing was, it was still embarrassing. And today it was making me angry. Pasha had dealt with bullets and shells and freezing and starvation, and it wasn't fair to make him the butt of a joke.

I was spared further discussion when we were interrupted by our new chief of staff. Everyone set down the magazines and scrambled to attention.

"As you were," said the chief of staff, adding, "Must you do that? I was training alongside you two weeks ago."

"Would you like a magazine?" asked Zhigli, handing her one. The officer rolled it up and tucked it in her pocket. "Duty before pleasure, I'm afraid. You girls have another training flight."

Groans and complaints arose from everyone except Galya.

"We're not here to train, we're here to fight," I said as we reluctantly fell in. "Not that Trud Gornyaka hasn't been relaxing . . ."

"Speak for yourself," said Zhigli. "You're in a house. We're holed up in a stable. We call it the Hotel Flying Horses."

". . . but I want to bomb something at some point."

"You know what I think?" said Galya. "I think the division commander doesn't like us."

Iskra stopped walking and looked at her. "You should have been a reconnaissance pilot with those observational skills."

Major Bershanskaya stood on the makeshift landing strip, a section of potato field marked out with kerosene lamps, talking to Captain Ilyushina. Ilyushina had sandy hair and the resigned air of someone who was constantly stepping in to fix other people's mistakes. She was saying, "Everything looks fine. I'll recalibrate the altimeters tonight before takeoff."

"Good. The meadow to the west should make a perfect auxiliary airfield. We don't need long runways like those heavy SBs. Good morning, girls. Go get started on your preflight checks. You're hedgehopping again. The division navigator says that your navigation skills are adequate at high elevations, but closer to the ground it's only a matter of time before one of you ends up wrapped in high-voltage wires."

The pilots and navigators dispersed to their U-2s. I lagged behind and asked Bershanskaya, "Ma'am, more training? I thought our first mission was tonight."

"You're not coming. Squadron commanders only."

"Why not?"

"It's too dangerous. There might be escorts," said Ilyushina.

"Male pilots go into combat with a few weeks of training. We've had six months. Is it so much to ask that we actually get to fight?" I protested.

Working ourselves to the bone in training only to get stonewalled at the end seemed a worse fate than never being recruited at all. Popov said we hadn't proved ourselves. But how could we prove ourselves if we never faced combat?

Bershanskaya told me kindly, "Koroleva, I know you want to be a daring eagle of the Red Army Air Force, but you're still an eaglet. Give it time."

Ilyushina told her, "It's like you have a hundred and twelve children."

"It's not—" began the major, but she was cut off by an explosion followed by a scream. The three of us ducked and covered our heads before it became apparent that we weren't under attack. The source of the noise was at the other end of the field, where a couple of dazed, dirt-speckled armorers stood around a small crater. One was holding a handkerchief to a laceration across her cheek and eyebrow.

"Well?" asked Bershanskaya.

"Only an accident, ma'am," said the uninjured one. "That fuze went off for no reason!"

Bershanskaya raised an eyebrow.

The uninjured armorer admitted, "We did throw a rock at it."

"We wondered if it could go off with the safety pin still in," said the injured one, a tiny girl named Masha.

"Turns out it can."

Bershanskaya put a hand on her forehead. Ilyushina looked from the crater to one armorer, then to the other, and shrugged. "Could have been worse. They could have tried hitting it with a hammer."

Bershanskaya turned to me. "You girls aren't ready."

★ EIGHTEEN ★

11 June 1942

Dear Pasha,

The night before last, we all gathered to see the commanders off: Bershanskaya and her navigator, our squadron commander Olkhovskaya and her navigator, and the command crew of the other squadron. After all our work, only six people got to fly.

The biplanes, each loaded with two bombs under each lower wing and two under the fuselage, left the light of the hooded kerosene lanterns and were immediately swallowed up by the darkness. Soon we could no longer hear their rattly engines.

As we waited out there in the cold night air, it sank in that this was not a training mission. Out there in their little planes, those women weren't concerned with regimental politics. They faced guns, maybe even fighters. And these fighters wouldn't just play with them. It was difficult not to spend the whole time thinking of the worst possible things that might happen. In the future I'll be flying and won't have time to worry about everyone else, but for the mechanics and armorers, every night will be like this.

And then came that familiar ticking in the distance. One of our "sewing machines" had returned. It came to a bumpy landing and Bershanskaya climbed out, along with the regimental navigator. Notwithstanding that the pilot was our superior officer, we mobbed them with hugs, kisses, and cheers. The 588th was combat active! Bershanskaya gave us a modest smile. Then the command crew of the second squadron arrived. They accepted our congratulations coolly.

A few more minutes passed before we realized that our celebration was premature. Olkhovskaya had not returned. The other crews hadn't seen her get shot down; she and her navigator had simply vanished. We spent the rest of the night and the next day waiting, hope glimmering whenever we thought we heard an engine or glimpsed movement in the sky. But there was nothing.

Olkhovskaya's mechanic went to Bershanskaya with tears streaming down her face. "Was it my fault? Did something go wrong with their plane? I checked everything so carefully. . . ."

Bershanskaya should've lied and told her that the plane was fine. Instead she said honestly, "I don't know."

We knew that this would happen someday. Not all of us would come home after the war. But I wasn't prepared. In our short months together, every girl in our regiment has come to feel like an essential part of it, someone without whom the 588th wouldn't be the 588th anymore.

Truthfully I didn't like Olkhovskaya much. She was strict and humorless. But now I remember the other things, like how she milked a cow the day before she disappeared and shared the milk with us. If Major Raskova had been here, she would have known what to say to raise our spirits, but Bershanskaya has no gift for speaking.

Gone without a trace. Do you know what that means, Pasha? It means that two airwomen who were eager to fight are now listed as deserters. It means that their families get nothing, not even the right to say that their daughters were killed in the Great Patriotic War.

It was a bitter consolation that they had successfully bombed their target. Bershanskaya assembled a glum and shell-shocked group of airwomen in the morning, her face an impassive mask shutting us out from her feelings.

She informed us that, despite our loss, the division commander judged the mission a success and was ready to declare us operational. "But," she added, "I'm prepared to request one additional week to prepare. It's been a difficult night. I don't want to send you into combat if you don't feel ready."

I felt anything but ready. But I imagined Popov's reaction when Bershanskaya made her request. Those little girls play at being pilots but go to pieces at their first casualty. It was the excuse he needed, proof that we lacked the mettle to be soldiers. So I asked, "What do the male regiments do when they lose someone? Do they take time off?"

The major bit her lip and said, "No. They don't."

Our decision was unanimous. If we wanted to be treated like the other regiments, we needed to act like them. If that meant flying our first operational mission the night after our first loss, then we would fly through the pain. So Bershanskaya appointed a new command crew for the second squadron: Zhenechka and her pilot, Dina. Zhenechka was distraught about receiving a promotion over the bodies of her comrades. She tried to turn it down. The major told her she had to obey orders. It was cruel, but the squadron needed a commander. I admit I'm glad it wasn't me, that I won't be the one stepping into a dead woman's boots, issuing the orders she would have issued and flying the missions she would have flown.

We flew our first combat mission last night in the rain. Popov had assigned us an easy target. Defenseless infantry. It would be a walk in the park, he said, something even a girl couldn't fail at.

The fields were all boggy. The vehicles' wheels kept sinking in. Our ground crews dismantled a fence and used the logs to make bumpy hardstands and runways for the planes, but our fuel truck kept getting mired down. After hauling it out of the mud twice, the girls gave up and carried the fuel to the planes in jerry cans.

Dina and Zhenechka left before us. We were to follow exactly three minutes later. Iskra kept track of the time on her watch. Two days ago we were overflowing with enthusiasm. Now I wasn't sure what I felt. Not nervous, exactly, though I should have been. Unsettled, I guess. I looked back at Iskra. Her face was pure focus, her mouth set in a line.

Just before we were set to take off, Bershanskaya came running up to the side of our plane, mindless of the rain. For an instant I panicked at the thought that she would change her mind and cancel our mission. A part of me hoped for it. But she only looked up at us and said, "Be careful."

"We will," I said, hoping I could keep that promise.

The Polikarpov's wheels skidded and slipped into the cracks between the wet logs, but I got her nose up and into the air before we hit the mud. The raindrops trickling up the windscreen made it hard to see, but it scarcely mattered, the night was so dark. I had to trust Iskra to somehow correlate the shadowy shapes we could see below us to the landmarks on her map. Trust. There it was again.

Before I knew it, I heard Iskra's voice, tinny and hollow through the speaking tube, telling me, "Target in sight."

Looking at the ground, I could make out the vague outlines of barracks, vehicles, and small human figures running here and there. Smoke rose from somewhere. Dina and Zhenechka had left their mark. And then I was struck with the knowledge of what we were doing. Images flashed into my mind: fires and figures lying motionless.

And then the image of Olkhovskaya's plane, spiraling to the ground.

"When you're ready, Iskra," I told my cousin.

"Bombs away," said Iskra. There was a click and the U-2 leaped forward, light and agile without its burden.

We were flying low. As the bombs detonated, a cloud of warm steam enveloped us; it was glowing with the light of the explosions. I brought the plane around to return to the auxiliary airfield. Our airfield lanterns, called "flying mice," shine in only one direction, so if you approach from any other, you can't see anything and could easily crash. I hadn't been afraid over the target, but now an irrational fear crept up on me, a feeling that I had done something wrong, a schoolchild's fear. I found myself second-guessing Iskra, wondering if it was taking longer for us to return, if we had already overshot the field, how we would ever find it again if we had.

But then I saw the little pinpricks of light marking the airfield. I touched down and felt our plane's tires sink into the soft ground. Dina and Zhenechka's U-2 was nearby. I could hear them talking quietly.

"There wasn't any flak," said Zhenechka, her voice tinged with disappointment. "It was like a training run."

"The flowers come first and the fruit comes later," was Dina's philosophical reply.

Our ground crew came alongside to get Number 41 armed and fueled again, and Galya brought us tin mugs of tea. There was no shelter at the auxiliary airfield, so we sat on the lower wing while we waited. The upper wing kept us a little bit drier.

Bershanskaya sat on the passenger seat of a bomb truck, her feet on the running board. She didn't say anything to us, but she gave us a smile—not a shy, crooked half smile but a proud smile.

I was still shaken and unsettled from that first mission when they got the plane turned around, but I had no choice; we did another run of the same target. We were never fired on. We returned to Trud Gornyaka as day dawned. Our host was already out. We stripped off our soaked uniforms and climbed the wooden ladder to the sleeping platform on the oven. I should have immediately fallen asleep after that long night, but an hour later, I found myself sitting up, trembling.

"Can't sleep?" said Iskra.

"No," I replied.

"Me neither." She was silent for a moment. And then, "Do you want to talk?"

"No."

"Me neither."

Our next sortie is tonight.

Yours,

Valka

★NINETEEN★

22 June 1942

Dear Valyushka,

The front has moved on and left us behind. We can't even hear the artillery anymore, but whenever there is dark red and purple thunder, I find myself ducking and trying to figure out where it's coming from. Pashkevich swears at me, calling me a baby who's afraid of storms. Petya isn't afraid of thunder, Pashkevich says, and he's ashamed to command a soldier who isn't even as brave as a little boy.

Petya has warmed to us, but I don't think he'll ever be like other children. He doesn't play or run around. Mostly he sticks close to me or Vakhromov. I wonder if it was right for us to force him into a life of military privation. And there's that knowledge in the back of my mind, Valyushka, that absolute certainty that this reprieve is only temporary. One day I will hear those red-orange dots and dashes and we'll be thrown back into combat. What happens to Petya then? Which is crueler, Valyushka, to abandon him or to bring him with us?

Vakhromov organized a summer school for him. I'm his music teacher. I teach him children's rhymes and folk songs, things I sang in choir when I was a little boy. He liked "Katyusha" but was confused by the line about the gray steppe eagle. He thought Katyusha's boyfriend was really an eagle. I laughed and told him no, it only meant that he was strong and brave, like an eagle.

"Like you?" he asked, to my bemusement.

I said, "I don't think so. I think he's more like this." And I showed him the picture of your airplane. I told him how you and Iskra dart into enemy territory and strike them from the sky when they least expect it. He liked that.

Teaching him gets my mind off how sick and miserable I am. We sit on the grass by the reservoir, draw notes in the dirt, and sing. Sometimes I accompany him on the harmonica. There's a book of music in my pocket, but I never use it. If I showed it to Petya, he might talk, and if the commissar found out, he might take it from me, and Rudenko gave it to me to protect.

The reservoir is beautiful in the summer. Sometimes it's

as still as a mirror and sometimes the wind breaks it up into ripples that make the sun sparkle off it. And when it rains, it makes a periwinkle pattering sound and you can't tell where the sky ends and the water begins. But Petya discovered that it has a secret. I was cleaning my gun by the bank when he ran over and said, "Danilin, come look." He calls us by our last names like a soldier.

I stood on the ruins of the church on the steep part of the bank and looked where he pointed. It was a calm day. The water was like green glass. Far out in the middle of it, beneath the water, there was a town. Dozens of houses, some destroyed, some intact. The roofs were thick with fuzzy green algae that waved gently with the current. Eerie dark windows and doorways. People lived there once until someone decided that we needed the water and electricity more than they needed their homes.

I imagined the water rising to fill the reservoir, overflowing the riverbanks, running down the streets, welling up around the foundations of the buildings, pouring in under the doors and through the windows. I wonder if the people who lived there watched as their former lives disappeared in the flood. How helpless they must have felt, the way I felt last summer, listening to the news.

"Did many people drown?" asked Petya.

"No. They evacuated the town first," I said, hoping that they had.

Petya pointed. "What about him?"

A body floated facedown near the bank on the far side of the reservoir, tangled in the reeds. It wore a waterlogged uniform. Wehrmacht gray? Russian khaki? I couldn't tell. A fat crow perched on its back, pecking at the exposed flesh of its neck. I pulled Petya close to me and told him we would practice inside today.

I wondered how long that body had been there, polluting the water. Had it been trapped in the ice upstream and floated down when the Volga melted? No. It wore a light summer uniform, not a heavy coat. All might be calm here at the reservoir, but to the east, at the town of Rzhev, men were still fighting and dying over a tiny strip of land.

I didn't want to know what else the river had sent us, but it had to be done. I smoked a quick cigarette to psych myself up and went walking upstream along the reservoir's twisty bank.

And there they were, piled up in a serpentine inlet where the current had washed them. Dozens of them tangled together, their bellies bloated, their vulnerable faces pecked away. The sight made my skin crawl. But we stopped drinking from the reservoir and now we're beginning to feel better.

Sometimes the whole world feels like a death trap.

Be safe, Valyushka. When you wrote your letter, you had flown two runs. You will have flown more by the time this reaches you. I'm keenly aware that any one could be your last. I know, you'll say it's silly of me to worry about you when I am in constant danger myself. Maybe it's just easier for me to dwell on what's happening to someone else.

I'll recite a chant from my liturgical music book for you. I *don't suppose there is any truth to all that, but what harm can it do?*

Yours,

Pasha

★

3 July 1942

Dear Pasha,

Only a few weeks and I feel like a seasoned veteran. There have been mistakes here and there, but we're learning. Not fast enough to please the division commander, though. To him, a dozen successful sorties can be outweighed by a single out-of-place jot in a logbook, at least if the offending jot was penned by a woman. Iskra says we can't expect someone his age who served under the Tsar to know any better. But he has not, so far, found cause to disband us.

There are two other night-bomber regiments in our division. The 459th flies the last of the big, broad-winged Tupolev SBs. The SB might look familiar to you: it is a descendant of the Rodina. They think of themselves as the real airmen who go on important bombing runs while we in the "broads' regiment" play with our toy planes.

And there's the 650th, which flies the Polikarpov R-5, another two-seater biplane slightly bigger and much uglier than the U-2. The men of the 650th have taken a liking to us. They call us their "little sisters." There's a friendly rivalry between our regiments. Their commander calls Major Bershanskaya in the middle of the night to tease her and compare how our regiments are doing. They're ahead by a solid margin. Their commander says not to worry; there's never been a women's regiment before, and all things considered we're doing well. Bershanskaya is not mollified.

Flying over occupied territory is difficult. Not because of the danger, but because of the destruction. When it's cloudy, it isn't so bad. Everything is indistinct, just specks of light. But then there are clear nights when the moon comes out and we can see everything: the fields churned up by tank treads and pockmarked with shell craters, thick plumes of smoke rising from burning farms and houses, cities reduced to nothing but a few isolated walls, black and gray and bathed with silver moonlight.

After one of those nights, I found Zhenechka crying on Dina's sturdy shoulder. She used to live here. I slid next to her and said, "We'll drive them off. We'll win it all back."

She said, "But it won't ever be like it was before."

And that made me feel out of touch and ashamed for being from a town that war has never touched, for knowing that I'll never see the remains of a place I loved as a burned-out ruin, not unless the entire country falls.

The first time we were fired on, I wasn't afraid, only confused. When the shells pass by you, they make a hissing sound and you see the trails of smoke from the tracers, and then boom, boom, earsplitting concussions as they explode. You can taste and smell the smoke and it chokes you. They can rip our fragile planes to pieces, but our stubborn mules keep flying with holes torn in the wings and shreds of canvas flapping in the wind. We haven't lost anyone since that first night.

Still, it's terrifying. I put fear from my mind while we're flying, but as soon as my feet touch ground, my hands start shaking and my legs melt. Bershanskaya says it's normal. It would be bad, I think, if I wasn't afraid. We're not immortal. We're so vulnerable up there in our fragile little planes. Especially since, after the first few nights, we stopped wearing parachutes. Foolish, I know. But without their weight, we can carry more bombs.

Worse than the guns are the searchlights. Nothing makes me feel more helpless. Sometimes four or five blind me from all directions and I can't tell up from down. Iskra is my salvation at those times. In combat she hasn't lost her presence of mind for even an instant. Once I felt the control stick squirm under my hands as she took over, and I only then realized that I had frozen up in a panic. I don't know what I'd do without her.

The rattling engines of our sewing machines were giving us away. The fascists heard us coming. I came up with the solution less by conscious choice than by instinct. I was approaching the target, getting tenser every second as I waited for the flak to begin, and the engine noise felt so painfully loud that I thought, "I wish I could shut it off!"

I thought of our old plane with the faulty engine and of all the times at our aeroclub when I'd killed the engine and had to land the plane like a glider. So I disengaged the engine and glided over the target while idling, making no sound except the whistle *of the wind through the control wires. I could hear the soldiers below speaking their ugly language. It nearly worked brilliantly. They didn't know we were there until we dropped our bombs. Then the searchlights swung around, looking for our silent plane. A clever pilot would have started up the engine and darted away before the searchlights had a chance to catch us. Unfortunately the pilot was me, so instead I attempted to hit the throttle and wondered why nothing was happening before I remembered that the engine was off. I managed to get it reengaged right as the searchlights settled on me, and we escaped with a lacerated horizontal stabilizer.*

I expected a reprimand when we reported at the end of the night. I'd disobeyed the flight plan and gotten shot up. But Bershanskaya said, "That's brilliant! Try it again tonight. If it works, I'll have everyone do it."

And that's how my momentary instinct became our regiment's official procedure.

Tanya perfected the technique. She and Vera have quickly proven themselves the best airwomen we have. Tanya puts her U-2 through aerobatic maneuvers that make me forget that she's flying the exact same plane as me. They get sent on all the most important runs, taking out bridges and crossings and running the occasional perilous daylight mission.

Their closest call came when we were bombing an ammunition dump. We saw their plane caught in the intersection of two beams. Tanya was flying straight, not even attempting to maneuver. Their rudder had been torn off in the barrage.

I remember thinking that the 588th could afford to lose me, but that Tanya and Vera had to make it back at all costs. So instead of dropping our bombs on the ammunition dump, I veered off, and Iskra dropped them over the searchlight battery. Brilliant flashes and showers of sparks, then darkness, wonderful darkness. Vera and Tanya slipped away and limped back to the airfield using only their ailerons. Vera said it was the longest three minutes of her life.

Can I blame the fascists for shooting at us? We're trying to harm them. I've killed people; I know I have. Some as evil as Hitler. Others, maybe, as innocent as you. It bothers me less than it should. The details are hidden from me. I don't know how many casualties I've caused, whether they died quickly or whether their deaths were long and lingering. Without knowing, without having to see my handiwork up close, it's easy to put it from my mind, easy to laugh and sing with my friends as we head back to the village at the end of a good night. I haven't told the others how effortless I've found it to become a killer. I'm afraid of what it says about me.

We've each been flying two or three runs a night. There's a chance to rest in between while the ground crew gets the plane turned around. Bershanskaya caught Vera and Ilyushina playing chess on the wing between missions and scolded them. "Don't you have anything better to do?"

"We're waiting for the armorers, ma'am," said Ilyushina.

Bershanskaya walked off with her brow furrowed, muttering, "There has to be a faster way to do this."

I think she's too hard on the ground crews. The click-snaps (that's what we call the armorers, after the sound of them loading ammo belts into the machine guns) have to wrangle 100-kilo bombs with only a flashlight for illumination, or sometimes nothing but the moon. They work bare-handed so that they can feel what they're doing. In the day, while the aircrews sleep, the mechanics and armorers are still up, cleaning the guns, patching the canvas, and getting the planes ready to fly again the next night.

We're packing up now to leave Trud Gornyaka, retreating along with the front. Temporary fences are being dismantled, trucks loaded, good-byes said. Soon we'll be sleeping in dugouts. "Like real airmen," say our big brothers in the 650th.

Despite all the noise and bother and our churning up their potato field beyond recognition, the villagers are sad to see us go. It pains me to think that tomorrow this place might be overrun by the fascists, to imagine that cozy little house where we slept on the brick oven burned to an empty husk or, worse, serving as a headquarters for those jackbooted thugs. Anna Aleksandrovna says she'll be fine. She's lived through two wars and a famine already, she says. This won't be the end of her.

How are you getting along, Pasha? I'm glad that you're out of danger for the moment, but I know how quickly that can change. Sometimes when Iskra and I are working out our flight plan on a map, I let my eyes stray off the edge and think about which way your reservoir is and how far. Too far. Impossibly far.

Yours,

Valka

★ TWENTY ★

WITH REDDISH-BROWN CLOUDS HIDING THE SETTING sun, I had to do the preflight check by the stark light of the "flying mice." Number 41 rested lightly on the crushed, rutted grass between the other two planes in my flight, wingtips rocking now and again when a gust caught them. Today I saw the three planes not as mules but as a line of cavalry horses lined up for the charge, stamping and pawing the ground in their impatience as we and the other aircrews circled around them.

The crew of armorers were struggling with a bomb. There was something odd about its shape and the style of its fins.

"What are you hanging on my plane?" I demanded.

"It's a German bomb," said Masha the armorer. "We captured a fascist munitions dump."

"Well, don't give it to me! I'll take real Soviet bombs, thanks. Put it on Tanya's plane."

"Belay that order!" said Tanya, appearing from behind her plane, which was Number 9. "I'm the flight commander and I shall take the Russian bombs."

Masha made a face. "You're both out of luck. These are all we have, unless you want concrete practice bombs."

One more way we were being treated like second-class citizens. I asked, "Do they even fit our planes?"

Masha waggled her hand noncommittally.

"Well. Life is life and we shall have to make do," said Tanya. She walked over to the navigators and I followed. They were clustered around a map planning our route. Iskra had out her little aeronavigation book.

"How's that going?" I asked.

"We've got a tricky job tonight, thanks to the clouds," said Zhigli, making a face. "I heard the division navigator asking Bershanskaya, 'Do your girls know how to navigate through clouds? Will they get lost if they can't see landmarks?'"

"On the bright side, not even an eagle would be able to spot us through that," said Tanya.

"You can be happy about it; you aren't concerned with trivialities like finding the target," said Vera.

Tanya rested her chin on her navigator's shoulder and put her arms around her. "Verok, darling, I trust you absolutely."

Galya, our aide-de-camp, vaulted onto Number 9 like the gymnast she was, a stack of letters in hand.

"Galya, our plane is not your climbing toy," said Vera.

Galya responded by flipping upside down with her knees hooked over the edge of the cockpit. She held up a battered envelope. "This is the closest I'll get to a plane while I'm in the VVS, apparently."

"Are you still sore about your assignment?" I asked.

"Don't I have a right? I have my pilot's license, but they didn't even make me a navigator."

"Someone has to be on staff," I said, privately thankful that it wasn't me.

Galya plopped onto the wing's leading edge and said forlornly, "I didn't even know there *were* staff positions in the army. I thought everyone carried guns and killed people."

"Truly this war has disillusioned us all," said Iskra.

Galya held up a battered letter. "Anyway, Valka, there's a letter for you."

I took the proffered envelope.

"News from Pasha?" said Iskra, and the rest of the flight perked up. None of them had boyfriends of their own, so they loved hearing about mine, no matter how many times I told them that he was nothing of the sort.

I had been hoping for something from Pasha, but I had no intention of betraying the depth of my disappointment. I said loftily, "For your information, this letter is from Lilya. I wrote to ask how things were going at the 586th."

"Lilya?" Interest piqued Iskra's voice. "How's she doing?"

I unfolded the letter and read. "'Hello, Valka! It's so nice to hear from you,' etc, etc. 'I've heard that you girls are wreaking havoc all over the front. But we became combat active first, and don't you forget it.'"

Tanya snorted. "Guarding an aircraft factory in Saratov across the river from where we trained doesn't count as being combat active."

"It's not a contest," said Vera.

"'The 586th had to compromise and hire some male mechanics because our girls don't have enough training to work on the complex Yak-1s by themselves. It's a good thing my hair is growing out. I looked terrible at Engels! I have decided to be in love with one of the mechanics. His name is Tolya.'"

Galya stifled a squeal of excitement. Zhigli said, "It's about time!"

"'I know you'll think I'm very silly, but that's because you have not seen Tolya. Anyway, you can hardly criticize me given all the time you spend writing to that dear boy of yours, who I sincerely hope you've . . .' I'm skipping that part."

A chorus of disappointed voices. Iskra tried to grab the letter. I slapped her hand away and continued reading. "'Is the 588th still untainted by menfolk, and if so, how are Iskra and Zhigli holding up?'"

"With difficulty," said Iskra.

The next paragraph ordered me to make up with Zhigli. I skipped that part, too. Never mind that Iskra wasn't permanently harmed, I still couldn't forgive Zhigli for what she'd tried to do. "'The men certainly aren't the problem around here. That would be Major Kazarinova.' No surprise there. 'Her leadership style consists of always finding something to berate us about. Our regiment came in first in the division for marksmanship, but all she had to say was that we were too slow recovering from dives!

"'If you ask me, she resents that we get to fly while she's permanently grounded with an injury. She says we ought to respect her because she spent ten years laying the groundwork for women in the VVS and none of us would be flying now if it weren't for her, not even Marina Raskova. As if that made her any better a commander. What she doesn't understand is that a leader is more than her technical qualifications. She needs to be someone we want to fight for.

"'The pyaterka and I have had enough. We went to the division commander and demanded that she be replaced.'"

Iskra whistled. "Insubordination!"

I kept reading. "'We didn't get our way, of course. But we are getting out of her crew-cut hair and reclaiming our natural place at the top of the aviation food chain: our regiment is being split up and I'm being transferred together with the pyaterka pilots and a couple of other girls. You'll never guess where we're going: Stalingrad. The hottest part of the front. . . .'" My voice stumbled. I hadn't read the letter ahead of time, and this part blindsided me. The letter had exclamation points, but I couldn't read it with the excitement Lilya seemed to have.

Everyone went quiet.

"'It isn't the most logical transfer. We're being sent to a regiment that flies LaGG-3s. How will my poor mechanic find Yak parts over there? I know perfectly well that Kazarinova is just breaking up the troublemakers. But so what? I'm going to shoot down some Fritzes!' And she ends with 'Give love and kisses to everyone.'"

The others had lost their smiles. Tanya and Vera edged closer to each other. Galya flipped awkwardly through her stack of letters, opening her mouth and closing it again, and finally said timidly, "Is she really going to Stalingrad?"

"That's what the letter says."

"'Hot,'" said Iskra. "That's one way to describe Stalingrad."

Tanya exclaimed, "Stalingrad's a death trap! We lose ten planes a day there. You send someone to the far east if you want them out of your hair. You send them to Stalingrad if you want them dead!"

"Maybe it will cool off," I said, knowing it wasn't true.

"Number 41 is all set," announced Masha, and we had to end our discussion and get into our planes.

We took off into a gloomy night, the cloud bank as thick and heavy as a gray wool blanket. Warm mist condensed on my face and trickled in droplets down the instrument panel. Our U-2 was its own tiny universe.

Lilya's letter occupied my mind. She was being sent to her death. And at Kazarinova's command. Once again I felt another friend being torn away from me.

The 586th was fragmenting before it had scored a single kill. The 587th was still training. Somehow the 588th, the regiment I had once considered a consolation prize, was the only one that had seen real combat.

Even that might not last if the division commander had his way. But at least I understood his prejudice against us. I still couldn't wrap my brain around Kazarinova. I thought of our own commander. No matter what the front threw at us, Bershanskaya protected us at all costs. If she were to give me an order like the one Kazarinova had given Lilya, it would be a betrayal.

"We're here," said Iskra.

We were still surrounded by featureless gray. I disengaged the engine and brought Number 41 down out of the clouds. Our target was a barracks, full of soft, unarmored targets, foreign invaders who wanted to enslave us. I had to think of them that way, because if I let myself imagine them as people like Pasha, even for an instant, then my feelings would rebel and I wouldn't be able to bring myself to complete the mission.

Better yet, think of them as nothing but a pattern of lights that I have been assigned to hit, a training exercise, a game.

"Bombs away," said Iskra as the plane gave a familiar lurch. The finned ends of the bombs disappeared into darkness. A cluster of plumes rose behind us, then died away quietly. I reengaged the rattly engine and pulled up the elevators. But Number 41 didn't come out of the glide as nimbly as usual. Something felt off.

"Do you feel that?" I asked.

"Yeah, our slug is a little sluggish," came Iskra's reply.

I looked over the edge of the cockpit. A dark, round shape clung to the bottom of the lower starboard wing. "I knew it! A bomb didn't release."

"No problem. Take us over that road. I don't want to waste it."

I obliged. There was a click, another click, and an exclamation of "That is one stuck bomb. Give the wings a waggle. Maybe you can jostle it loose."

I rocked the aircraft, but the last bomb stubbornly refused to fall. My initial thought of "I knew captured bombs didn't fit right" was quickly overwhelmed with uneasiness. I licked my dry lips and said, "Iskra, this is a problem."

"I'm aware. Do you think you could land her?"

I was good at landing, but one false move and that bomb would detonate. I thought of the planes crowded on the airfield, mechanics checking the instruments, pilots and navigators waiting in their cockpits or getting out and stretching while armorers surrounded their aircraft, Galya running around delivering tea and letters. And us landing in the middle of that, carrying death. "It's too big a risk. You'll have to release it manually."

"Manually, as in . . ."

"As in with your hands."

"Are you crazy?" Iskra was losing her cool. Iskra never lost her cool.

I tried to speak with the authority of an aircraft commander instead of a nervous cousin. "You're over the lower wing. I'll keep her level. Go."

The ticking engine slowed as I throttled it back as far as I could without stalling the plane. I heard the click of my cousin's harness being released. Glancing back, I glimpsed Iskra putting a leg over the edge of the cockpit and onto the wing's ribbed surface. She slipped between the control wires and stepped out onto the middle of the wing, clinging to a wooden strut with one hand while holding out the other for balance. She stood over the remaining bomb.

Cupping a hand around my mouth, I yelled, "Try bouncing!"

"Bouncing?" The wind nearly whipped away Iskra's reply.

"Jump on the wing. Gently! Don't put your foot through the canvas!"

The biplane shuddered. When I looked back again, to my relief Iskra was still there. So was the bomb. Iskra knelt, then lay flat on the wing. Still gripping the strut with her left hand, she reached out over the front edge of the wing and felt for the manual release.

We had been following a pale ribbon of muddy road speckled with black water-filled craters, but now I spied a dark obstruction ahead, small and distant, but growing quickly. It resolved itself into barracks, tents, vehicles. I yelled, "Iskra, I have to turn!"

"No!" Iskra screamed. I could only make out half her words. ". . . barely holding on . . . bank . . . I'll . . . and die!" And, raising her voice, "And then I'll kill you!"

"Then hurry up! There's an encampment ahead."

Iskra tremblingly let go of the strut. She pulled herself forward so that she could reach farther under the wing and fumbled with the bomb rack. The encampment loomed. A row of flak guns stabbed the sky. Were they manned? I couldn't tell. No searchlight beams cut through the darkness, but they could light up in an instant when the operators heard our rattling engine. My instinctive fear of the guns vied with the need to protect my cousin. I risked a look at the wing. Iskra brought her hand to her mouth and pulled off her soft leather glove with her teeth. She reached down again.

I cut the engine. My fingers dug into my palms, numb with the effort of holding back my fear, of not grabbing the control stick and pulling us out of there. As dead silence enveloped our little aircraft, voices rose from below. The guns were manned. I held my breath. Surely they couldn't spot the plane in the darkness. Nothing up here, just endless black sky.

As Number 41 reached the encampment, there was a jolt. The bomb fell.

It detonated with a bright flash. The plane shuddered from the impact of the hot air. The searchlights came on as their crews scrambled into position. I reengaged the engine and gunned the U-2 forward. I tensed, waiting for the shells to rip into Number 41's fragile canvas skin.

A scream rang out. Iskra had slipped. She was clinging to the back strut, one hand gloved and the other bare, her legs hanging over the edge. In a moment of panic, I had to suppress the urge to climb out of the cockpit and help her. All I could do was fly straight and level. Iskra got a footing on the wing with one leg, then the other, until she could reach forward far enough for me to grab her forearm. She had lost her glove. I pulled her up so she could clamber into her cockpit.

At first there was no sound but the two of us catching our breath, and then we burst into relieved laughter. Iskra looked back. "I think we hit one of the guns."

★ TWENTY-ONE ★

16 July 1942

Dear Valyushka,

We captured a couple of German scouts yesterday. Not spies, just regular soldiers in faded camouflage. They were about my age, proper blond Aryan boys, but ragged and scrawny as starved rats. I expected them to be defiant. They weren't. They seemed dazed, like they weren't sure what had happened or how they had ended up here.

It was impossible not to see myself in them. I wondered if they had enlisted or been drafted, whether they fought because they truly believed in fascist ideals or because they were made to fight, or simply because Germany was their home and they didn't know what else to do.

Pashkevich interrogated them himself. I don't know if he was supposed to or if he just wanted to. Of course they didn't speak Russian. Pashkevich berated them and smacked them around a bit for that and then found someone to translate. Petya clung to Vakhromov, who whisked him away, muttering, "The child doesn't need to see this."

Turns out they didn't have anything to tell us that we didn't already know. Pashkevich refused to believe that. He took out his service pistol and struck one of them across the mouth. It broke his jaw. The other begged him to stop and swore that they had already told him everything. So Pashkevich shot them. First the wounded one while his comrade watched. Then the other. One bright orange gunshot after another.

Pashkevich saw me staring at the bodies. He said, "Do you have a problem, Danilin?"

I said, "No, sir."

He said, "Good. Now take out this trash and bury it." And I did.

I could make excuses. I could say that it wasn't my place to say anything or that it wouldn't have made any difference. But the truth is that he was hurting them and I was afraid that if I tried to stop him, he would hurt me.

Or worse, give me the pistol.

I keep thinking about what I would have done if he had ordered me to shoot them. I wish I could say I don't know. But

I do. I would have done it. I would never have forgiven myself but I would have pulled the trigger. I wouldn't have had the courage not to.

You worry about what bombing the enemy says about you. But you're doing what must be done in a time of war. If no one was willing to drop bombs, we would lose the war and we would all be enslaved or slaughtered at the hands of the fascists. Those scouts, though, their deaths helped no one. And I allowed it to happen. What does that say about me?

Our vacation by the reservoir will come to an end soon. We're awaiting orders. I'm reluctant to touch my radio for fear of what I'll hear. Do you remember the troops encircled at Rzhev, how they bravely held out for all those months? They're gone now. Wiped out. If they weren't important enough to save, I have no illusions about what will happen to us.

Yours,

Pasha

★

29 July 1942

Dear Pasha,

Part of me wants to ask how Pashkevich ever became an NCO, but I know. The Red Army likes them that way. Hard and angry and ready to do anything. But we can't let ourselves become like that, not even to win the war. If I were there, I would straighten him out. And he would have to listen to me, because I outrank him.

I don't want to hear you agonizing over what you should have done or what you didn't do, and especially not what you might have done under other circumstances. You can't change what's already happened. All you can control is what you do next.

I'm keenly aware of this. Our regiment has suffered two disasters, and the second one was entirely my fault.

The first was a freak accident amid the chaos of rebasing. The fascists are still pushing us back. Every few days we're forced to move again, flying through skies thick with smoke from fields set alight by fleeing peasants who had no time to harvest them. There's a rumor that the village of Trud Gornyaka was burned to the ground. I feel sick thinking about what might have happened to Anna Alexandrovna and the other peasants. Iskra saw me poking at my kasha at breakfast and she gave my hand a squeeze, too quick for the others to notice. She knows when to not say anything.

Moving around as much as we do, we can't always tell what parts of a particular field are for planes, what parts are for vehicles, and what parts are for people. That's what caused the accident. Iskra and I were reporting after a third sortie when there was a scream and a squeal of brakes. We dashed over. Galya, worn out from running errands around the airfield all night, had lain down for a short rest. A fuel truck was rushing to the planes. The driver didn't see her until the wheels met her.

Galya was alive, but in bad shape. Her face had lost its usual color and was very, very pale. Sweat broke out on her forehead with every ragged breath she fought to draw as they lifted her onto a stretcher to await the air ambulance. We held her hands and told her, "You'll be okay, Galya, just hold on," even though we were far from sure.

I've never seen Bershanskaya so furious. I can only hope her fury is never directed at me. She ripped into the already-miserable driver and threatened to have him court-martialed.

When she came alongside Galya's stretcher, Galya grabbed her sleeve and, struggling with each word, said, "Promise me that when I come back you'll let me fly."

I was amazed. Lying there grievously wounded and she was thinking about what she'd do when she returned. Of course Bershanskaya promised.

We slept very little the next day as we awaited news. The call that came from the hospital, to our surprise, was good. Galya had injured her spine, but it wasn't broken, as they had feared. The doctors were impressed by her resilience. If all went well, they said, she'd be fit to return to duty in a month. She had a message for Bershanskaya: "Remember your promise!"

It was such a relief to know that we wouldn't lose our precious Galya. The accident was a reminder of what could happen to any of us at any time. I resolved to take special care of Iskra the next time we flew, and I slept extra close to her afterward beneath the aircraft's wing.

Sometimes we relocate so hastily that there is no time to

construct dugouts and we sleep on the airfield under the wings of our planes. The ground crews thoughtfully park the planes on high spots to keep us from getting soaked if it rains. But it's hard to sleep in broad daylight with only a cockpit cover hung over the edge of the wing, especially when a mechanic starts banging around on the engine right above you. One benefit of canvas: it hurts less than aluminum when you sit up too fast.

One of those days I woke and Iskra was gone.

I found her on a hill near the airfield, stretched out on the grass with her eyes closed. Sunlight bathed her delicate face. I lay down next to her and whispered, "Trying to get a tan?"

She laughed without opening her eyes. "No. I'm just enjoying it. I spent weeks in a cell, two meters by three. Sometimes I wondered if I'd ever see this again." She gestured broadly at the sun and the sky and the rolling grass of the steppe.

She acts so normal, I almost forget that anything had happened to her. But Iskra doesn't have the luxury of forgetting. I asked, "Do you want to tell me what happened? I hate that you have to carry that alone."

"No, baby cousin," she replied. "I just want to feel the sun."

Amid everything, it's amazing that we get any flying done at all. But we do. And that brings me to the second incident.

I really don't want to tell you about this one. I'd rather let you keep telling everyone how proud you are of me, your hotshot pilot friend. But however much I hate to disappoint you, lying to you is even more unthinkable.

It goes back to the partisans. There are thousands of them

in fascist territory, from bands of a few dozen furtively cutting telephone lines in occupied cities to brigades with hundreds of fighting men and women. Surrounded by fascist forces, they have only air supply as their lifeline. Our agile biplanes can dart in and out of their forest hideaways, dropping ammunition and medical supplies or airlifting out wounded men.

The partisans light signal fires to guide us, but the crafty fascists light their own fires to draw us off. We get around this by prearranging a signal pattern. One night the partisans will place the fires in a triangle. Another night it will be a cross. Tonight it was three fires in a row along the patch of clear ground that served as a runway.

Something else was different today: Zhigli flew as a pilot. Bershanskaya has promoted her. She was a cautious navigator, but in the front cockpit, she's fearless. The only thing she worries about is what might happen to her former pilot if she's not around to take care of her.

The weather was foul. There was rain and a difficult headwind that kicked up into gusts strong enough to wrench the controls from my hands. Zhigli was flying ahead of us, but we couldn't see a thing through the lashing rain.

We caught a glimpse of her as we neared the drop zone. She should have already dropped her cargo and gone, but instead she was circling the clearing. I waited for the white shapes of parachutes to pop open underneath her plane. None appeared. After a couple of circles, her U-2 peeled away. But it didn't head back to the airfield. It passed us and Zhigli waggled its still fully loaded wings, then turned north—the opposite direction she should have gone.

"She wants us to follow her," said Iskra, as if I didn't know what a wing waggle meant.

"I know," I said a little defensively. "But what is she doing?"

Iskra sounded doubtful. "Something must have gone wrong with the drop."

We were over the clearing. I spotted a line of three lights, flaring up and dying down erratically in the wind. Everything looked fine, and I told my cousin so.

She said, "It's the right signal, but . . ."

I didn't have time for Iskra's waffling. I brought Number 41 down to the right altitude for a drop.

Iskra didn't pull the release. She said, "Maybe we should follow Zhigli."

"I have no idea what she's up to and I won't follow her to find out. Come on, Iskra, you know Zhigli gets ideas. She doesn't want to fly if she hears a dog howling because she thinks it's a bad omen. Stick to the flight plan."

"She must have had a reason."

I'd had enough. I wanted to mark off that fiftieth sortie. So I said, "Junior Lieutenant, I'm the commanding officer of this vessel and I'm ordering you to make the drop."

We're real soldiers now, not play soldiers. She obeyed my order.

When we were back at the airfield, trying not to slip on the wet canvas as we climbed out of our cockpits, Iskra said, "I can't believe you pulled rank on me!"

"Sorry," I replied. "The middle of a sortie is not a good time for a sudden change of plan. Please don't be angry."

"But Zhigli . . ."

Her plane came in just then, still laden with supplies. "She's all right. And see? She failed to make the drop."

Water streamed down the stairs of the plank-roofed command dugout as we headed to our debrief. We waded in, trying not to splash.

We found Zhigli there, doing what she does best: getting other people in trouble.

". . . north to south. But the partisans' runway runs east to west!"

Bershanskaya riffled through the papers on her desk and found an aerial photo of the partisan camp. The makeshift buildings and paths that made up the partisan camp reminded me of the pattern of wires and tacks on your homemade radio. "Look at that—you're right! What were the exact instructions?"

Our head of communications said, "'Three fires in a line along the runway.' Not 'three fires in a line east to west.'"

"Right, so any Germans who intercepted the message wouldn't know which way to line them up," said Zhigli.

Bershanskaya asked, "Did you find the real drop site?"

A small mercy for me, Zhigli hadn't.

"We'll try again when the weather clears up. No harm done."

"No harm done by me," said Zhigli. She pointed at me. "I tried to warn her, but she ignored me! You made the drop, didn't you, Valka?"

I said sharply, "I completed the mission. It wasn't my job to follow you on your flight to nowhere."

"And it never occurred to you that I might have had a reason? You thought I was going for a joyride in a rainstorm carrying a hundred kilos of ammunition?" Zhigli's dark-lashed eyes narrowed. "Or did you think I was leading you into a trap?"

"You can't expect me to trust you," I said.

"You should have," said Bershanskaya. Her face was stern, with no hint of the good humor that usually danced beneath the surface. "It was a copycat signal."

I had a sinking feeling in my stomach as I realized what that meant.

Zhigli crossed her arms. "You dropped your cargo in the middle of a German camp. The fascists just got an early New Year's present."

"'I'm the commanding officer of this vessel and I'm ordering you to make the drop,'" muttered Iskra, mimicking my voice.

"You're not in trouble for making the drop, Koroleva," said Bershanskaya. "You had no way of knowing. It was an accident. Two heavy machine guns and ten SMGs' worth of accident, but still. The real issue is why you ignored Zhigulenko's attempt to alert you."

Zhigli began, "Because she's convinced I'm—"

Bershanskaya held up a hand to silence her. "I know there's bad blood between the two of you. It doesn't matter why. But you need to work it out. Short of pistols at dawn, I don't care how, just deal with it. I can't have two pilots in my regiment who won't work together, and I won't separate you like squabbling schoolchildren. Understood?"

"Yes, ma'am," I said, gritting my teeth. I couldn't explain that this was more than a playground fight.

The major dismissed Zhigli, but told me, "One moment, Koroleva. There's one more thing you need to do."

She made me tell the division commander.

Heading to that meeting felt like being sent to the principal's office after picking a fight with the boys at school; and like my defiant preteen self, I made up a long list of excuses, blaming Zhigli or the partisans or the weather. Except then I realized who would most easily take the blame for me. Iskra. There was an entirely different way to look at the fiasco: a questionably loyal navigator with known ties to wreckers deliberately drops weapons into enemy territory, despite clear indications that it is the wrong location.

No. No one could be given cause to look into Iskra and her past. She might have escaped unscathed last time, but the arrest was a permanent black mark on her record. She would never be truly out of danger. And that meant I had to take the fall, completely and unequivocally. I had messed up due to pure stupidity and that was the whole story.

You can imagine how that went. The division commander has been waiting for a mistake like this since we arrived. I got a long lecture in which the words "girls" and "useless" frequently coincided. Bershanskaya managed to cool him off a bit, but in the worst possible way: by pointing out that Zhigli hadn't made my mistake and that it was therefore a single pilot's isolated error, not representative of the whole regiment.

He didn't disband us on the spot, though he wanted to, but he did ground me for two days. It would be longer, but we're at war and we can't spare pilots, even censured ones. Worse, he's contacting his superiors. Says he's willing to go all the way to the top if that's what it takes to get rid of us. However that goes, it's safe to say that I've set our regiment's efforts to prove our competence back to zero.

I guess the list of people who believe in me is back down to just you.

Yours,
Valka

★ TWENTY-TWO ★

2 August 1942

Dear Pasha,

Galya can barely sit up, but already she can't wait to be back with the regiment. Every day she asks when she'll be well enough to return. She's bored out of her mind at the hospital. She and Zhenechka write each other poems and stories and Zhenechka reads them to the rest of us. It keeps Galya occupied—and us too, because we're rained out.

Last week's rain kicked up into a beautiful summer thunderstorm. Lightning flashed and the downpour was so torrential that we couldn't see a meter ahead. Lucky me: I was grounded on days when there was no possibility of flying anyway.

There was also no chance to rest or relax. Thunder constantly boomed overhead. Our dugouts were half flooded. Vera, in the bed by the doorway, would put out her hand to test the depth of the water during the night. If it was only a few centimeters deep, she'd say, "It's fine, go back to sleep." But when it got shin deep, she'd throw on a coat and wade out to the pump truck to get them to pump it out.

Colonel Popov made good on his threat: he complained about us to the marshal in command of the front. Turns out the marshal and Major Raskova go way back. Keen to see how her regiments were faring, he arranged an inspection the day the weather cleared up. And, he told us, he was bringing a friend.

I was nervous about the inspection, in part because of our damp and bedraggled state, but mainly because I was convinced Germans would show up somewhere armed with Russian SG-43s at that exact moment. It didn't help that his friend turned out to be Tamara Kazarinova.

Kazarinova, wearing her customary frown, immediately stalked, or rather limped, over to Bershanskaya.

Bershanskaya said truthfully, "Major. This is a surprise."

"I've been hearing so much about your regiment that I wanted to see it for myself," said Kazarinova. "I would have thought that a brand-new commander might take it slow and spend more time learning how things are done, but you've jumped in as though you've commanded your whole life." Her tone left no question as to how she felt about this upstart civilian.

"During wartime, we must all step up to greater responsibility," said Bershanskaya.

"What's this I hear about your girls gliding? Your mechanics didn't have trouble installing their engines, did they?"

Bershanskaya replied that our gliding technique was strategic and had, so far, been highly effective.

"Frankly, I'm impressed by what you've accomplished here," said Kazarinova. "Given your level of experience, it's amazing that you've even gotten those trainers off the ground."

That was enough for Bershanskaya. She said in a tone of carefully controlled politeness, "How's the aircraft factory? Still unthreatened, I hope? It must be nice having such a relaxing assignment that you can afford to take a few days off to visit an old friend. But I suppose your regiment can spare you easily enough, since you can't fly anyway."

Kazarinova glowered, but she only said, "Knowing Marina Raskova doesn't make you untouchable. Remember that."

She retreated to rejoin the marshal. Bershanskaya bit her lip while the rest of us sneaked nervous glances at each other, trying to gauge how much trouble she had just gotten us into. She's made us a very dangerous enemy.

But I can't say that any of us blamed her.

To my astonishment, the marshal actually seemed pleased with us. He's the same man who inspected us in Engels all those months ago. He praised us for how far we'd come, saying that Raskova's girls were all grown up. Then he turned to Popov and said, "But it's probably hard for the girls in the ground crews to *do everything themselves. Why don't we send them ten or twenty men to do the heavy work?"*

Our infuriated armorers yelled, "We don't need any help! We're fine on our own!"

The marshal smiled indulgently and said that of course we were.

Popov broke in to say, "They may look like soldiers, but they've been a disaster. They mistook their own escorts for enemy aircraft and they accidentally delivered an airdrop to the fascists—at least I hope it was an accident. They're a danger to themselves and a liability to the rest of the division."

"This is what happens when you put a civilian in command of rookies," said Kazarinova.

The marshal brushed them off. "Cut them some slack— you have to remember that you're dealing with young girls, not battle-hardened men. All things considered, I think they're doing very well."

So our regiment will not be punished for my mistake. Yet the inspection left a bad taste in my mouth. I don't want to be treated like a girl if it means what that marshal meant by it, being handled gently and forgiven when I mess up because I can't be expected to do better.

Major Bershanskaya agreed. When the marshal was gone, she addressed us. "There you have it, eaglets—he says you're doing well . . . for girls. Do you know how often I hear that? 'Your pilots fly so well for women.' 'Your girls are doing such a great job, almost as good as the men.' I'm not satisfied with that. Are you?"

Of course no one was.

She turned to me. "Junior Lieutenant, how many sorties did you fly on the seventeenth?"

I checked my logbook. "Two, ma'am."

She said, "Your big brothers in the 650th all flew at least three."

I ventured that their planes were faster.

Ilyushina put her hands on her hips. "And if they become elite Guards and we don't, I'm sure you'll find it adequate consolation that you were outflown by the mighty Polikarpov R-5."

Bershanskaya asked her how quickly a ground crew could turn a U-2 around. Ilyushina said it could take as little as five minutes.

"Explain to me how we're only fitting in two sorties a night," said Bershanskaya.

Ilyushina shrugged. "Maybe they can't cut it in the field."

Protests broke out up and down the line from the mechanics and armorers. Bershanskaya asked a click-snap, "I won't accept that what takes you five minutes in theory takes an hour when you're under stress. What's the real problem?"

She had singled out Masha, the girl who'd had the accident with the detonator. Masha still has a white scar on her forehead. She stammered and said, "It doesn't take that long—I mean, it shouldn't. But everyone is trying to get to the fuel truck or the truck carrying the bombs and we get in each other's way." In an even smaller voice, she added, "Also, ma'am, I'm not complaining or anything—we all want to do everything we can for the war effort—but we load and fuel the planes all night, and we service the weapons during the day. We never have a real chance to sleep."

That day, we discovered the genius hiding beneath Bershanskaya's reserved exterior. She conferred with Ilyushina and this is what they came up with: No more ground crews for each plane. Instead she divided the mechanics and armorers into groups and assigned each group a specific duty. One group would meet the planes and bring them to their hardstands, another would refuel them, and so on.

The next morning at breakfast I sat down next to a pilot from the 650th and asked him how many sorties he'd flown that night. He proudly told me that he had flown four. I got a long explanation of his heroic bombing missions and a generous offer to take me up in his R-5 and give me a few pointers before he got around to asking me how many I'd flown. I offhandly told him, "Seven. But I was last in the flight order."

Next thing I knew he was wiping tea off the table.

Our competition with our big brothers is not a competition any longer. Now we outstrip our objectives every night and they find many different ways to say "What?" "How?" "That's not possible!" We run out of bombs and our armorers have to beg, borrow, or trick their way into getting more.

In a few months we've cracked a problem that no one at the VVS had been able to solve. Bershanskaya told Ilyushina to write up a report for the division engineer so the other regiments could adopt our procedure. But instead of accolades, Ilyushina acquired a reprimand for violating the Technical Maintenance Manual and Bershanskaya got a strongly worded letter from Popov warning her that if she didn't follow regulations, our flying days would be over regardless of how much the marshal liked us.

"Predictable," said Ilyushina.

Bershanskaya asked her, "How often do you actually see the division engineer?"

"Not since we first arrived," replied the captain. "He's too busy keeping those obsolete Tupolev SBs in the air."

"So he has no way of knowing if we're following the manual or not."

"I . . . suppose not," said Ilyushina, who had figured out where the conversation was going and didn't look completely on board. "But if Popov catches on, it's all over."

Bershanskaya thought it over. She said, "I'd rather spend a few weeks as an excellent regiment than the whole war as a mediocre one."

And so she made a pragmatic decision: Ignore the reprimand and keep doing it our way.

Yours,

Valka

P.S. Have your orders come through yet? Tell me the instant they do. Maybe they'll bring you closer to my edge of the map.

★

14 August 1942

Dear Valyushka,

Yes, our new orders came through. I felt nauseous as I decoded them. Rzhev. Even the name is the color of blood. My friends on the radio call it the "meat grinder."

The first thing we saw when we arrived at the salient was a battery of armored trucks carrying big racks of parallel rails for launching rockets. When Pashkevich saw them, his face split into a feral grin and he yelled, "All right! Those will send the Fritzes running scared!" And to me, "You've finally met the Katyushas."

That night, the Katyushas fired.

Why did the army give such a pretty name to such a horrible machine? When those rockets lit up in a salvo, they made a sound so unearthly that its color was not a real color: blindingly bright, yet black, pure jet black. As they screamed overhead, Pashkevich sat on the roof over the dugout door and laughed. "Eat rockets!" he shouted at the Germans.

I retreated to the far end of our dugout and huddled there, trembling, my eyes squeezed shut and my arms covering my head. You'd be ashamed of me.

Another voice joined the cacophany. Petya was screaming. A piercing, prolonged scream, breaking only for an occasional gasp of air. Vakhromov sat on the bed next to me, cradling the boy in his arms and speaking soothingly. Deep creases lined his forehead. The war is wearing him down.

Pashkevich reentered the dugout and caught me cowering.

He backhanded me and shouted not to be such a coward. I'm nearly as frightened of him as I am of the Hitlerites, even though they're the ones who will kill me. Then he turned to Vakhromov and ordered, "Shut that kid up!"

"I'm trying, but he's frightened," said Vakhromov.

Pashkevich drew his sidearm. He said through clenched teeth, "Shut him up or I will."

Vakhromov drew the boy closer to him, his eyes darting back to the officer with the gun. "Petya? Petenka, listen to me. You have to quiet down now. I know you're scared, but . . ."

Petya kept screaming. I took his hand. He dug his nails into my palm. I searched for words, anything that could reassure him, but couldn't find any.

But I did have a song.

I opened my mouth, but choked on the sound. I cleared my throat and tried again. "Apple and pear trees were blooming." At first my voice was barely audible, but as I continued that familiar song, it grew stronger. Soft gold tones began to paint over the piercing black.

Petya cracked one eye open a sliver. His screaming diminished to whimpering. Another volley of rockets howled outside. Their noise sliced through the music, so sharp it felt like physical pain. I faltered. Then a new color entered the song, sky blue, timid and quiet.

Petya was singing. I found my voice again and sang with new strength. We finished the last verse together.

One side of Pashkevich's mouth tightened, but he said

nothing, holstered his pistol, and left the dugout. Petya looked up at me, showing his big front teeth biting his lip in a hesitant semblance of a smile. Vakhromov said, "That was brave."

He's wrong. Even while I sang, my heart was pounding and my cheeks were wet with tears. The truth is, I'm anything but brave.

I'm scared, Valyushka, so scared, and it feels all the worse because you are always so bold. Please don't hate me. Please don't think I'm a coward. I don't want to be even though I probably am. I shouldn't be writing this to you but I have to talk to someone and I wouldn't dare say so to Pashkevich or Vakhromov or even my radio friends. Maybe I won't send this letter. Maybe I won't get a chance.

Yours,

Pasha

★ TWENTY-THREE ★

IT WAS MIDMORNING, OR THE BEGINNING OF THE NIGHT for the 588th. I was snapping open and closed one of the hair slides that had proliferated everywhere as the other girls grew out their hair and trying, not very successfully, to fall asleep. My nerves were still shot from the night before. It had been a creepy night. An eclipse had turned the moon a sullen red. Zhenechka said it was beautiful. Zhigli said it was bad luck. I only knew that I hated flying beneath it.

And then there were the dark blue pills. The regimental doctor gave them to us pilots to keep us alert. They keep us alert, all right, and narrow our irises down to nothing so that our eyes look dark and strange. I had taken one before my last flight of the night and now the thin stripe of light that fell through the crack in the shutters seemed unbearably bright.

It was not a good night to be struck with insomnia. The words of Pasha's last letter ran circles inside my brain. His hopelessness was beginning to scare me. But anything I might say to console him would feel empty or, worse, falsely cheerful, because he really was staring a horror in the face, and my words couldn't shield him from it.

I sighed and propped myself up on my elbows.

We were based in a schoolhouse, the only intact building in a bombed-out town long since evacuated. The other girls' sides gently rose and fell under their blankets. Vera was sitting at the teacher's desk, rolling cigarettes out of coarse military-issue tobacco. I raised myself onto my elbows and said quietly, "You might as well get some sleep if you can. She'll be fine. That mission will be easy compared to those daylight bombing runs you love so much."

Vera asked, "If it was Iskra, would you be sleeping?"

"Of course not."

Tanya entered the classroom, pulling off her leather flight helmet and unbuckling the belt around her baggy flight suit. She was a willowy young woman with heavy-lidded eyes and a long face usually decked out, as then, with a big, sloppy smile. Vera looked up and relief flashed across her face.

"Did you stay up all this time waiting for me? You're not my babysitter!" Tanya laughed.

"I'm not? Then why do I spend all my time keeping you out of trouble?" Vera got up, pulled her pilot close, and kissed her.

They stayed like that for a long moment, eyes closed, arms resting lightly around each other's waists, before Tanya pulled away. "Not in front of everyone, Verok. You're embarrassing me."

"They're all asleep."

"Not Valka. I can see you watching us, you voyeur!"

"Am not. I just can't sleep," I mumbled, covering my eyes with the crook of my arm. Seeing them filled me with a forlorn feeling. How nice it must be to serve alongside the person you loved. To see them and know that they were safe and well every day, not just through an occasional letter. To draw strength from them.

Vera asked her pilot, "How was the morning bus to headquarters? Did Number 9 get shot full of holes?"

"You'll be happy to know that I brought our baby home completely unscathed."

"Good." They sat down on Tanya's bed, which creaked under their weight. Vera's voice turned serious. "Tatiana, I want you to stop flying these solo missions."

Tanya laughed. "I was ferrying a political officer. It was the safest thing I've ever done."

"I understand that. But anything can happen. And if it does . . . I want us to be together."

"Verok. Don't talk about that. It's bad luck." A pause. "But I'll stop."

"Tanya. Vera. Go to sleep!" hissed Iskra.

They dropped off into silence, but sleep still eluded me. I rubbed my eyes with the heels of my hands hard enough to make myself see spots, even though I knew from experience that nothing would make the effects wear off faster. I grew acutely aware of every bruise and ache I'd acquired being jounced around in my plane's hard seat.

A curling paper border of capital and lowercase letters ran along the top of a green chalkboard so worn its plywood backing showed through. The wooden desks and chairs, marred with ink spills and carved initials, were stacked against the back wall to make room for our cots. It was strange to remember that I'd been a student scarcely more than a year ago. I'd struggled with algebra and complained when my parents made me miss a flight because I hadn't finished my math homework.

The memories were like watching a film about someone else's life. I'd never be that schoolgirl again. When Raskova said she'd make us into soldiers, I hadn't realized I'd be giving up my old self. The one who could sit beside Pasha in the cockpit of our little plane as easy as anything. We could never have a moment like that again, not now that planes had become killing machines.

We might save our Motherland and our homes, but we could never really return.

★TWENTY-FOUR★

I LEANED MY HEAD BACK AGAINST THE LEATHER RIM of the cockpit and closed my eyes to catch a moment's rest before takeoff. I liked this moment, when the planes were in place but their engines were still off and I could hear the familiar noises up and down the flight line.

Behind me, using her map light for illumination, Iskra flipped through the pages of her aeronavigation book. I couldn't figure out why she was so attached to that book. It wasn't because she needed to brush up on her navigation skills, that was for sure.

For once, I'd ended up at the front of my flight, though the other flight in our squadron was ahead of me. Two planes back, Zhenechka amused Dina, the squadron commander, by telling her a fairy tale. In the plane ahead of us, the pilot, Sofiya, played with a kitten she'd found in a pile of rubble; it had been the village's sole remaining inhabitant. "No, you mustn't grab that! That's the throttle. Leave it alone. You're doing it again! What did I just tell you?"

The middle of the flight order was the best place to be, I decided. I felt secure there, with friends in front of me and friends behind me, ready to swoop in and help me if anything should happen.

I opened my eyes at the sound of someone walking up to our plane. It was Galya, sporting a flight suit, a helmet, and a million-ruble smile. She had just returned to our regiment the day before, wincing with pain every time she took a step but undaunted in her ambitions.

"Look at you, wearing big-girl clothes!" I teased, flicking her helmet's dangling buckle with one finger. She was my age and almost my height, but in her flight gear she still managed to look like a kid playing dress-up. It saddened me to see her moving stiffly and not bounding across the airfield with her former energy. Galya the gymnast was gone forever.

"Bershanskaya says I can navigate tonight if I can find a pilot to take me," she said.

"Sorry, darling, you'll have to look elsewhere. Valka is bound to get into trouble if she flies without me," said Iskra, shooing Galya away. But her voice was kind.

A minute later a cry of excitement announced that Galya had found a pilot: Zhigli's former pilot Polina, just behind us. She climbed into the rear cockpit while the displaced navigator stood nearby, arms akimbo, complaining, "Kicked out of my own plane. How do you like that?"

I laughed inwardly. I was barely more than a rookie myself, but already I felt a big-sister affection for the newer airwomen as I watched them reach the goals that I'd passed only a few months earlier. Galya especially. Her effervescent cheer would brighten up the airfield.

The armorers spun up our engines. The cacophony of propellers surrounded me. One by one, the planes ahead of me took off. Sofiya handed off her kitten to an armorer and roared down the runway. I sat up and took the controls. Exactly three minutes later, we followed.

It was a perfectly clear night, the indigo sky resplendent with a million stars. Clear enough to see for kilometers. Clear enough to see everything.

The searchlight beams came into view ahead of us. They looked eager. There were so many, a whole forest of them, roving back and forth and then converging on a single spot with startling speed. Transfixed in the beams was a bright speck, first white, then red. Fire. No! My heart plummeted. I pointed and shouted, "Iskra, that's one of ours!"

My mind refused to accept what I was seeing. We had lived through countless missions and no one had been shot down. Not since that first night. They would shake off the lights. I was convinced of it, although they were already burning. Somehow they would escape, cheat death, and we would laugh on our way back from the airfield in the morning. I was sure of it, absolutely sure, even as the bright spot spiraled toward the ground and vanished, two lives with it. Gone. Just like that.

I was still reeling, unable to accept what had happened, when the second aircraft was shot down. It sparkled with flashes of red, white, and green, grotesquely reminiscent of fireworks on the anniversary of the Revolution. The signal flares were exploding. The plane came apart as it fell, all in flames, the wings, the tail, the wooden frame already stripped of its delicate canvas, and the two girls. In powerless horror, I watched my friends burning, tumbling free of the wreckage, and I tried as hard as I could not to think of the flight order, not to match names and faces to those burning figures.

Fire! My hands froze in place. Why were my friends not dodging the guns and escaping? And then a sudden realization: Where were the guns? Their concussions should have cut sharply through the silence of the night, but there was nothing.

The beam of the searchlight momentarily illuminated another shape, not the angular double cross of a biplane but a broad-winged plane with a big, tapered belly and twin engines the shape of bullets. I could plainly make out the black crosses on its wings. A night fighter. We were easy prey. We were going to burn!

And then it was Sofiya, straight ahead of me. Her U-2 seemed so close. It was like one of the demonstrations our instructors used to do with model planes, and I couldn't shake the idea that I could have reached out and plucked the aircraft from the sky if my hands had been willing to move. The fighter dived greedily, mindless of the frantic, ineffectual burst of machine-gun fire from Sofiya's desperate navigator. The plane barely caught fire. A hint of yellow licked it here and there; then the wings neatly divided from the fuselage and fluttered down like whirligig seeds. The broken craft plummeted out of the beams and into darkness.

We were next. We approached those stripes of light, which slowly pivoted in search of their next victim. Sweat beaded on my forehead as though I could already feel the heat of fire consuming the cockpit around me. I needed to do something. I would die if I didn't. I would take Iskra to her death as surely as the three planes ahead of me, but my hands wouldn't respond.

"Valka." Iskra's voice coming through the speaking tube was a hoarse whisper, as though she feared that the fighter pilot might overhear us. Then, louder, "Valyushka, are you all right? Focus, baby cousin. We need to complete the mission."

I tried to think. I tried to remember what we had learned about fighters, how to outmaneuver them, but everything had been forced out of my mind except one single word: Fire!

The stick moved under my hand. Iskra had taken the controls. She cut the engine and went into a glide. "Don't worry, baby cousin. I promised to take care of you."

Through the fog enveloping my mind, I remembered our flight plan. We were supposed to drop our bombs on our way out. That meant circling around and passing over the target again after bombing. Two passes among the beams. Two chances for the fighter's cannon to rip us apart.

We were almost there. Somewhere in the darkness the fighter

waited for us. Iskra veered a little way off course and circled around, approaching the target from the far side. We were still gliding. She put us into a gentle dive, eight hundred meters, five hundred, three hundred. It was risky. At that altitude, we could easily be caught in the blast when our bombs landed.

And suddenly, through the fog in my mind, I saw what Iskra was doing. When the searchlight operators looked for us, they would look too high.

The pair of chalk marks on the wing lined up with the target. A jolt. The bombs dropped. Iskra barely had time to reengage the engine before a hot shock wave hit us. It tossed us through the air. The plane's controls jerked wildly. For a moment I thought that fire had caught us after all, that we had evaded the fighter only to be destroyed by our own bombs. But we were undamaged. As Iskra brought us level, there were the searchlight beams—crossing above us! I could hear the drone of the fighter, searching for us where he had found the others. But we were already away. Safe.

Galya and Polina. They were behind us. Polina must have seen what Iskra had done. I found myself pleading aloud as though they could hear, my throat dry and hoarse. "Please don't drop your bombs yet. Do what we did." But then came the explosion as their bombs fell and my instrument panel was illuminated with yellow light. I glanced back. There was their plane, transfixed by the searchlights, its crew blinded and disoriented. And half the squadron was still behind them.

It would be classified as an accidental collision in the official report, but as I craned my neck to catch a glimpse of them, I was sure they were making a choice. I could see Polina, her brows low-ered in intense focus. And on Galya's young face, the hard look of a warrior. She wanted to be a real airwoman. She knew what that entailed.

As the fighter swooped in for the kill, their U-2 pulled up sharply, straight into its path. The little biplane and the sleek fighter, locked together, fell out of the sky.

We landed and stumbled numbly out of our cockpits. Our mechanic's sturdy arm steadied me. We had made it. Why? We weren't the best aircrew and I certainly wasn't the best pilot, not the fastest or the boldest or the cleverest. I was the one who froze in the face of danger. Polina and Galya were the ones who saw what to do and did it without hesitation, and it had cost them their lives.

Our chief of staff held the map with the flight times noted on it, tears welling up in her eyes. She knew who each explosion represented. I foolishly wanted to ask if there had been any sur-vivors, but I had witnessed the crashes myself. At the sight of us, a wavering smile fought through her tears. She grabbed us like she was pulling us from a shipwreck. "Valka? Iskra? You made it! You're alive!"

I was. Useless and worthless and alive.

I couldn't face the rest of the regiment. I feared those looks of hope when they saw that someone had returned and how they would fade into dismay when they realized it was only me. Pasha was the only person I could face. So I grabbed pen and paper and wandered aimlessly down the street and into the remains of the village until I found a quiet spot where I could sit and write to him.

It didn't go well.

I couldn't get my thoughts in order. My feelings came piling out one on top of another and I couldn't make sense of the jumble. I wasn't good at being sad. I didn't know how. When something upset me, I channeled it into anger. Anger at the world, at the fascists, at myself.

I leaned against the charred frame of a wall from which all the plaster had flaked away and stared up at the gray predawn sky. Splinters tangled my hair. It had been a short night, but I was exhausted, not as if I needed to rest but as if the vitality had permanently drained out of me and I would never feel like myself again.

I wrote a few words and scratched them out. My bleary eyes could barely make out the sheet of paper in front of me, so I wiped them, which probably left ink marks on my face, but I didn't care. When I picked my pen back up, I immediately smeared the ink with my wet hand. I crumpled the paper and dropped it onto the uneven floor of the burned-out house. It hadn't said anything anyway.

Had the fascist pilot known he was killing girls? Maybe. But he hadn't seen Sofiya playing with her kitten before takeoff. He didn't know that Polina pasted cutouts from Zhigli's silly magazines in her cockpit. He didn't know that Galya had a slip of paper in her pocket granting her six months of leave, which she'd refused to take.

And there at last was the anger, bursting out in a flood. I got up and screamed and kicked the house's blackened hearth. I pounded it with my fists. The crumbling brick ripped the skin from my knuckles. When I had worn myself out, breathing hard, my shoulders slumped, blood trickling down my hands, Iskra was there in the doorway.

She didn't say anything, just put her arms around me and leaned her head on my chest. I clung to her solidity, digging my fingers into her so hard it must have hurt. No one would tear Iskra away from me. They had taken my other friends but they would never take her. Never. Not unless they took me too.

Iskra led me to the school and I broke down again the instant I stepped inside. Against the wall, eight camp beds, folded. I tried not to look at them. The schoolroom felt very quiet without Galya's laughter. Everyone stuck close together as though we feared that someone else might vanish. Tanya held Vera's hand, their fingers threaded together.

Zhigli sat curled on her bed surrounded by friends, her eyes red and puffy from crying over Polina. Her voice broke as she said, "It's my fault. I knew as soon as I met her that she was destined to die young. It was her fate, and I was the only thing protecting her, the thread by which she was hanging on to life. So many times we had close calls and by sheer luck we pulled through unharmed, time and again. And then we parted and the thread snapped."

I'd never seen her looking so vulnerable. I couldn't harbor any anger toward her. At that moment it was impossible to see anyone in the regiment as a rival or an enemy, but I wasn't ready to talk to her, either. I sat in the corner by the blackboard and focused on Pasha's gentle presence. Pasha, who sang in the face of fear. He'd faced his own losses. He would understand. How I needed him right then. But I needed him to be really here, to hear his voice and feel his touch. I wanted to bury my face in his chest and let him put his arms around me, and then I'd be able to face what I needed to tell him.

TWENTY-FIVE

2 September 1942

Dear Pasha,

We've returned to something approximating life as usual, if life can ever be usual again. I don't remember what I ended up writing to you that night, whether it was coherent or even legible through the tear stains. You're the only person I can spill my guts to like that. We've seen each other at our best and worst and I don't need to pretend to be a cool, collected military pilot around you.

Bershanskaya appointed navigators as replacement pilots and mechanics as replacement navigators. She's the only person

I haven't seen cry. She just frowns and squints into the distance. She thinks she can't show weakness, either for our sake or because of her superior, watching, waiting for us to crack from the strain so he can send us home. Those girls didn't give their lives to become proof that women can't handle combat.

But that, at least, has not happened. We took our suffering and kept fighting, and we will keep on doing it as long as any of us are left to fight.

Our regimental navigator was among the casualties. Bershanskaya appointed Zhenechka to replace her and and assigned her to train the new navigators. Zhenechka was dismayed that her promotion again came in the wake of tragedy.

Over the next few days, I kept hanging on to the stupidest threads of hope, telling myself that my own eyes were mistaken, that my friends would show up the next day, whole and well, and that entire night would turn out to have been a bad dream. But the Soviet infantry found their aircraft scattered on the steppe like broken toys. The crews were identified only by the serial numbers on the planes' engines.

We have little time for formalities out here in the field. The major said a few words about each girl and we put them in the ground. Mourning them was no easier the second time. Soon we'll move on and those eight graves will be left alone near an abandoned village in the war-torn steppe. Will anyone visit them? Will anyone remember that they're here?

The next morning, I found Zhigli outside, kneeling on the wing of her U-2 with buckets of white and red paint. She had written on the fuselage "REVENGE FOR POLINA." I felt I should say something, but I didn't know what. Finally I simply asked her if she would write something on our plane. She nodded and wrote, in swooping white cursive, the words "TO AVENGE OUR COMRADES."

The other airwomen and mechanics copied her. Soon half the aircraft in the regiment bore messages. Some the names of our friends. Some patriotic messages, like "FOR THE MOTHERLAND." One mechanic painted "FOR STALIN" on a plane. When the plane's pilot saw, her face went dark. She grabbed the brush and, in front of everyone, smeared out the message with one smooth motion, saying, "I fight for my country, but I don't fight for Stalin! He's a man—let him fight for himself!"

Never in my life have I heard someone say such a thing out loud. She could have been shot on the spot. But nobody stopped her, nobody reprimanded her. Iskra looked stunned, but instead of launching into a lecture about politics, she only said quietly, "That was foolish." She's definitely changed.

Zhigli saw the whole thing. A bit of me honestly expected her to run off to the MPs and report that there was a traitor in our midst. But another part of me said that I knew Zhigli, and that nothing I've ever seen suggested that she would do such a thing. And she didn't.

At the moment, I was too distressed to make anything of it. But now I see the incontrovertible proof that I am among friends. That the women around me would support each other to the death and would never, ever betray one of their own, not for all the fame and money the Soviet Union would heap on them. I found myself thinking over everything Zhigli had done and wondering if I hadn't been, all this time, seeing something that wasn't there.

When Colonel Popov ordered us to assemble, I didn't have the strength to muster my usual indignation. Mostly I felt resignation when he told us, "Well, girls, I'll finally be rid of you." So I almost didn't register what he told us next. We're not being disbanded, as I expected—we're being transferred. You've heard that the fascists have stormed the Caucasus, heading for the oil fields, and that the Red Army is throwing everything it's got in their way to stop them. Apparently that includes us. We've graduated from a valueless regiment suitable only for the most routine, unimportant missions to an actual strategic resource. Figures that it happens when we're too broken up to care. Join the VVS, see the world, so the posters say. But it troubles me to be moving even farther away from you.

Please write. There's been no word since you arrived at Rzhev. I keep thinking of reasons why. Excuses, really. You ran out of paper. The mail isn't getting through. If this letter makes it, or even if it doesn't, know that this Katyusha remembers you, like the song says.

Yours,
Valka

★

Dear Pasha,

I'm writing to you from our new base in the Caucasus, despite the fact that you still haven't written back and I am getting cross about it.

I've missed mountains. The Caucasus Mountains are a jagged pale blue range with deep valleys and streams cutting through it. On clear, moonlit nights, the view from the air is breathtaking: the stark mountains jutting up from below, the deep blue sky speckled with stars, and the dark expanse of the Black Sea.

While we were packing up to rebase, I found Galya's headband. The silly polka-dotted one with the bow. It was hanging on the clothesline, and I guess we missed it when we packed up our friends' things to send home to their families. That had been hard. Blinking back the moisture that had gotten into my eyes, I tucked the headband into my kit bag. I couldn't let go of this unexpected reminder. Galya wouldn't make it to the Caucasus, but this would. Zhigli would call it an omen.

Our new division commander is a harried colonel who always looks like he was just unexpectedly awakened. He warned us that the Transcaucasian Front wasn't playtime. They were fighting a war here and he didn't have time to babysit us or coddle us with safe missions. He didn't know what we'd been doing in the steppe, but here, we would fly real, dangerous combat missions from our first night onward, and he hoped we were prepared.

A few months ago, I would have taken that as a challenge. Now it feels like an insult. As if he knows what we've been through.

Our base is a sleepy resort town on the Black Sea. The sea is a nice change from up north, where we were sometimes reduced to washing in puddles. The Red Army didn't give much thought to hygiene when it sent women to the front. Bershanskaya does her best to keep us supplied with cotton wool, but like all other supplies, it's not always easy to get.

We're staying in a sanitarium, sleeping in real beds with pillows and sheets. Such luxury! Ilyushina says it'll turn us soft, but I don't see her volunteering to sleep under the wing of a plane. Zhenechka is sitting under the window, writing a fairy tale that begins "Once upon a time beside the blue sea there lived a female night bomber regiment." How she plans to end it I can't imagine. Our time at the front has been nothing like a fairy tale.

Our airfield is on a cliff above the village. Our planes look proud and formidable lined up in their green and tan and black camouflage. But the weather is treacherous. Gales blow in off the sea. The wind howls and our planes rock as each gust threatens to rip them off their anchors. The ground crews have to run up to the cliff and hang on to the wings of the aircraft to keep them from being tossed through the air like dry leaves.

The worst are the impenetrable fogs that roll in from the sea and engulf us. Sometimes a night begins clear, but fog swallows up our airfield while we're away, and everyone has to find somewhere else to land. We sleep huddled under our planes' wings and fly home in the morning, wet and shivering. Major Bershanskaya is always out on the airfield those days, counting each plane as it returns and resembling a mother duck making sure all her ducklings have safely crossed a road. At breakfast, we lay out places for the girls who aren't there. It's our way of assuring that they will come back.

The fascists have fortified the Taman Peninsula with everything they've got. Around the fascist-held territory is one solid wall of flak after another. They're firing a new kind of multicolored tracer, red, white, and green. Each shell breaks up into dozens of smaller shells, like a flower blooming. It's dazzling and beautiful and very, very dangerous.

It's taking a toll, not so much physically as emotionally. It's hard to go to sleep in the morning knowing that you'll have to face it again the next night.

When we showed up at Engels in high spirits, keen to defend the Motherland, we had no idea what we were getting into. Sometimes I wonder how many of us still would have volunteered if we had known.

War is not natural for women—that's what the other girls say. We are made to create and nurture life, and to destroy it goes against our fundamental nature. They're right that war is unnatural, but I think of you singing or quietly reading and it seems to me that nobody could be less suited for combat than you. I don't mean that as an insult. No one should find war easy. When I'm on a mission, I feel that hardness slipping over me and

I realize I'm getting accustomed to this. That I'm good at this. And I don't want to be.

Do you remember how I begged you to play Nadezhda Durova with me? I would hide my hair under a hat and be Nadya the cavalry maiden, and you, of course, had to play everyone else. You didn't like playing the French dragoons that I drove off with my broomstick lance. But you liked being the wounded officer who I put on the back of my horse (my father's bicycle) so that it could carry you to safety. And you liked the end of the game, when you got to play the tsar and I confessed to being a woman and then you pinned my mother's brooch on me and pretended it was the Cross of St. George.

War was heroic back then. Banners and pageantry. Or do we only think that because we're far away from it, because we can't hear the cannons or smell the smoke and the blood? Is it possible that Nadezhda Durova felt as useless and miserable as I do?

Damn, will people in the future think of us the way we think of her? Will there be films and plays about the heroic 588th Night Bomber Regiment? I hope someone survives the war to set the record straight.

Stay safe.

Yours,
Valka

★

Dear Valyushka,

I'm still here. Despite everything, I'm still here. That's good; I didn't want that other letter to be the last one I ever sent you. Truthfully, after I sent it, I hoped it would get lost. I didn't want you to know those things about me.

I'm sorry about your friends. I know what it's like to lose a friend, that space inside you that can never be filled by anyone else. Those unique things about friends, the way they walked or the colors of their voices, things you might have hardly noticed when they were there, but you miss keenly once they're gone. Rudenko was like that. Vakhromov does the work he used to do without complaint, and when he and I are carrying the radio equipment and Petya is walking between us we form a sort of family, but our squad will always feel incomplete.

Why does the army encourage us to form bonds like that? Why do they want us to be close when they know what will happen to us?

Petya is still with us. Bringing a child here is insanity. Pashkevich said as much, but Vakhromov and I couldn't think of parting with the boy who to me is a little brother and to Vakhromov another son. It's selfish of us. If we really cared about his welfare, we would send him away. But if we even mention the idea, he throws a fit and says he won't go.

Most children don't like bedtime, but Petya is particularly intractable. Last night he, Vakhromov, our commissar, and I were sitting around the fire. I was playing "Katyusha" by the flickery red light. My harmonica's colors are sliding from bright to dull as the stressed metal loses its pitch. Vakhromov told Petya that it was bedtime, but the boy ignored him. He repeated himself increasingly firmly, but Petya kept refusing and finally burst into tears.

"That boy needs a spanking," said Pashkevich, who was cleaning his gun nearby.

I offered to sing Petya something, but he wasn't interested. I asked if he was afraid of his dreams. He nodded.

I asked, "What do you see?"

Petya's voice was very quiet. "Houses burning. Guns shooting. The soldier girl."

"What soldier girl?"

"The one they killed."

Our commissar looked up sharply. "Killed? By the Hitlerites?"

Petya nodded again.

He came around to Petya's side of the fire and went down on one knee so that he could look him in the face. "Tell me what happened."

In bits and pieces, Petya's story came out.

He remembered the night only in fragments. A noise awakening him. Fire everywhere. Fascists running and yelling, then emerging from behind a stable with a captive.

"They thought she was a boy at first. She was wearing men's

clothes and she had short hair. They took her into a house and made the people leave. There was a light on in the window all night. Sometimes they took her outside in her underwear and made her walk around barefoot. There was snow. She never made a sound.

"In the morning they put a sign around her neck and marched her around town. There were burns and bruises on her face and blood on her fingers. They made us all come out and watch. She was brave. She didn't cry. They made her stand on a box and put the rope around her neck and she talked to us the whole time. She said she wasn't afraid to die. She told us to keep fighting.

"One fascist set up a camera and took pictures. The executioner yelled at him because he was being too slow and the soldier girl kept talking and threatening them. Finally he was done. Mama covered my eyes with my hands.

"After she was dead, they were very happy. They got drunk. They pulled her shirt open and stabbed her with bayonets. They were laughing. Mama wanted to take her down and bury her, but they wouldn't let her. They said she had to stay there as an example. That's when Mama decided we couldn't live there anymore."

Petya didn't cry while he related this story, but told it matter-of-factly, as if watching a girl be executed was just part of life. I suppose, for him, it is. I wish I could pick him up and carry him away to safety, to Stakhanovo maybe, where my sister *could teach him all the things he's forgotten about being a child.*

The commissar said, "What was the name of your village?"

"Petrishchevo," said the boy.

"Petrishchevo," echoed the commissar. "The town where Zoya Kosmodemyanskaya was sent. You saw them kill her. And you said that the fascists had a camera."

Another nod.

The commissar looked up at Vakhromov. "Do you know what this means? There are pictures of the execution. Of the war crimes they committed. We have photos of the body, but the fascists will just deny that they had anything to do with it." And to Petya he said, "Do you think you'd know the man with the camera if you saw him again?"

Petya thought he would.

Vakhromov said, "If you are thinking of doing anything that will put this boy into more danger, I won't allow it."

The commissar replied, "There's a nasty rumor about Kosmodemyanskaya going around. People are saying that she wasn't killed by Hitlerites at all. The story is that the villagers executed her themselves because they were angry at her for burning their houses. Is that how you want her to be remembered? As an arsonist killed by her own people?"

She was an arsonist no matter what account you listen to, but I knew better than to argue with a commissar.

He went on, "Private, if those photos exist, they can prove how she died. We can put names and faces to this atrocity. The world needs to see them!"

I hope he's just talking. He's no commander, after all; he has no authority to send us anywhere. But I'm afraid of what he might have begun. What it might mean for Petya. What it might mean for me.

Yours,
Pasha

★ TWENTY-SIX ★

25 September 1942

Dear Pasha,

I can picture the confusion and worry that will cross your face when you open this letter and see tidy cursive instead of my usual sloppy handwriting. Your first thought will be that I've been killed in action. That's what I'd think if I received this letter. Don't worry. This letter really is from me, only a nurse is taking dictation. As to why . . . I'll explain from the beginning.

We had just rebased to an auxiliary airfield nestled in a fortresslike gorge with only a narrow opening to the south. We hadn't had a chance to camouflage the airfield when a squadron of Stukas bore down on us. The instant the major saw those gull-winged black silhouettes in the sky, she yelled, "Everyone in the air—now!"

The fear never goes away, but you get used to it. As that familiar wave of adrenaline hit me, I jumped into the plane and Iskra followed. Masha the armorer spun our propeller. I grabbed her arm, pulled her up after me, and lifted off as a line of cannon fire ripped up the ground behind us. The shadow of one of the attack aircraft passed over us. Its wheel spats seemed close enough to knock my head on. The other U-2s took off like a startled flock of birds. A German tail gunner opened fire on Zhigli. Gasoline sprayed her plane's canvas side. Her fuel line was hit. My throat tightened. For a moment, I thought I would see two more friends die. And one of them, I realized at that moment, I desperately needed to talk to. I'd left something important unsaid.

Half the regiment was still on the ground, dashing for cover behind the trucks or hitting the ground where they were. The Stukas formed up for another pass. Then, mercifully, a roar of engines, and a flight of Soviet fighters soared over the trees. Cannon fire cut the air. The air was thick with planes, ours, our friends', our enemies'.

Stukas are deadly against targets on the ground but sluggish and ungainly in air combat. A stricken one spiraled into the cliff side and exploded in a shower of torn metal, forcing the women below to duck and cover their heads. A bent wing slammed into the ground where Masha had been standing. The rest of the fascist squadron scattered. The fighters waggled their wings at us in greeting before they departed. We waved and blew them kisses.

Zhigli had maintained control. She brought her airplane limping back down, gushing gasoline like blood from a wound. Then the rest of us landed our sewing machines one at a time, looking for safe spots amid the rubble.

As I helped the trembling Masha out of the cockpit, I clapped her on the shoulder and told her, "Congratulations, now you've flown in combat!"

"I think I prefer to stay on the ground," she said with a nervous laugh.

Zhigli's shot-up plane was wheeled off to a hardstand and her mechanic replaced the fuel line by the light of a couple of flying mice placed a safe distance away from the gasoline-soaked aircraft. The damage was more serious than it initially looked. The mechanic had to fetch Ilyushina, who then sat nearby, alternately instructing and berating her, a blanket wrapped around her shoulders, less for warmth than to remind everyone that she could have been sleeping if they knew how to do their jobs.

Zhigli paced around her plane impatiently. Her navigator napped.

I wanted to talk to her, but there were preflight checks to be done and flight plans to be reviewed and I didn't have a chance.

The night's mission was an important one. We were bombing the airfield in the occupied city of Armavir, the very airfield the fascists have been launching their attacks from. If we could put enough holes in the runway to keep their planes grounded, that might give our forces the edge they needed to kick the Wehrmacht out of its toehold in the Caucasus.

Bershanskaya's final words to us before we departed were "Watch out. There will be flak."

I told her, "We've flown over a hundred missions. What are the odds that this one will finish us off?"

Iskra said statistics don't work that way.

We crossed the front lines low. I called down to the soldiers on the ground, "Stand firm, brothers!" and they yelled and cheered in reply.

When we got to Armavir, it was dead black except for a wooly white spot where the clouds hid the full moon. Iskra said, "We could fit in ten runs tonight at this speed," and I remember breaking into a smirk, thinking how furious Zhigli would be at the time she was wasting.

Tanya and Vera were flying ahead of us. As they reached the parallel lines of lights that unmistakably marked an airfield, a cacophony of shells burst around them. Searchlights swung this way and that in an attempt to pin them down. Tanya banked and peeled away, the bright orange explosions following the sound of Number 9's ticking engine. I admired the way she flew, smooth and graceful as a ballet.

I slipped Number 41 in between the beams and over the target. I could just make out the shiny snub noses of a line of Junker bombers. KG 51, I recalled from the briefing, was a bomber wing with the sigil of an eidelweiss. We were about to knock a few petals off that flower.

Iskra saw them too. "The nerve of them, parked on a Soviet airfield!"

I cut my engine and crept over the airfield. The gunners were still following Tanya, who dived and darted amid the deadly flowers. All this was according to plan. Our sky slugs would never survive the heavy defenses here in the Caucasus, so Bershanskaya had come up with another one of her ideas: decoys.

Yes, that is what it sounds like.

We have no radios, so there's no way to confirm what the other pilot will do or to let her know if there's a problem. You need to get inside the other girl's head. Our squadron has flown so many missions together that this is second nature: I can tell when Tanya is about to climb or bank or dive before she begins. Of course there's a major flaw to this strategy: you'd have to be crazy to actually try it. Luckily the women of the 588th have all been blessed with a complete and utter lack of better judgment— and a fierce desire to defend our friends.

A navigator needs twenty seconds to aim or she'll miss the target and the whole sortie will be in vain. You have to defy every natural instinct in order to keep your bomber steady while shells explode next to your ears. I anxiously watched our friends' plane evade the guns as Iskra aimed. We dropped our bombs.

The guns snapped away from Tanya and onto us. As I banked to draw them away, everything behind me grew bright. Not the clean white of an illumination flare, but a flickery red. The aircraft came around and a giant plume of thick, oily smoke met us. I turned into the wind and climbed until we were clear of it. We were over the airport again. And it was up in flames.

The pillar of smoke rose from a battery of fuel trucks, engulfed in fire. Bright yellow trails licked out from them, following the spilled gasoline as it snaked its way in patterns across the tarmac and pooled in the craters left by the other bombers in our squadron. The ground crew scrambled to put it out. Little white puffs from fire extinguishers mingled with the smoke, but when the flames didn't subside, the crew gave up and ran.

In another instant the fire had spread to the line of aircraft. One of the hulking bombers was burning. Glass sparkled as the panels of its canopy shattered. Then the fire claimed another bomber. And it was still spreading.

I gave a whoop of excitement. Iskra's voice came through the speaking tube. "Go, team Koroleva! Now let's go have a victory dance at the aerodrome!"

"You got it!" I told her. Then Number 9 was beside us. Tanya saluted me.

Had the big explosion made me forget that it was my turn to act as decoy? Had I foolishly assumed that all the searchlights had been taken out in the explosion? It doesn't matter.

One way or another, the searchlight caught me.

Every detail of Number 41 lit up in bright white, with ink-black shadows cut out in sharp relief. There was a blinding reflection off the windscreen. I instinctively held up a hand to block it. A tracer bullet hissed past me in a stripe of smoke. I bit my lip. A burst of flak fire rang out, tearing through the port wings. The U-2 faltered, the air slipping through the ragged *holes. I fought to keep it level.*

"We're hit!" screamed Iskra. It was the least helpful comment she has ever made.

"I noticed!" I yelled back.

We escaped the searchlight beam, but flames were flickering around the tip of the bottom wing. They swiftly licked their way toward the fuselage, making the fragile canvas crumble away into ash. My hands clenched the controls. The voice in my head screamed, "Fire, fire, fire!"

"You have to sideslip!" said Iskra. "It's the only way to put the fire out!"

She coughed and choked, enveloped by the plume of smoke, which had to be stinging her eyes and making it hard to breathe. She wouldn't be able to see anything from back there. If anyone was going to land this plane, it would be me. Iskra had brought me home safely once. I had to do the same for her. But when I tried to think about flying the plane, the voice in my head shouted me down. I needed something to focus on, anything but those terrible flames.

The words found me, unsought and unbidden. Your words. "Apple and pear trees were blooming, mist creeping on the river . . ."

I let the song fill my mind and drown out the voice of terror.

And then, amid the chaos, it was like you were there in the cockpit with me. I swear I could feel you beside me, hear you breathing, calm and steady. I had a sense of your hand over mine, forcing the control stick to move. The entire lower port aileron was gone, but I had three left. I banked starboard and jammed the rudder to port. Number 41 glided sideways. The flames wavered, then flared up brighter than ever.

Our friends' airplane was sticking close to us, even though there was nothing they could do to help. They hadn't been hit; we'd played our role as decoys. We were losing altitude. All around us, unforgiving rocks. The only safe landing spot was our airfield.

The wing was nothing but a charred wooden frame. The fuselage was beginning to catch. I could feel heat on my leg. "Fire, fire, fire!" screamed the voice. The song returned, louder. I felt you next to me, the side of your face touching mine, your hands on my shoulders, steadying me.

My face and neck grew moist with sweat, whether from heat or fear I don't know. I forced myself to keep my eyes on the terrain ahead. The jagged mountain that hid the airfield rose before us. I had to bring the plane around to the right, the only side from which the airfield could be approached, but the control stick kept tugging to the left. My hands ached from fighting it.

There it was, a narrow path to safety amid boulders and craters. We were going to make it. But I couldn't keep her steady any longer. Half the control surfaces were gone. The stick in my hand did not respond. At that moment, everything was outside my control. Nothing is more terrifying for a pilot than having no control.

Number 41 rolled on its lopsided wings. It coasted along the runway, sharp rubble ripping the skeletal port wings clean off.

One wheel met the ground as my cockpit erupted in flames. Iskra was already jumping free. For a moment, it seemed as though our U-2 might right itself, but then it rocked and came to a skidding halt on its side, plowing a deep furrow in the field. My head cracked against the edge of the cockpit. My vision swam with hazy colors.

When I could see again, I tried to unbuckle my harness, only to find that it was on fire. It came apart in my hands. There should have been pain, I realized abstractly as I watched the flames crawling up and down the side of my flight suit, there should have been and there wasn't and that worried me. The choking smoke made it difficult to think. A pop and a hiss and a blinding white flash nearby. Then a green flash. I knew I needed to move, but I had lost track of which way was up. A voice, Iskra's voice, yelled my name from nowhere in particular.

Through the fire, I could see the indistinct shape of a plane on its hardstand, and another shape bounding toward me. Strong hands grabbed me under the arms and dragged me free from the burning wreck. My rescuer threw me to the ground. She wrapped something soft around me and rolled me roughly on the grass until the flames were out.

As my shock wore off and my blurry vision cleared, I found myself wrapped in a singed blanket. Zhigli was looking down at me. And there, finally, was the pain, an agonizing searing spreading from my thigh all up and down my left side. It was a moment before I realized that I was screaming.

The next few hours were a blur. I'm in the field hospital

now, half mummied in bandages. The doctor says a minute longer and I'd have lost my leg. Not that it would have mattered; a minute longer and I'd have lost the entire plane, me and Iskra with it.

It had to be burns when I finally got injured. A bullet wound I could have handled, I think, although maybe I'm only saying that because it hasn't happened. But burns! Remember the time you touched the flame on the Primus stove, Pasha, and how it kept you up all night? Now imagine that's running from your calf all the way to your shoulder. The word "pain" doesn't begin to describe it. I'll admit I did my share of writhing and crying before morphine reduced me to a haze.

I'm trying not to look at the other patients in the ward. They make me feel like a faker. I know that's silly considering I was literally on fire and I thought I was going to die. You can't be dying and faking at the same time. But I'm going to walk out of here and rejoin my regiment. Most of them won't.

My hands are blistered from touching the harness's hot metal buckles, which is why a nurse is writing for me. The doctor won't clear me to fly for six weeks. Six weeks! I'll miss dozens of sorties. I don't know how I'll manage. But the only actual loss was Number 41. Our faithful winged friend is a charred husk, fit only to be stripped for parts. I wasn't prepared for how hard that news hit me. We went through a lot with her.

Aside from the nurse, your letters are my only company. I've been spending my downtime rereading them. Our letters got us both through the war this far. You made it clear how much my *letters meant to you, but I'm not sure if I ever told you how much strength yours gave me.*

My eyes keep returning to your last letter, to the part about Zoya Kosmodemyanskaya. It's one of those stories that you can never get out of your head. She died bravely, like a soldier. Back in Engels, I used to wonder if I would be as brave as her in the face of death. Now I know. I wasn't stoic and silent and I don't expect to be on the front page of Pravda, *but I brought us home. I did what I needed to do. I can be proud of that.*

Zoya's story made you fear for me. But you're a radio operator. You know everything that goes on in your area, and you've told me how you overhear things you shouldn't know. The Germans know that. If they caught you, they would know how much information they could get out of you. All this time you've been worried about what they might do to me when I should be worrying about what they might do to you.

The truth is that in a war like this there's no separating out who is in danger and who isn't. The risk falls on all of us, men and women, soldiers and civilians. So does the responsibility.

Please send me another letter, a long one. I need something to occupy me and I want to know that my Pashenka is safe.

Yours,

Valka

I heard voices outside and looked up to see Iskra entering the tent on her left foot, balancing with a crutch. Her other foot was splinted. Zhigli followed, a copy of the military newspaper *Red*

Star tucked under her arm.

Iskra ruffled my hair like I was a small child. "How are you feeling, baby cousin?"

"By normal standards or by the standards of someone who was on fire?" I asked. "What happened to you, bunny rabbit?"

"Funny story. I jumped out of a moving airplane. Sprained my ankle when I hit the ground, but it's not bad. And one of the flares got me." She held up a bandaged forearm. "The worst part was that you were burning right there in front of me and I couldn't help."

"But I had Zhigli." I looked up at her. Her dark-lashed eyes were full of earnest concern. "I didn't deserve it."

"Maybe not," said Zhigli, "But it was fated. I was grounded so that I could help you. See?"

I wasn't superstitious, but I couldn't deny that if Zhigli hadn't been grounded, I wouldn't have survived. Twice she'd been delayed from flying, and both times she'd ended up exactly where she needed to be. I wondered if fate would someday put me in the right place when someone needed me.

The fight that I'd kept going for so long seemed unbelievably petty. It was time to end it. "What a day. First you almost get shot down, then me. I'd better say this before either of us has another brush with death." I took a deep breath. "Look, when Iskra was arrested, I couldn't make any sense of it. I needed someone to blame, a villain for the story I was telling myself. And I picked you. That was wrong of me. I know you didn't turn her in. I think I've always known. You don't have to forgive me, because I've been really awful to you, but I'm sorry."

Zhigli threw herself on the bed and hugged me, but she quickly let go at my involuntary squeal of pain. "I knew we couldn't stay enemies. We were always destined to be friends."

Thinking back on everything that had happened since we'd first sat next to each other on the train, I decided she was right.

She added, "Captain Ilyushina says you owe her a new blanket."

That made me smile.

"I have something for you," said Iskra.

"A letter?" I asked, trying not to sound too hopeful.

"No, baby cousin, there hasn't been anything from Pasha," said Iskra. "He's probably fine. You need to give that boy more credit. He's been out there for more than a year. He's a survivor, like you. And look what you got!"

She handed me a small strip of cloth, khaki with a yellow stripe.

I turned it over in my hands. "A wound stripe? I don't know . . ."

"I can sew it for you," Zhigli offered.

"It's not that. It's just . . . I don't want to show off that I've been wounded. I don't want my defining achievement to be catching on fire."

"I'm wearing mine," said Iskra, pointing to a red stripe sewn prominently over her left pocket. "I earned it; why shouldn't I be proud to wear it? But I only got the one for light wounds. You got the prestigious one."

"You weren't the one who crashed the plane," I pointed out.

"Believe me, Valka, the crash isn't the part people are going to remember," said Zhigli, sitting down on the side of my bed. "Hitting that airfield was incredible! They're still tallying up the damages, but I'm sure the Luftwaffe won't forget it in a hurry. Bershanskaya was over the moon—once she found out that you were going to be all right, that is. The girls of Aviation Group 122 are turning into real war heroes!"

"Aviation Group 122? What have the other regiments done?" I asked.

"We're not the only ones who've been keeping busy," said Iskra.

She and Zhigli grinned at each other and Zhigli held up the newspaper. "Now this you're going to love." She began to read. "'While the 437th IAP was engaged in the defense of Stalingrad—' Why do newspapers always find the dullest possible ways to recount everything? I can tell this story much better."

She set down the newspaper and launched into a highly animated narration, punctuated with many gestures of her long-fingered hands. "High over Stalingrad, an Me 109 flashes through the sky like a streak of deadly lightning. Its target, a Yak-1—one of our very own pyaterka pilots, valiantly engaged in the defense of the city. The Messerschmitt's pilot, Luftwaffe ace Erwin Meier. Three iron crosses adorn his uniform. Meier has brought no fewer than eleven planes plummeting from the sky in flames, and his appetite is already whetted for a twelfth. The pyaterka pilot maneuvers with all the skill of her aerobatics training but cannot evade him. Soon she is in his sights. A smile creeps across his face, the smile of a ravenous wolf. Cannon fire rings out."

Zhigli's eyes widened in pretend shock. "But what's this? The Yak is still flying. It's the Messerschmitt that has been raked with bullets. Another Yak-1 has appeared out of nowhere on his six. It's fresh off shooting a German bomber and the taste of victory is in the pilot's mouth. Meier dodges this way and that, but the agile Soviet fighter remains on his tail. Clearly he has met his match! Who is this mysterious pilot? He can't make out the tail number, but over its regulation camouflage, this Yak's fuselage bears a picture of beautiful white flowers!

"Another barrage rips through his plane, tearing the engine to pieces. 'Impossible!' thinks Meier. 'I am invincible!' But his aircraft is in flames and he has no choice but to bail out and accept defeat.

"On the ground and captured by the Soviets, Meier requests the honor of meeting the pilot who defeated him. And who do you think is brought forward?"

I shrugged.

Iskra said, "She's blond, she's cocky, and she keeps flowers in the cockpit of her plane."

My jaw dropped in a combination of a gape and a delighted grin. "You're kidding! She only transferred three days ago!"

Iskra held up the newspaper, pointing to a small photo of Lilya in her flight gear, leaning against her fighter's fuselage and looking understandably self-satisfied.

Zhigli said, "Meier, presented with this petite and beautiful young girl, refuses to believe his eyes. 'You're playing a cruel joke on me!' he rages. 'How can this girl fly a fighter? She's a child!'"

I smiled. I'd thought that once, but heaven help an enemy pilot who made the same mistake.

"But Lilya recounts their dogfight to him in vivid detail, and eventually Meier is forced to concede that he has been bested by a girl. He drops to one knee, slips his gold watch from his wrist, and presents it to her in recognition of her honorable victory. And how does Lilya respond? Looking him dead in the eye, she says coldly, 'I do not accept gifts from my enemies.' And she turns on her heel and strides away."

I said, "That sounds like Lilya. Did she really paint flowers on her airplane?"

"Lilies, naturally," said Zhigli. "They're calling her the White Lily of Stalingrad."

★ TWENTY-SEVEN ★

5 October 1942

Dear Valyushka,

You're hurt! I knew this would happen. Even as your accomplishments fill me with pride, I'm always terrified about how it all might end. Every night as the sun sets, I think of you taking off and of the danger you will be in. Sometimes it wakes me at night. It's almost too much to bear. I wish I could have really been there with you. Of course in reality I don't know anything about airplanes and would only have made things worse.

I have little enough control over anything here. Petya has attracted attention. That's not a good thing. Our commissar took him to headquarters to tell his story. A few days later, a new member joined our squad. A woman. She showed up while Petya was helping me divide the loaf of hard black bread for lunch. I cut the bread and Petya calls out the name of each soldier in his childish cyan voice. He takes this duty very seriously.

Vakhromov was preoccupied with his own thoughts and missed his name, which according to Pashkevich's rules means that he misses the whole meal. I sneaked him a slice anyway and asked what was on his mind.

"My daughter," he said. "Her birthday was a few days ago."

Have we really been out there that long? It seems impossible.

Vakhromov said, "I keep thinking about that first year with my son. Every day when I came home he'd learned something new. With my daughter, I've missed all of that."

"It will all be over soon. I mean, it has to be, right?" I said without much certainty. Even with the lend-lease supplies that are now trickling steadily in, it's hard to imagine the Red Army persevering for another year like this one, Leningrad besieged and starving, desperate building-to-building fighting in Stalingrad, an endless impasse here at the Rzhev salient.

That's when the new woman showed up. She had a PPSh-41 slung over her shoulder and her hair was pulled into a severe braid. Our commissar interrupted the bread ritual to bring Petya to her. He said, "Petya, this is Comrade Stepanova. She wants you to tell her your story."

Petya said, "I don't want to," and Vakhromov said, "You're making him relive the worst day of his life," but Stepanova said, "Tell me." Her voice was cold crystal blue.

So he did. She listened intently, not betraying any hint of emotion. She made him describe everything: Zoya, what she looked like, what she was wearing when she was caught, her tormentors, their uniforms, what they did to her and how she responded.

When he was finished, she said, "There's no doubt about it. He was there."

Petya ran back to me and clung to my dirty tunic. I gave him a piece of bread and took the heel for myself while I listened to Stepanova and the commissar's conversation. I only understood half of it, and that half I didn't like.

"Are you sure you want the kid?" the commissar asked Stepanova. "The villagers are willing to help."

She said, "Zoya burned their village. They're not reliable allies. The kid we can control. You see how he trusts those soldiers."

"Do you think an eight-year-old's memory is reliable?"

"He described everything perfectly," said Stepanova. "How's the intelligence report coming?"

"It's hit a snag. You remember Malakhov? He's been convicted of antigovernment activities."

"Wrecker?"

"Worse than that. Trotskyist."

The only crime worse than sabotaging the state: supporting Stalin's greatest rival. I'm redacting Stepanova's reply, a word no woman ought to use.

The commissar said, "I know. But he was our main contact in that area. We'll find them, don't worry. It'll just take time."

Pashkevich broke in and demanded to know what this was all about.

"We're recovering the photos," said Stepanova, as though no further explanation was required.

"Like hell we are. Who's in charge here?" Pashkevich demanded.

"I am," said Stepanova, crossing her arms. "Or are you blind as well as stupid?"

Her collar tabs bore a T-shaped gold insignia. She was a starshina, the squad's ranking NCO. When Pashkevich saw that, he threw down his rifle and yelled, "That's it! I won't take orders from a woman!"

"I'll give you thirty seconds to rethink that statement before I arrest you," said our commissar.

Pashkevich glared, muttered something that might have been an apology, and stalked away.

Petya was still clinging to me and listlessly nibbling his piece of bread. Vakhromov came over and picked him up. The boy said, "Why does everyone want to hear that story? It's not a nice story."

Vakhromov chewed his lip while contemplating his reply. He said, "Those fascists did some very bad things. We think everyone *should know about it, so that everyone will know what bad people they are."*

That was enough to satisfy a kid, maybe, but after everything I've been through, this felt too neat, too heroic. Once Petya was tucked into bed, I found Stepanova and asked, "The fascists commit atrocities every day. You could walk through any occupied city and find a story like this. Why this one? Why us?"

Stepanova said, "It's true. You could find something like this anywhere. But if you looked for a hundred years, you wouldn't find someone like Zoya."

I know you asked for a long letter, but you can see from my spotty writing that I'm running out of ink. Please send more so I can keep writing to you.

Yours,

Pasha

P.S. You called me Pashenka.

★

8 November 1942

Dear Pasha,

Did I? It must have been the morphine.

Thank you for writing. I couldn't lay my hands on any extra ink, but enclosed please find a pencil. Writing in pencil is an insult to your beautiful handwriting, but pencils don't leak or jam, and if they break, you have two pencils, and you can erase if you make a mistake. No need to thank me; I assure you I'm being entirely self-serving in allowing you to keep writing. Your letters are essential to preserving my morale.

In some ways, being forcibly bedridden was worse than being on fire. All that time I had nothing to do except worry. Sometimes I worried about Iskra and the girls. But mostly I worried about you. I think about those troops who were encircled and how the army decided that they were not worth saving and I constantly fear that you will be swallowed next.

And every time I fell asleep, I dreamed of fire. Not of my burning plane, though sometimes I thought I heard its ticking engine in the background, but of the barracks at Stakhanovo and of being a little girl again, trying to back away from the flames but unable to because they were everywhere.

Those dreams were the last straw. I declared myself better, despite the protests of the doctors, and went to rejoin my regiment. My hands have healed, but my left side is scarring from my shoulder to my knee. Another reason you wouldn't want a picture of me. It was hard getting my uniform on, but I thought of all the sorties Iskra was flying without me and I forced myself through it. I'm not jealous that she flew with other pilots, but now her count is ahead of mine!

When I arrived at our aerodrome, I grabbed Iskra and pulled her into a bear hug and we kissed each other on the cheeks. She said with a laugh that happy reunions after near disaster were becoming a hallmark of our relationship. I said that I would never let her fly with anyone else again. When

I asked her what she thought of the other pilots, she said she doesn't fly and tell.

Bershanskaya took one look at me and ordered me back to the hospital. I told her I felt fine. She poked me in the leg. I yelped. She said, "No you aren't. Get back to the hospital." But I begged until she relented.

I got to meet my new sewing machine. It's Number 18. I'm not sure I like her as much as our beloved Number 41. Same model, same specs, but the engine has a different pitch and rhythm. Will this plane bring me home safe with one wing shredded and on fire?

Iskra assured me that, once I got in the air, it would be like I'd never been gone, but it was still with trepidation that I put my hands on the controls to take our new plane for a test flight. I taxied her slowly and took off carefully, as though I were back in flight school. And then the thought struck me: What was the worst that could happen? The worst had already happened! And I had survived! I broke into a maniacal grin and thought that I would never be afraid of anything again.

The girls had tons of gossip to catch me up on. Of course everyone wanted to talk about the Armavir sortie. According to records, Iskra and I took out six planes all together. The KG 51 bomber wing has decided to judiciously withdraw from the Taman Peninsula. "Meaning they're running away with their tails between their legs," said Zhigli.

I thought it was only fair to say that taking out the bomber wing would have done me no good if it hadn't been for Zhigli.

She's earned her share of the praise, both for saving me and for putting up with me.

No, we didn't singlehandedly liberate Armavir or even its airport, but we did receive decorations. Would you believe it, Pasha, your Valka is a war hero! The Red Army thinks so, anyway.

But being a hero should feel like something, shouldn't it? I ought to feel proud and brave. But I feel the same as yesterday. Helpless in the face of a war too big and too cruel for one bomber pilot to matter. Worried about you. Keenly aware that, even with a medal, I can't save you from the danger you face.

There was a ceremony yesterday on the anniversary of the Revolution. Ten of us, me and Iskra among them, were given the Order of the Red Star, and many others got engraved watches. Almost all pilots. I looked guiltily at our armorers as I marched past them to receive my medal. We'd all die without good armorers, but they are never decorated and they get lower pay and worse food. It doesn't seem fair.

But there's no resentment between the girls who got medals and the girls who got watches and the girls who got nothing. How could there be when we know that any of us might not return from the next mission?

There's a tradition that when you receive a decoration, you have to drop the medal into a glass of vodka and then drain the glass. Bershanskaya made an exception to her usual rule against alcohol. We didn't have any glasses, so we had to drop our red stars into empty rations cans. But drinking didn't unknot the worry inside me. Iskra said I should let myself relax and have fun for one day. I told her it's hard to, knowing you're still out there.

Our humble night-bomber regiment is finally attracting attention. The higher-ups, the ones who wondered if we needed a few big men to help us, have noticed that we fly twice as many sorties as everyone else. We're being rebased north to rejoin our old division, not as helpless rookies but as full-fledged airwomen. Something big is in the works, an offensive that requires all the best air support available. If you can believe it, that means us.

It even has a name: Operation Mars. Do you know about it? The name sends a thrill of excitement through me. Mars, the god of war. This is the big one, the turning point, or so I've heard. And it all begins with smashing the Rzhev salient.

You can imagine my feelings when I heard the word "Rzhev." I could barely sit still for our briefing. I'm coming to you, Pasha, after all this time! We'll be together again! It's not likely that you'll actually spot me and even less likely that I'll see you, but if you hear an overgrown sewing machine overhead, look up. If there's an 18 on the tail, it's me!

But not all the news that greeted me was so rosy.

Khomyakova, one of the pyaterka pilots from the 586th, was killed in a crash. She wasn't in combat. A few days before, she'd shot down a bomber, the regiment's first kill and a real point of honor for our women's regiments. She'd been in Moscow receiving a decoration. When she got off the train that night, tired from traveling, Major Kazarinova let her take a nap in the dugout while her mechanic warmed up her plane. But then

Khomyakova got scrambled—ordered to take off immediately—and she ran to the plane, still half asleep, took off, and crashed straight into a hangar.

Her death was ruled a combat casualty, so there won't be an investigation. Meanwhile, Major Kazarinova has been removed from command, officially because of failing health. That war wound, you know. Iskra, would you believe it, stubbornly maintains that it's a coincidence.

You might think that, with everything going on in the women's regiments, I wouldn't have time to worry about anything else, but I keep thinking of you and Petya. You're right—attracting attention isn't a good thing. Khomyakova found that out, not that the knowledge will do her any good. I don't know what that starshina of yours is planning, but the fascists won't hand her those photos tied with a bow.

Yours,

Valka

★ TWENTY-EIGHT ★

THE LAST OF MY STITCHES WERE OUT. I'D BEEN DECLARED fully recovered. I locked myself in the bathroom and took off my clothes so that I could get a good look at myself, or as good a look as I could in the rusty, pitted steel mirror.

It wasn't pretty.

My left side was covered with a wide swath of mottled red, broken up by irregularly placed skin grafts I only hazily remembered getting. Those scars would be with me for life. At least they were covered by my uniform. I couldn't bear to let anyone see me like this. A few months ago Pasha had gushed about my beauty. He was in for a rude surprise if I ever saw him again.

I could imagine Iskra saying, "That's my vain baby cousin,"

but it wasn't vanity. This war had put its mark on me. I'd never be able to put it behind me when it was over, not now that the reminder was physically stamped on my body.

When I emerged from the bathroom, the other girls were still discussing Khomyakova's death. The conversation had been going in circles for an hour.

"It's a weird story all over," said Tanya as she pulled her long-sleeved undershirt over her head. Our flight shared one sanitarium ward, a cheerful room with yellow wallpaper, a row of neat iron bedsteads, and a view of the sea. "Why put her on night duty when she'd been traveling all day? Why let her rest if she was going to be scrambled?"

"You can't fly while you're asleep," said Zhigli's young navigator.

Iskra and I exchanged glances. She said, "*My* pilot certainly doesn't."

"Absolutely not," I concurred, putting on my most innocent face.

"It does cast serious doubts on Kazarinova's judgment," said Vera. "A disciplinarian who gets results is one thing. But a disciplinarian who lets her own pilots die in preventable accidents is unacceptable."

"Accidents?" said Zhigli.

Everyone paused in their various states of dress and stared at her.

"What's that supposed to mean?" asked Iskra sharply.

Zhigli said, "The pyaterka wanted Kazarinova removed from

command. Kazarinova has probably been harboring a grudge against them. An insubordinate pilot becomes the hero of the regiment and then turns up dead in a fluke accident a few days later?"

"You can't just throw around a claim like that," said Vera.

"It's not beyond Kazarinova," I said. "Nothing is."

Zhigli sat on the edge of her bed and tied her portyanki, which had daisies embroidered on them. She said, "Everything makes perfect sense when you look at it in that light. Which pilots opposed Kazarinova's appointment?"

I thought back. "The pyaterka and Lilya."

"Right. So isn't it suspicious that half of that group got transferred to an underequipped regiment flying the wrong planes in the hottest part of the front? And one of the two who stayed at the 586th ended up dead? Kazarinova only has one name left on her list."

One of the rods used to clean the guns rested on top of the cast-iron stove. Iskra took it and delicately began curling the ends of her hair. She said, "Zhigli. These ideas you're entertaining are horrendous."

"What happened is horrendous!" I snapped.

Iskra pointed the hot metal rod at me and then at Zhigli. "Kazarinova made a mistake, plain and simple. These wild speculations are . . . they're borderline treasonous, is what they are."

"You wouldn't say all this if our commissar were here," agreed Vera.

"Not to mention they're completely bizarre," continued Iskra. She returned her makeshift curling iron to the stove and slipped on her flight helmet, taking care not to disturb her hair. "Now, are we going to stand around making up conspiracy theories or are we going to fly some slugs?"

She headed out of the room without waiting for a reply. I followed, fastening my own well-worn leather flight helmet under my chin and putting on my goggles. I told my cousin, "I can't believe you're defending Kazarinova. She *arrested* you. She had you *thrown in prison*."

Iskra paused, holding open the front door. "You may have noticed she didn't *murder* me."

Remembering what had happened last time we argued and what we were headed into, I pulled her into a protective squeeze. "No. And I'm glad she didn't."

15 November 1942

Dear Valyushka,

To think that you're coming here—and you'll be wearing that beautiful red star! How can you think you're ugly, Valyushka, when you have that? You are a hero and that makes you beautiful, no matter what your body looks like.

Thanks to Operation Mars, I could see you very soon. It isn't likely, but it's something I can hope for. And I desperately need something to hope for.

We're not supposed to talk about the offensive on the radio for security reasons, but everyone is. This is the important one, they're saying, the final assault. The one that will wipe out the

Rzhev salient once and for all. I'll have to hope they're right, because I'll be in the middle of it.

The intelligence report finally came through. Pashkevich swore when he saw it. They've found the German cavalry regiment, the one that was in Petrishchevo. They're in the salient.

Stepanova considered the report stoically. She said, "It should be manageable. We'll accompany the offensive. The bombers and Katyushas should do most of the work for us. We'll have to hope that our man is alive when we get there. I have . . . questions for him."

I tried to hide my feelings as I asked, "We're going in during the offensive? Under the Katyushas?"

"Yes, Danilin, under the Katyushas," she said, like I was an idiot. My skin prickled, and not just because of the winter air.

Stepanova has been with us for a month now, yet she has made no attempt to get acquainted with us. I don't even know her first name. She sits by herself during meals. It seemed wrong to me to face death alongside a total stranger. So I sought her out.

She sat on a crumbled remnant of wall, paring her nails with her combat knife. I sat beside her, half expecting her to order me away, but she didn't. I nodded at the submachine gun leaning against the wall. "That's a beautiful gun. Sure beats our old Mosin-Nagants."

"If you're about to suggest a trade, forget it," she said without looking up.

I gave a short laugh. A better weapon would be wasted on me. I said, "No, it's just that we don't see many PPSh-41s in the *infantry. But sometimes I see photos of partisans carrying them."*

Stepanova said, "It's been useful."

Our commissar had told me that Stepanova had been a partisan once. I told her as much.

She replied, "Might have been."

"And that you served during the defense of Moscow."

"Might have. What's it to you?"

I lit a cigarette and told her, "That was Kosmodemyanskaya's assignment, too. You would have trained alongside her. You knew her."

There was a long silence. Finally, without looking at me, Stepanova said, "Yes, I knew Zoya."

"So this mission is personal."

"My country has been invaded. The whole war is personal for me."

"Are you out for revenge?"

She asked what business of mine that was.

I said, "I could sacrifice my life for it. Petya's, too."

Stepanova flipped her knife between her fingers. Her face was still impassive. She said, "Zoya and I were schoolchildren together. We trained together. We crossed the lines together. Except for the caprices of fate we would have died together. They took her from me and they will get what's coming to them. Call it revenge if you like. I call it justice."

It frightens me to be under the command of someone like her. Yet a part of me understands. Reports are coming in about the POW camp in Vyazma. Tens of thousands of men are crowded into an unfinished slaughterhouse with no water, sanitation, or protection from the elements. The prisoners fight over frozen chunks of raw, rotten meat flung to them by the guards. Hundreds die every day. Their bodies are thrown into mass graves.

If you get shot down in the offensive and have to land behind enemy lines, that could be you.

If I found out something like that had happened to you, I'd forget all my conflicting feelings about being part of this war. I wouldn't think of anything except how to make them pay.

Tell me it won't come to that.

Yours,

Pasha

Captain Ilyushina had her hands full checking out the aircraft before their journey north. Number 18 had acquired a winter coat of hastily applied white paint. I'd grown fond of her. She wasn't fierce and gutsy like her predecessor, but hardy and reliable. The longer I was in the field, the more I appreciated that.

While Ilyushina worked, I regaled her with the story of our aeroclub's temperamental plane. The longer the war dragged on, the more I found myself reminiscing about life back in Stakhanovo.

"A steel fuselage and a wooden wing?" came the engineer's echoey voice from inside the fuselage. "I know Yakovlev designed some mixed-material light aircraft before the war."

"If that's it, ours must have been some kind of failed prototype. It had a problem with the engine conking out. You could fly all day without a problem, but if you went into a dive at the wrong angle . . ."

Ilyushina's tousled blond head emerged from the front cockpit and she rested her grease-spotted arms along its edge. "You, my friend, had something loose in your fuel tank. A ball bearing, I'd guess. The perfect size to cover the fuel line when it rolls into exactly the right place."

"You're kidding!" I said, almost laughing at my own stupidity. "We spent four years trying to fix that plane and all along it was that simple? You must think I'm an idiot."

Ilyushina shook her head. "You're a good airwoman. You all are."

"Why, captain, did you just say something nice about us?"

"You can call me Klava. I don't want to be the last person in the regiment known only by her rank." The engineer sat beside me on the wet grass at the edge of the airstrip. Before us, the ground dropped away into bottle-green sea wrinkled with waves. The air tasted of salt and pine and oily exhaust from Ilyushina's testing aircraft engines.

I asked, "So you're no longer sore about having to spend the war serving with a bunch of girls?"

"I'm glad I'm not still at the airport factory. Nothing is as infuriating as doing quality control when you want to be at the front." She put a cigarette in her mouth and lit it with a lighter made from a copper-washed cartridge case. "I wish I could have served with my husband's unit, though."

Surprised, I glanced down at the plain gold band on Ilyushina's right hand, noticing it for the first time. "I don't think you've ever mentioned that you're married."

"Was married," Ilyushina corrected.

"Oh," I said quietly. "What happened?"

"He was sent to the front. What do you think happened?"

"I'm sorry."

Ilyushina shrugged just like I did when I was trying to pretend I wasn't worried about Pasha. "There's no time for love during a war, anyway."

"What was he like?"

Ilyushina considered. "What I remember most is how much he cared about things. He treated whatever he was doing as if it was the most important thing in the world. His schoolwork. His military duties. Us."

"Was that why you wanted to go to the front?" I asked, thinking of what I would have done in her place, then realizing with a pang that I might end up in her place. "Because of what happened to him?"

Ilyushina nodded. "Stupid of me, isn't it? Being here doesn't help him." She lapsed into silence and looked out at the water. "You have a boy, don't you? The one you're always writing to."

"Yes, Pasha." The reply came naturally to me without thought.

"Take care of him, Valka. If you can."

That was apparently as much relationship talk as the engineer had in her. She stood up and ground the cigarette out under her boot heel. "Enough chitchat. I've got nineteen other planes to look at."

She climbed into the next plane. I stayed by the cliff edge, lost in thought. I had admitted something to Ilyushina that I hadn't even admitted to myself. I'd spent so much effort quashing rumors about Pasha, telling everyone that he was only a friend. Even though I anticipated his letters and tore them open eagerly, yet carefully, for fear of tearing the paper inside. Even though I daydreamed about meeting him when we rebased, inventing elaborate scenarios involving forced landings in friendly territory. I'd see him first. Then he would turn and there would be that moment of recognition. His soft brown eyes would light up. I'd throw my arms around him and, regardless of who was watching, kiss him the way I should have kissed him on the barge all those months ago.

No. Pasha was not just a friend. Pasha was mine. The thought fit me as comfortably as a favorite pair of slippers, yet it was heavy with responsibility. Because if he was mine, then Ilyushina was right. I needed to take care of him.

20 November 1942

Dear Pasha,

Promises are cheap. There are many promises I could have made you once in all earnestness that I would have broken by now: that you'd be home in a year, that we'd see each other again soon, that I'd take care of myself and not get hurt. But as I make you this promise, I want to believe it more than anything: One way or another, we're making it out of the meat grinder alive.

Faithful Number 18 brought us to our new aerodrome east

of Rzhev. We're rejoining our first division, the one we served with in Trud Gornyaka. We formed up on the airfield, standing straight at attention, our chests spangled with stars and medals. Colonel Dmitry Dmitrievich Popov was there to meet us.

He stalked down the line, his face more worn and weary than I remembered, but frowning just as deeply. He stopped in front of me and asked, "Junior Lieutenant, what is that you're wearing?"

I said, "The Order of the Red Star, sir."

"How did you get it?"

I told him about the Armavir airfield.

He furrowed his brow and looked at me intently, as if he thought I might be lying, but only said, "Your big brothers at the 650th have three red stars among them. Half of you have them."

When he reached Bershanskaya, she saluted and greeted him with "Well, colonel, we've been foisted on you again."

He cleared his throat awkwardly and said, "Actually, I requested you."

Bershanskaya's eyes widened with innocent surprise. "Really? Are we the last U-2 regiment in the Soviet Union?"

The colonel looked everywhere but at Bershanskaya. "No. I asked the commander of the Transcaucasian Front for the 588th specifically. He didn't want to give you up. He offered me two male regiments instead, but I insisted."

"I was under the impression that you were displeased with our performance when we served under you." Bershanskaya kept her face serious, but her green eyes twinkled. She was enjoying this conversation immensely.

"I was. But I've been forced to reevaluate. We need to hammer the Wehrmacht infantry as hard as we can before the offensive. Especially at night. The less sleep they get, the lower their morale, and the better our troops will do."

Bershanskaya asked what that had to do with us.

Popov said, "There have been reports from Wehrmacht soldiers captured in your operational area. You've gained a reputation. The Hitlerites, you see, have very traditional views about men and women. For a fascist soldier to be terrified of a bunch of girls . . . it's humiliating."

"So what you're saying is . . ."

He forced out the next sentence as if it took physical effort. "I'm saying that being women makes you better harassment bombers."

Objective accomplished.

But now is not the time to lord it over our division commander. I've heard rumors about Operation Mars. Rumors about our men being outnumbered and underequipped. Rumors that all the air support in the world won't save the offensive.

What about you, Pasha? Your band will be delving straight through the worst of it. Are they sending you into the grinder with a scant handful of bullets and no choice but to charge blindly in and hope for the best? Finally we'll be fighting side by side, and yet there might as well still be an ocean between us.

Yours,

Valka

★ TWENTY-NINE ★

THE COMMAND DUGOUT, LIT ONLY BY A COUPLE OF artillery-shell lamps, was even darker than the evening outside. Other airwomen had already claimed the miscellaneous crates and boxes scattered about the dugout in lieu of chairs; they were not talking and joking as they usually did, but sitting tense and quiet. As I entered, I gave a start. Bershanskaya was not in her usual spot but stood off to the side with her arms crossed. At her desk sat Tamara Kazarinova.

"Glad you decided to join us, Koroleva," she said. I bit back the desire to point out that I wasn't even late. She hadn't changed a bit. Same crew cut, same stern crease between her eyes.

My heart instinctively sped up with the knowledge that

something was wrong. Everyone said she'd left the 586th in disgrace, headed for a desk job and an early retirement. What was she doing there? Had she come after Iskra? I turned a searching look to Bershanskaya, who shook her head silently. No, we would not get an explanation.

Kazarinova didn't seem interested in my cousin. She turned her attention to the marked-up map spread across the desk as if this were a regular briefing and her presence didn't signify anything out of the ordinary. "There is a small partisan camp located here in the ruins of an abandoned village. There are about two hundred partisans there at the moment."

Tanya grumbled something about wasting bombers on supply runs. I asked, "What's the signal-fire pattern?"

"Junior Lieutenant, you will not interrupt during a briefing," snapped Kazarinova. "And this is not a resupply mission."

She slid the map to the side, revealing a photo of a bearded middle-aged man in a long leather coat and a flat cap, brandishing a submachine gun. "This is Viktor Malakhov, the leader of the company. They have been operating with apparent success since summer, but recent intelligence has proved that Malakhov is a Trotskyist saboteur."

Malakhov. The name nibbled at my memory. Where had I heard it before?

"Their supplies have already been cut off in the hope that they would weaken and be overrun, but they've proven to be a resilient bunch, so more direct intervention is required. We've been ordered to make sure that they don't survive the war. Malakhov, in case you should spot him, is the primary objective, but all the partisans are secondary objectives. If we can disperse the camp, the Hitlerites ought to do the clean-up work for us. No flak is anticipated, naturally, so I expect you to keep it neat and accurate. You are dismissed."

I wanted to dart away immediately, but I waited for Iskra, afraid to let her out of my sight while Kazarinova was around. We stood in the long shadow our plane's tail cast in the dying light as if we were hiding.

"What's she doing here?" I asked in a low voice. "She's not . . . she's not replacing Bershanskaya, is she?"

"Not as far as I know," said Iskra carefully. "Bershanskaya just said she'd be with our regiment for a while and that she would brief us on tonight's mission."

"Well, it's safe to say she has a plan. And she's not wasting any time. This mission has her fingerprints all over it." My fingers sought my mouth. "Those are Russians we'll be bombing. Our own people."

"Valka, you would say that *anything* you didn't like had her fingerprints all over it," said Iskra, adding, "Did she mention the bombing altitude?"

"I don't think so."

"Then go ask."

I would have said, "Go ask yourself," but I figured Iskra had earned the right to avoid Kazarinova.

When I reentered the dugout, I found Kazarinova with her boot off, massaging her injured leg. I'd known there must be a scar, but the size of it startled me. An irregular patch of red slashed diagonally from her knee to her ankle and was crisscrossed with several deep, straight surgery scars. She was looking at a photo on the desk that had nothing to do with the night's mission. It depicted a sleek, clean-lined interbellum biplane. A young pilot stood straight and tall next to it and a beaming teenage girl with messy bobbed hair sat on the lower wing.

I recognized the look in that young pilot's eyes. It was the same look that had shone from the face of every girl in Aviation Group 122 on that very first day in Moscow. That look said, *I've made it. I worked so hard and so many people tried tried to stop me, but I've finally made it.*

Kazarinova's gaze broke away from the photo. "What is it, Koroleva?" she asked in her usual businesslike tone.

"Oh, um, my navigator wanted to know the bombing altitude."

"Six hundred meters, standard procedure," said Kazarinova, then looked at me like she was wondering why I was still there. I momentarily wanted to say something like "I'm sorry about what happened to you," but her stern expression silenced me.

As I rejoined the other pilots, I couldn't get the image of that jagged scar out of my mind. I thought about my own accident and the doctor telling me that in another minute I would have lost my leg, and I found that, despite everything, I couldn't hate Tamara Kazarinova.

As we did our preflight check by the raking orange light of the setting sun, Iskra asked me, "Any word from Pasha?"

I took the cap off the fuel tank so I could double-check the fuel level. The smell of gasoline bit my nose. "Why are you asking me? The entire regiment knows every time I get a letter from him. Sometimes before I do."

"Only because we love you, baby cousin."

"Does the concept of privacy mean nothing to you?" I asked as I replaced the cap. My tone was harsher than I meant. Tonight's bizarre mission had me on edge.

"Are you seriously asking that question after a year in the military?" Iskra replied, adding, "Valyushka, I know you better than you think. I can tell that you're worried. It might help to talk about it. Believe it or not, you aren't the only person who cares what happens to Pasha."

I *was* worried, even though it had been less than a week since Pasha's last letter. He was caught up in something that neither he nor I could control. Anything could have happened since his last letter. When I was feeling good, I entertained the happier possibilities. The photos had already been recovered by someone else. The mission had been a resounding success and no one had been hurt and the whole squad were being named Heroes of the Soviet Union for their valor. (I couldn't entertain *that* idea for long before it collapsed under its own improbability.)

In darker moods, other possibilities came to mind. The worst was one where the letters simply stopped coming. Days pass into weeks, then months. How long would I wait? When would I stop hoping that the next day a letter would come?

But it was none of Iskra's business. I glared at my cousin

through the propeller and said, "Don't call me Valyushka."

We were first in the flight order, a treat under normal circumstances, more like a punishment today. Bershanskaya came up to us, looked at me, looked harder at Iskra, and told us, "This is a sortie like any other, girls. Complete the mission."

We took off, our wheels skidding on the icy ground. A light snow had begun to fall. The snowflakes that settled on our noses and lips melted into speckles of cold water. Those that settled on our goggles remained snowflakes. Operation Mars would launch in a few days, and by the looks of it, it would launch in the middle of a snowstorm.

"How many soldiers do you think were encircled here at the salient?" I asked Iskra. An unhappy realization had crept into my head.

Iskra replied with uncharacteristic indifference. "I don't know. Half a million? Why do we care?"

Because they were ordinary people who did not deserve their fate. Because they had families and futures and maybe even girls who loved them but had never quite worked up the nerve to say so. "What would you do if you were a Red Army man trapped behind the lines? You'd join the partisans."

"Oh, that's what this is about, baby cousin." The pet name sounded weary, not affectionate. "I promise, we can't possibly end up dropping bombs on Pasha. The offensive hasn't even started. He's still safe behind the Russian lines."

"But all those other soldiers . . ."

"I don't like this mission any more than you do, so drop it," said Iskra curtly. "I get to nap on the way there. You nap on the way back. That was our agreement. Your heading is 290 degrees. Wake me if anything changes." She pulled the speaking tube out of her ear so I couldn't reply.

A layer of white blanketed everything, fields and trees, rubble and ditches and craters. It blunted the edges of the tank stoppers and quietly disguised the husks of damaged houses. The snowfall melted the horizon into a uniform white haze. I should have felt reassured by this tranquil isolation, but in the silence, with Iskra asleep, I found myself thinking about the mission, and that was unwise. I could have raised an objection. I could have refused to go. They would have court-martialed me, but at least I would have been able to live with myself. When had I become this person? I repeated Bershanskaya's words to myself: "a sortie like any other."

An expanse of rugged evergreens, their branches sagging under the weight of the snow, came into view ahead. "Target in sight, Iskra," I called, loud enough to be heard over the engine and the wind. "Is that our forest?"

"Yeah, that's it," came my cousin's groggy voice as she replaced her speaking tube.

We circled over the woods. Iskra spotted a clearing dotted with the remains of a village. We passed over again, lower, barely clearing the treetops. Snow made everything bright, even on a cloudy night. I could clearly make out the tumbledown stone walls of a few dozen buildings, some roofed over with rude boards or corrugated iron to provide a modicum of shelter. The ground was smooth and white. There was a fire in the middle of the clearing, visible by the flickery orange light it cast on the snow, and a cluster of figures standing around it. Malakhov? I didn't think so. They looked too small. But everyone was an objective.

I tried to slip into my night-bomber mind-set, to see them as nothing but shapes on the ground, a meaningless training exercise. I couldn't. They were people, our people. The thought of what we were about to do sickened me. And another part of me berated myself for feeling no compassion for the fascists, as if they were not also people who had futures and families and girls who loved them.

"It's time," I told Iskra as the houses came in line with the chalk marks on the wing.

"Wait." Iskra's voice had none of its usual confidence. She sounded hesitant, lost.

Twenty seconds over the target. "Now or never."

The bombs did not fall. I muttered a curse under my breath and reached for the bomb release. Ten seconds left. I didn't need to pull the release, I told myself. It was Iskra's mistake, not mine. We could drop the bombs harmlessly in the forest and mark it in our flight logs as a miss. Bombers missed all the time.

Iskra's mistake. And Kazarinova was at the airfield. Watching us. Waiting for mistakes. Five seconds left.

I pulled the release. The bombs fell away. That's it, it's out of your hands now, I told myself as I averted my eyes. The heat and pressure of the blast hit us. A direct hit, clean and accurate and entirely my doing. I was suddenly angry at Iskra, as if the whole mission had been her fault. "Dammit, Iskra, do your job!"

"But those were . . ."

I said spitefully, "I sleep on the way back, remember?"

We didn't speak on the way back, didn't say a word to the armorers as they met us on the airstrip and turned the plane around. When we neared the target the second time, I only broke the silence to ask, "Have you got it this time?"

"Yes," said Iskra. Those were the last words we exchanged all night.

We had left our mark. Messy dark splotches marked where bombs had blasted away the snow to reveal the earth below. I spotted one figure crumpled on the ground and two others carrying a third. It was easier that time. The damage was already done.

The winter night felt interminable as we flew, bombed, refueled, and flew again, long after I was sure nothing could have survived. By the end of the night, hardly anything could be distinguished of what had once been the partisan camp. Snow and dirt and stone and wood had blended together like a smeared finger painting.

We were bone tired when Number 18 rolled onto her hardstand for the day. Iskra had taken a couple of the dark blue pills to get through the night, and she massaged her temples through her hand-dyed lavender cap comforter as we stumbled into the command dugout to report. But inside, voices rose.

". . . hearing disturbing reports about this regiment. Disobedience, lack of discipline, defacing aircraft . . . But that isn't your biggest breach of regulations, is it?"

"I don't know what you're talking about," said Bershanskaya.

She sat across from her own desk like a child being scolded by her teacher. Her voice was quiet, but not its usual controlled quiet. This was a cowed quiet.

"Don't play games with me. I've been here all night. I've confirmed that you aren't following standard turnaround procedures. Adopting your unauthorized procedure in the first place might generously be considered a lapse of judgment. Continuing after an official reprimand? That's insubordination." Kazarinova laboriously got to her feet, leaning heavily on the desk. Pain flashed across her face as she put weight on her bad leg. She said, "I'll be watching you carefully, Major. If you step out of line, headquarters will hear about it."

She limped out of the dugout.

Bershanskaya raked a hand through her hair. She turned to us with a pleading look. "Tell me you completed the mission."

"Yes, ma'am," I said, suddenly glad for euphemistic military language. "The objective has been accomplished."

"Good." Her green eyes softened with regret. "Dear eaglets, I'm so sorry. I didn't want to accept that mission, but I had no choice. I'm under a lot of pressure right now."

I glanced out the dugout door. "What does she want?"

"To break me," said Bershanskaya. "To prove I'm not fit for the job. I don't know if she wants the command for herself or if she just wants us to fail because she failed. Either way, Iskra, I'm afraid you're the weak spot she needs."

I reflexively put a protective arm around my cousin. "Are you going to . . . ?"

"No. It'll be all right. Follow orders, fly your missions, and, whatever you do, don't break rules while Kazarinova is around."

Suddenly the whole miserable night made a bitter kind of sense. I said, "It was a test."

Bershanskaya nodded. "A loyalty test. Iskra's name was cleared once, but she'll never be completely free of suspicion. If you hadn't dropped those bombs, you would have been aiding a known wrecker. Drawing a connection between Malakhov and Iskra's parents would be easy. I'd be implicated for keeping you here even though I knew your past. It would be enough pressure to crack the 588th apart." That distant look entered her eyes. I wondered if she was thinking what I was thinking, wondering if the lives of the partisans were a price worth paying. She said, "You're dismissed. Go get some sleep."

We returned to our own dugout. Most of the other girls in our flight were already asleep. Night bombers learned to drop off instantly. I kicked off my boots and threw myself gratefully onto the hard mattress without bothering to undress, but before I could fall asleep, Iskra whispered, "Valka. I told you to wait."

In my exhaustion, it took me a moment to figure out the context. I muttered, "What did you want me to do?"

"I . . ." Iskra's voice faltered. "I don't know. Drop the bombs somewhere else, I guess. Onto the fascists. They'd deserve it. I know it's what Kazarinova wanted, but . . ."

"You think Viktor Malakhov didn't deserve it?"

"Do you think he did?"

I considered. "No. But I'd've thought you would. He's a

Trotskyist and a traitor. I'd expect you'd be lining up to drop bombs on him."

"Malakhov, maybe," said Iskra without much conviction. "But . . . that wasn't Malakhov out there when we were on our first run. I got a good look at them, Valka. Some of them were young. Just kids."

"Did we kill them?"

"I don't know. Someone must have survived, because there were no bodies outside at the end of the night."

"We're worthless either way, aren't we? If we didn't disperse the camp, our mission failed. If we did, we killed a bunch of teenagers fighting on our side."

"Yeah." Iskra's voice sounded hollow, and I thought she might start to cry.

I crawled into her plank bed and snuggled close and warm beside her. She was holding her aeronavigation book in both hands like a talisman. I'd never seen her like this. Even after she lost her parents, she'd been so confident, so sure that she understood the world and her place within it. Stripped of all that, she seemed exposed. So small. So delicate.

"Do you want to see it?" she asked, offering me the book.

Iskra hadn't let me anywhere near that book since it had mysteriously showed up in her possession. I gingerly took it. I'd half expected it to contain some kind of secret, but no, it was exactly what it looked like, a slim, well-worn volume with nothing on the white cover except the words *Aeronavigation: Third Edition*.

"Where did you get it?" I asked softly.

"It was after I was arrested, while they were . . ."

Iskra's voice faded. She searched the dugout's rough plank ceiling with her eyes. "You can't understand what imprisonment does to you. The isolation. I could feel my mind eating itself alive for lack of anything to occupy it. God, I missed you so badly."

I found her hand and squeezed it.

"One day a guard passed this book through the opening in the door. Didn't say a word. But look!"

She opened the book to the front flyleaf. Written across it in quick, confident cursive were the words *Keep studying*.

"That book saved my life, baby cousin, and I'm not exaggerating. Without it, I don't know how much longer I would have lasted before there was . . . permanent damage. I was holding something in my hands that someone else had held in their hands, had read and thought about and written in and knocked the corners off. It gave me something to focus on during those endless days alone in that empty cell."

"And nobody ever owned up to it? No one ever told you, 'I was the one who sent you that book'?"

She shook her head. "How could they? What if I were arrested again and it came out that they'd helped me when I was imprisoned before? They'd be putting themselves in danger."

I parted my lips and said thoughtfully, "It would make sense if it was owned by . . . a navigator."

"I'd thought of that."

"But you lied to me. You said that no one had secured your release."

"I don't know that anyone did. Only that someone sent the book."

I gave her a reproachful look. "Of course they were the same person. Why would she tell you to keep studying if she wasn't working to get you out?"

Iskra waved me off. "I know, it looks obvious. But I had a long time to think about it. Maybe the note wasn't even meant for me. Maybe it was written in that book years ago when it was given to its original owner. And . . ." Her shoulders rose and fell in a sigh. "All right, I'll admit it: I wanted to be acquitted properly, because then I'd know that people could be found innocent and that would mean that if someone was found guilty, he was really guilty. Because if I allowed that what happened to me was unjust, then the whole house of cards would come falling down. But today, I saw those children and all I could think was 'family members of a traitor to the Motherland.' From this side, I couldn't pretend that there was some hidden reason why this should be happening. There was no possibility of justice."

"Your parents," I said, fumbling for a silver lining. "They're almost halfway done serving their sentences. When you see them again, you'll be able to tell them that you understand. That you know they were innocent. Hearing that will mean so much to them."

"Oh, Valka." Iskra looked at me with sadness in her soft blue eyes. "You really don't know what 'without the right of correspondence' means, do you? They've been dead this whole time."

★ THIRTY ★

20 November 1942

Dear Valyushka,

Five days until the assault. I feel unprepared. Like the first day of school, or more like the dreams you have before the first day of school where you don't have your books and you don't know where your classes are and it turns out there was an assignment you were supposed to do over the summer.

Have I really been out here for more than a year? Can I be an experienced veteran when I'm barely nineteen and have never fired my gun in combat? It seems impossible that I've survived that long. But then I try to remember what normal life *was like and I barely can.*

When they issued us our winter uniforms, there weren't enough to go around. I got a quilted coat and trousers and an ushanka but no warm valenki to put over my leaky high boots. The snowmelt numbs my toes. I wrap my feet in extra layers of portyanki and stuff rags and newspaper into the ends of my boots but it doesn't help much. We're short of ammunition, too. We're going into this operation cold, tired, and underequipped.

I took the little cartridge-shaped capsule out of my pocket, uncorked it, and unrolled the bit of paper inside. Vakhromov said filling it out was signing your own death warrant, but as I stare Operation Mars in the face, I feel like it has already been signed and this is only a formality.

I may die, but I won't die unknown and anonymous.

When I got to "next of kin," I didn't even think about it: "Junior Lieutenant Valentina Sergeevna Koroleva, 588th Night Bomber Regiment, 325th Night Bomber Division, Fourth Air Army." Whatever happens, I want you to be the first to know. I want my family back home to find out from you, not from an impersonal telegram.

Stepanova surprised me today. I was lying by the fire, reading Rudenko's book. I don't mind having it out now, with this commissar. She came over to warm her hands and asked, "Do you like poetry?"

The book wasn't poetry, but this was the first friendly gesture Stepanova had ever made to me, so I said, "Yes. I'm very fond of it."

"Do you know Mayakovsky?"

I smiled, because every Soviet loves Mayakovsky, and I recited the first poem that came to my head, the one that goes, "Here in four years' time from now, there'll be a garden-town."

Stepanova looked at me very hard and said, "Why did you choose that poem?"

Mayakovsky wrote many poems more fitting to our circumstances, poems about war, about fear and loss and meaningless suffering. But those weren't the words I wanted to say. I wanted to speak about building and planting and hope. About a time when war won't divide us.

Stepanova said, "I was sitting by a campfire the last time I heard that poem. We were behind the lines near Moscow. Zoya was reciting it."

Her face in the firelight did not betray how the poet's words made her feel, whether the memory of her courageous friend saddened her or stirred a flame of pride.

This will be my last letter before the offensive, maybe my last letter ever. I don't know if you'll receive it or not. Your letters get delivered erratically, nothing for a month or two, then a couple of letters at once. I haven't heard anything from you since the seventh of November. It isn't really likely that all the pieces will fall into place and you'll swoop in to deliver me. Chances are I'll be cut down in the first wave of the assault.

I have so many regrets. This whole time I've written around my feelings for you. I've talked about everything else, but never what was most on my mind. I was frightened. I didn't know how *you'd react, if you'd laugh at me or brush me off or, worst of all, stop writing. But it won't matter now.*

I love you, Valyushka. I have since I was a child. You're everything I'm not: daring when I'm afraid, bright and hopeful when I'm despondent, willing to fly across a country to pursue your dreams while I helplessly wait for the inevitable.

All these years I haven't told you. And yet, here at the end, I want more than anything for you to know.

Yours always,

Pasha

"Is it still snowing?"

"Valka," said Iskra. "It was snowing a week ago. It was snowing a day ago. It was snowing five minutes ago. *It's not going to stop snowing.*"

I paced in the narrow dugout, my hands tucked underneath my arms in an attempt to get the blood flowing into my fingertips. I could see my breath. The dugout floor was icy at the end near the door and muddy at the end near the oil-drum stove, no middle ground. Vera and Tanya were sitting in front of the stove and passing their last cigarette back and forth, their bare feet up on the cinder blocks the stove was set on while their boots and portyanki dried.

"An offensive in the middle of a snowstorm," said Tanya. "It's insane. No air support, no way to sight for the artillery. Those boys are as good as dead out there."

"Tanya, stop. Valka's keyed up enough already," scolded Iskra.

"They should have delayed the offensive," said Zhigli.

"Why didn't they?" asked Zhigli's young navigator, cocooned in several blankets at the other end of the dugout.

"Pride," said Zhigli. The word hung in the freezing air.

Iskra stuck out her foot in front of me. "Stop pacing. It's annoying."

I plopped onto Iskra's bed. "I feel so useless."

"Pasha will be all right." How could Iskra sound so sure of herself?

"He doesn't have valenki," I whimpered. "There's a blizzard and he doesn't even have proper warm boots."

"He's from the Urals. You guys are built tough."

I gave her a pointed look. "Iskra. You've *met* Pasha."

Pasha's missing boots weren't the part of his last letter that was most on my mind. The surprise wasn't what he said, it was that he said it. Not a revelation, but a breakthrough. But instead of speeding off through the sky to take him in my arms, I was grounded in a dugout.

All our time together flicked through my mind. I wished I could reach out and reshape those memories.

"Iskra?"

"Yeah?"

"You want to know something terrible? When we were kids, I only wanted to be friends with Pasha so I could listen to his radio. I've known him since he was born but I only cared about the goddamn radio."

Iskra gave my shoulders a squeeze. "Baby cousin, this will

come as a shock to you, but everyone is terrible when they're thir-teen."

"Pasha wasn't."

"No. He was a sweet kid."

Zhigli, who was lying on the next bed over, said, "You need to stop worrying, Valka. It won't help him."

I asked her, "You know about destiny and stuff. Pasha . . . he filled out his identity capsule. That's bad, isn't it?"

She drew in her breath through her teeth. "Yeah. I've heard that."

"Is there a counteraction? Can you fix it if you throw the cap-sule away, or erase it?"

"Fate doesn't work that way," she replied, looking up at me with sadness in her dark blue eyes. "If something is going to hap-pen, it will happen. You can't trick it or find a way around it. I thought I could change Polina's fate, thought I could hold her back from the brink. I was wrong."

I wrapped my arms around my knees, feeling like a stalling plane, dropping from the sky.

★ THIRTY-ONE ★

27 November 1942—never mailed

Dear Valyushka,

I am alone.

It's been a long time since I was well and truly alone. One doesn't have much privacy in the army or sharing a one-room apartment with three other people. But now, if I were under orders to get up and go find someone, anyone alive, I couldn't do it.

Vakhromov is a little ways from my grove. He lies on his back, his body bent unnaturally over the radio battery. He stares sightlessly into the sky, his lips ash gray, frost forming on his eyelashes, a fresh layer of snow gradually softening the shape of his body. That's what courage looks like.

As for me, I can't so much as bring myself to dash across that open space. I haven't even checked whether Vakhromov is dead. Oh, god, my friend could have been lying there unconscious for a night and a day, slowly freezing to death.

I close my eyes and focus on the colors. White. White. For a moment the rustle of the branches above me creates a streak of muted green. Then it fades. I couldn't break that oppressive blankness, not even if I spoke, for my speaking voice has no color, not even white. My voice is like me: nothing and no one, a thing that can be added or subtracted without changing the result.

Only my singing voice has color. But I can't find it in myself to sing.

I want to talk to you so badly it hurts. I spent the last few days before the assault knotted up with anxiety about my foolish, heartfelt words to you, in addition to my anxiety about the mission. Did that letter reach you? How did you respond—did you cry or laugh at my earnestness? What would you say to me if you were here now? I'll never know. I'll never see you again.

And so I decided to write to you. I'll never have a chance to deliver this letter, not even a romantic silver-screen moment where it is found on my body and given to you so that you can tearfully read it after my death, not that I can imagine you sorrowfully dabbing your eyes with a handkerchief under any circumstances. But it makes me feel like I'm not so completely and utterly alone.

I'm having trouble putting my thoughts in order, but what does it matter? No one will ever read this letter anyway. I don't need to worry about wasting paper or about whether my words make sense to anyone but me. So I'll simply begin where my mind takes me, to the start of the offensive, the crossing of the Volga.

I was carrying my rifle. I was running in the snow. It was white and thick as a blanket and its sound would have been green if it hadn't been buried beneath all the other sounds. The heavy radio was strapped to my chest like a suicide bomb. Its steel case was cold. So was my helmet where it pressed against my forehead. I wished I could wear my ushanka instead. Snow leaked into my high boots and melted, soaking my portyanki with icy water. My feet prickled with pain every time they touched the ground.

I hadn't fired. There were only three bullets in my magazine and there was nothing to fire at anyway. I was crossing a frozen river, slick and featureless. Five meters ahead everything disappeared into a white void. The world was a blank canvas painted with sounds: bright orange gunshots, yellow-green hissing bullets, rumbling burgundy artillery.

And the Katyushas. When they fired, the whole canvas was splashed with their unearthly color. Their voices got brighter and sharper and more terrifying as we closed in on the enemy lines. They made my feet root themselves to the ground. I forced myself to pick up my lead-heavy legs and keep moving.

Vakhromov was to my left, clutching Petya's hand. The boy's short legs couldn't keep up. Vakhromov knelt and let him climb onto his back on top of his kit bag. He got up and kept running, carrying the battery and his rifle and the piggyback child all at once.

On my other side, our medic and the NCOs. Pashkevich charged ahead with a wide, crazy smile. This was the most fun he'd had since the war started. Stepanova's mouth was set in a thin line. She held her submachine gun, but she didn't fire, even though only she had enough ammunition. She was saving it.

More streaks of light green. I wanted to curl up on the ground and make myself as small as I could. But there was our commissar, sidearm drawn, faintly visible through the whirling snow. The pistol wasn't for the fascists. It was for anyone who turned back.

The fascists aren't aiming at me, I told myself. If I can't see them, they can't see me, either. But not every bullet misses, even if fired at random. There was a brief, choking cry, and the commissar collapsed. Our medic tried to stop, but Stepanova shouted, "Keep moving!"

Then she staggered as though she had run into a wall. Pain cracked her emotionless facade, but she didn't fall. She regained her footing and kept running.

I nearly fell into a hole in the ice where a bomb or shell had broken through and exposed dark water, gaping in the snow like an open wound. Vakhromov and I stayed close to each other. Petya's eyes squeezed shut against the storm, or maybe out of pure terror. The boy buried his face in the shoulder of Vakhromov's quilted coat and grabbed his own wrist around the soldier's neck so he wouldn't fall.

Tears froze to my cheeks. Ice clumped on my eyelashes, forcing me to wipe my eyes on my sleeve so they didn't freeze shut. A fresh gust of wind engulfed us, kicking up the snow on the ground. I lowered my head against it and whispered in a fear-cracked voice, "May he save our Motherland as Katyusha saves their love. . . ."

Six of us made it across the front lines to collapse breathlessly against the wall of a gutted house. Stepanova was holding her side.

"Let me look at that," said our medic.

"You'd like that, wouldn't you," said Stepanova through clenched teeth, waving him away.

He offered her morphine.

She said, "No. I need my head about me."

But she should have accepted his help, because as the day wore on, her gait grew unsteady and her face flushed and feverish.

The blizzard had died down, but snow still swirled around us, giving the battlefield an unearthly feel. Shapes approached us like dark paper cutouts before resolving into solid objects. Craters. Tank stoppers. Twisted human figures, some in gray Wehrmacht uniforms, more in padded Russian coats.

Stepanova led the way through the macabre scene. The battle raged on every side, heard but not seen. Gunshots echoed deceptively. Once we walked blindly into the middle of a *firefight. We hit the ground and scrambled for the Russian side. A bullet ricocheted off Pashkevich's helmet.*

"Help or get lost," said an officer.

On the map, the salient looks small. From the inside, it's an endless wasteland. We picked our way laboriously through, clambering over a tangled pile of tanks, belly-crawling across a stretch of open ground. Darkness fell before we reached our destination. As Vakhromov and I hunted for a spot free of corpses where we could make camp, I felt I was on some sort of gruesome picnic.

The next morning, we reached a patch of forest. I found it difficult to believe that a forest had survived and that every tree was not smashed to splinters. Vakhromov handed his canteen to Petya, then took a drink from it himself. Stepanova took out her map and compass.

"Can we cut through the forest?" asked Vakhromov. "It would be safer."

The starshina frowned at the map. "We got turned around back there. If we're where I think we are . . ."

"Women have no sense of direction," said Pashkevich. "Give me that."

Stepanova bristled and held the map away. She said, "The town we're assigned to burn down should be on the other side of the trees."

"What are you talking about?" Pashkevich demanded.

"Ma'am, we're not burning anything. We're here for the photos," I said.

"But . . ." Stepanova furrowed her feverish brow. "We just left Moscow."

I shook my head. "We aren't near Moscow. We're near Rzhev."

"Rzhev. Of course. I misspoke."

The medic ventured, "Ma'am, are you feeling all right?"

Stepanova curtly told us to keep moving.

We smelled the stable before we saw it. The artillery had opened it like a greedy child ripping open a present. The fire had burned itself out, for the most part, except for a few wan flames flickering among the butchered horses. One man was alive. We found him cowering in the corner, his face slashed by shrapnel. Pashkevich finished him off with his bayonet. Stepanova rounded on the sergeant and demanded, "What did you do that for? We might have needed him!"

"A dead fascist is a safe fascist," grunted Pashkevich.

Stepanova stumbled to what once had been the doorway and leaned on what had once been the frame. Sweat glistened on her forehead, despite the cold. She looked around, her eyes not quite focused. "Zoya? Where are you?"

Vakhromov and I gathered around her. I tried to hide my trepidation about our rapidly unraveling mission as I said, "Ma'am, you've got to stay with us. We're not looking for Zoya. We're looking for the pictures of her."

"She's gone off to burn the stables. She told me to keep watch."

"Look at me, ma'am," said Vakhromov, grabbing Stepanova's

chin and pointing her face at his. Her eyes slid off him. He said, "Zoya is dead! She was killed a year ago. She isn't here!"

"Great. We're under the command of a delirious woman," said Pashkevich.

And then my stomach dropped. I said, "Where's Petya?"

There was an awful moment while the two of us looked frantically around and I thought of the countless things that could have happened to him, from being accosted by the fascists to stepping on a mine. How could I have let him out of my sight for even an instant?

Then I spotted him. He was standing some distance away, looking solemnly down at the torn body of a German officer. Vakhromov stood beside him and put his big hands on Petya's thin shoulders, trying to explain that it was war and these things happened.

"I know," said the boy. "That's him."

"That's . . . ?" Vakhromov began. He yelled, "Stepanova! Pashkevich! Petya's found him."

What was left of our squad gathered around the partial body. Pashkevich said, "I hope the photos are on this half of him."

Our medic crouched so that he could go through the officer's blood-soaked bread bag, which was still on his belt. Then he recoiled as though he'd found a snake in the bag. He dropped what he was holding. Photos.

Stepanova knelt and picked them up. As her eyes flicked over them, her expression did not change. She said, "Zoya. Here you are. It's been a long time."

She grimaced and grabbed her wound. Vakhromov and I had to catch her to keep her from falling. He helped her sit down.

"It's all true," said the medic, his voice hoarse. "Everything that they said happened to her. I was telling myself that it was just propaganda. But it all really happened. What about everything else, is it true, too? About the camps? The things they've done?"

Pashkevich said, "Save your personal crisis. We've got what we came for. Danilin, you're the only man in this squad who's acting normal. Hold on to these." He took the photos from Stepanova's weak fingers and gave them to me.

The girl's defiant gray eyes challenged me, as though looking made me party to the crime. I wanted to apologize for seeing her when she was so vulnerable, for seeing her when she couldn't prevent me from looking because she was only a silver nitrate image, and because her hands were tied.

Pashkevich said, "Set up the radio so we can get the hell out of here."

Stepanova, her head lolling back, told him not to bother.

Pashkevich gave her a sharp look. "What does that mean?"

Stepanova said, "This was never what you'd call an official mission."

A barrage of gunfire interrupted us. Our medic's neck jerked around and a spray of blood burst from the side of his head. The rest of us ducked behind the scorched remains of a horse, Vakhromov shielding Petya with his body. I fumblingly tucked the photos into my bag of spare radio parts. Dull thuds as rounds hit the dead animal's back. The fascists were firing out of the dark doorway of a barracks. Pashkevich shot back, then swore and tossed his Mosin-Nagant aside. "I'm empty. Stepanova, give me yours."

Stepanova, staring into the middle distance and still trying to talk to Zoya, allowed him to lift the strap of her SMG over her head. He rattled off a burst of gunfire, but the Germans kept shooting. I looked around. There wasn't enough of the stable left to protect us. Behind us was nothing but open steppe. To get to shelter, we'd have to run toward the Germans.

"Grenade?" asked Vakhromov.

Pashkevich shook his head. "Not unless you've got superhuman aim. If you miss that doorway and it bounces off the wall, we'll all end up like Fritz there."

Stepanova finally smiled. It was an abstract, contemplative smile. She murmured, "Well, Zoya, this is where it ends," and she pulled something tiny off her belt and tossed it and I reflexively caught it, and when I opened my glove I found a metal ring. Stepanova was across the open space and through the doorway before anyone could stop her. I barely had time to lower Petya's head and mine before the sharp, yellow-edged white concussion hit us.

And then quiet. No more shooting. No more Germans. No more Stepanova.

Pashkevich wasted no tears on her. While I was still reeling, unable to accept what had just happened, he announced, "I'm in charge now. Find cover and then get that goddamn radio set up so we can get out of here."

We made for the woods, hoping that we could find our way through the thick-falling snow. The dark outline of a patch of trees appeared out of the white as the rumble of an engine interrupted us. We whirled around. A German truck.

Vakhromov didn't hesitate. He yelled "Run, Petya!" and opened fire as the boy ran for the woods. He shot once, twice, three times.

Three bullets for each rifle. Vakhromov shook as the fascists returned fire. The empty gun fell from his hands.

I attempted to fix one of the swastika-clad figures in my shaking sight, trying to hit but hoping to miss. My finger curled around the trigger. The butt of my rifle recoiled into my shoulder. My ears rang a bright, piercing yellow from Pashkevich firing Stepanova's submachine gun beside me. As I fired another ineffectual shot, a slug slammed into my chest.

"That's it for me," I thought, dropping to my knees because that was what you did when you were shot. Dying didn't hurt. That surprised me. But I didn't lose consciousness, or see a bright tunnel. It wasn't until Pashkevich took out the last man in the truck and we found shelter under the trees that I figured out what had happened. I wasn't wounded. My radio was. A bullet had pierced its case and shattered the vacuum tube.

"Don't you have a spare?" asked Pashkevich.

I'd used it three months ago.

Pashkevich sighed resignedly.

I said, "We need to find Petya."

"Kid's got a better chance without us," said Pashkevich. "If he can get out of that uniform, he'll pass for a civilian. Our priority is our own survival. You stay here and guard the stuff, Choir Boy. I'll scout for a safe route. I'll be back in a couple of hours."

Now that the tire tracks have long since disappeared into the white, I am forced to accept that Pashkevich will not return. Taking the truck was a mistake. The Soviets would have fired on it. It wouldn't have fooled the Germans for long. I wonder how many fascists he took with him. It was a good end for Pashkevich. Heroic. What he wanted. But there will be no blaze of glory for me.

I've created a little nest in the depression beneath the pine trees. The branches help block the wind, but the cold of the frozen ground seeps up through the needle litter and the rain cape I'm using as a ground cloth. I pull my torn coat about my body as tightly as I can to compensate for its missing buttons. I can't feel my feet. Occasionally I get up and stomp around until they started tingling, but they only go numb again a few minutes later.

Just now I picked up my rifle and examined it. My hands have stopped shaking. That's good. I unchambered my single remaining round and rolled it around on my palm. It was a bottleneck cartridge about as long as my gloved hand was wide, with a rim a little wider than the rest. I said, "It's just me and you now, buddy."

I needed to use it wisely. But what was wisely? If I ran into

Germans, there was no hope for a lone soldier with scarcely any training. One bullet wouldn't change that. I made a mental list: "Consequences of Firing the Bullet," by Pavel Kirillovich Danilin.

Things It Will Do:
- Leave me unarmed
- Give away my position
- Make the fascists angry
- Kill one person (maybe)

Things It Won't Do:
- Kill more than one person
- Prevent me from getting killed
- Get me home

I omitted one item from the first list. There were ideological reasons for leaving it off (I had to complete the mission) and practical ones (I had no sidearm and suicide by rifle was a tricky business), but the truth is that I was afraid to consider it.

It would have been a more sensible choice than what I actually did, which was to take the cartridge and fling it as far as I could. For an instant its brass jacket glinted in the cold winter light. Then it disappeared into the endless snow. I felt a moment of blissful relief. And then, "Shit! What am I doing?"

I ran over to the place where the cartridge had fallen and dug through the snow until I reached the dirt and dead grass underneath. *Nothing.* In a few minutes, I gave up the search as hopeless. *Nice job, Pasha. Now you're not only lost and alone behind enemy lines, but you're completely unarmed.*

I have to do something. The knowledge frightens me. I've spent so long repeating Morse code orders that I'm at a loss for ideas of my own. Finding Petya was my first thought, but I'm far more likely to stumble onto the Germans than to find him if I go looking. Besides, Pashkevich was right: Petya's best chance is to get rid of his uniform and become just another peasant child. Or maybe I'm only telling myself that because I'm too scared to move.

I smoked the last of my cigarettes and strung out the radio antennae out of habit, one along the ground, the other up one of the snow-laden pine trees. That occupied me for a few minutes. Now I once again have no orders and no plan.

So here I am, Valyushka, writing to you. It's helped. I feel a little better now, calmer. Things could be worse. At least you sent me a pencil.

A pencil.

I have an idea.

★ THIRTY-TWO ★

WAKING A SLEEPING AIRCREW IN THE MIDDLE OF THE DAY usually required a death wish, but when Masha the armorer invaded our dugout, she said the magic words: "It's stopped snowing!"

We all awoke instantly. Zhigli threw up her hands. "There is a God!"

"If there was a God, it would have stopped snowing on the twenty-fifth of November," I said.

Beautiful sunlight blinded us as we emerged from the dim dugout. Our eyes adjusted to meet a flat expanse of white sparkling beneath a liquid blue sky. The snow was waist deep, broken up by hummocks covering planes and vehicles and by narrow paths where people had struggled through from one dugout to the next. The ground crews, armed with shovels, were excavating the aircraft. We joined them unbidden. Iskra and I clambered on top of Number 18 and kicked away the snow until the cover was light enough to pull off. It was refreshing to be outside doing something.

The hardy little plane sat at the wrong angle, its propeller pointed at the sky, its tail balanced on its horizontal stabilizer. The tail skid, stressed by the cold, had snapped under the weight of the snow. Captain Ilyushina regarded the damage, arms akimbo. "That's not so bad. I can replace it in a few minutes. You'll be clear to fly tonight, no problem."

The mail truck had finally made it through. Our new aide-de-camp, who I've never quite forgiven for not being Galya, doled out creased, water-stained letters. I gave her a pleading look. She held out her hands helplessly. "I'm sorry, Valka, there's nothing from Pasha. But that doesn't mean anything. The storm delayed the mail all over."

I hung my head. I unfairly resented the other airwomen, greedily tearing open letters from parents and sweethearts safe at home. They got news about meaningless village gossip while I didn't know if Pasha was alive or dead.

Major Bershanskaya, the rest of her staff in tow, threaded her way through the mechanics and click-snaps. She found Dina and Zhenechka circling their plane, looking for damage. "Lieutenant. I need an aircrew for a special assignment tonight. We just got notified about an evacuation from the salient. Apparently a radio operator got stranded there with some sensitive materials."

An evacuation . . . Pasha! He was alive. Excitement and relief collided and caught me in the middle. I vaulted out of my plane, onto the wing, and then onto the ground, and saluted. "Ma'am, requesting permission to take this mission."

Bershanskaya gave me a long look of dawning comprehension. "Is your Pasha one Pavel Kirillovich Danilin of the 336th Rifle Regiment?"

I nodded. I was trying to stand at attention properly, which was difficult when I wanted to grab my commanding officer and beg her for whatever she knew.

"And you know about his assignment." Bershanskaya shook her head. "Do the censors catch anything anymore?"

"Please, ma'am." I didn't even try to hide my anxiety. It felt like there was a nest of ants running around inside me.

Bershanskaya looked at Dina. "What do you think, Nikulina? Are they up to it?"

"Sure. Iskra is a strong navigator."

"Then it's all yours, Koroleva." Bershanskaya walked over and spread out her map on Number 18's wing while Iskra and I looked on, leaning our arms on the canvas. I tried to focus on the lines and dots, but the knowledge that Pasha was alive pushed all other thoughts from my head. "You know by now that the salient is still holding. Our ground forces attempted to attack it at once from every side, but it was difficult for them to maintain an even line, with the confusion and the lack of visibility. Some regiments drove ahead of the others and were cut off. Unfortunately, Danilin's squad was accompanying one of them. Apparently they laid their hands on some sensitive materials that headquarters is keen to acquire, but the rest of the squad was killed and Danilin has no return route except by aircraft."

The major traced her finger across the map. "Danilin knows his approximate position, but it'll be up to you, Iskra, to locate him precisely. Take care: The battle is still in progress and troops may move unpredictably. He has no way to signal you or to provide light to land by, but you may drop an illumination flare. Watch out for the depth of the snow. Naturally there won't be any defenses at Danilin's location, so as long as you can slip past the front lines safely, you can dart in, pick him up, and return in time to rejoin the squadron later tonight. And, Junior Lieutenant"—Bershanskaya gave me a serious look—"I understand that this mission is personal to you, but you must promise me that you will approach it like a soldier. People die when feelings get in the way."

"I promise," I lied, unable to keep a massive grin from creeping onto my face. I felt lighter, as if my fear for Pasha was a literal weight that had been taken from me.

"Belay that order." Once again I hadn't seen where Kazarinova had come from, but there she was, leaning on the opposite side of the wing, her stern dark eyes pinned on me and Iskra. Helpless outrage flooded me. She couldn't do this. She could ground us and court-martial us and systematically dismantle our regiments to keep us from succeeding where she had failed, but I wouldn't let her sign Pasha's death warrant.

Bershanskaya squinted up at her. "Do you need something, Major?"

"This mission is canceled." Kazarinova stated it as an incontrovertible fact.

"What? Why?" I demanded.

She raised her chin so she could look down her nose at me. "Order 270. That soldier is a traitor."

"He's not a—" I broke in, my face hot. Bershanskaya quieted me with a motion of her hand and said, "He was on assignment."

"Check again. No superior officer ordered that mission. Officially, his squad disobeyed orders and fled in the middle of an offensive. You've defended your regiment's past irregularities by claiming that they are benign or beneficial. Sending a suspected wrecker to aid a traitor to the Motherland: That's anything but benign, wouldn't you say?"

Sharp black eyes met soft green ones. I held my breath. The green ones fell.

"I'm glad we are in agreement, Major," said Kazarinova. She told our head of communications, "Inform the boy that his ride has been canceled."

Kazarinova stalked away. The image of Pasha flashed in my mind, his gentle face falling when he learned that I was abandoning him and that he was alone in the salient, it so vast and he so very small. I begged my commander, "You can't cancel the mission! I *need* this."

Bershanskaya said with carefully controlled calm, "You'll be flying with the rest of the first squadron. Report for your briefing at seventeen hundred hours."

My legs had gone wobbly and I thought I was going to throw up. I protested, "You can't let her push you around. She doesn't outrank you. She has no authority to—"

"Junior Lieutenant, just because I don't discipline you doesn't mean I can't," said Bershanskaya, folding her map.

I threw her one last look of despair and stumbled into the empty dugout. Lacking the energy to walk over to my own bed, I threw myself on Iskra's. My throat knotted into a lump that made my breath come in shuddering gasps. I jammed the middle two fingers of my left hand into my mouth and gnawed them.

The unattended stove had burned down to a few sullen red embers. Iskra tossed in a new log. She sat silently on a crate and took off her gloves so that she could warm her fingers as the fire crackled and flared up.

I said, "Did you ever notice his hands?"

"No, baby cousin, this may surprise you, but I never paid any particular attention to Pasha's hands."

"He has beautiful hands. I can't bear the thought of anything happening to them. How can I leave him there, Iskra, how can I let them hurt Pasha's hands?"

Iskra stroked my face with a fire-warm hand. "He made it through the offensive and got what he went for. He's a survivor, Valyushka. A hero."

I tried unsuccessfully to swallow the lump and choked out, "If they hurt him, he'll talk. He's not Zoya Kosmodemyanskaya. He's not independent and stubborn and driven, he's honest and open and kind. And I want him to be that way. Why should someone have to act like a soldier to be a good Soviet, Iskra? Don't we need people like Pasha, people who can be vulnerable?"

Iskra said, "They won't torture him. He's a soldier, not a spy. If the fascists run across him, they'll only take him as a POW."

"As a POW," I echoed. "To Vyazma. Do you know what's in Vyazma?"

Iskra silently prodded the fire with a gun-cleaning rod. She knew.

"I guess it doesn't matter," I said. "Court-martialed as a traitor and sent to our camps or captured and sent to the fascist camps. What's the difference?"

"Valka. No." Iskra looked up. Flickering yellow firelight illuminated the curve of her cheek. "I don't want to hear you talking like that."

"It's true."

Iskra wetted her lips. "There have been injustices on both sides. I know that better than anyone. But that doesn't mean there's no such thing as justice. I don't want to hear for a second that we don't have the moral high ground. What you do still matters. It may not win the war, it may not bring about the utopia we keep waiting for, but it matters."

"It might matter if there was anything I could do! I would go through fire and water for Pasha. If I only had . . ." My voice faded into a whisper as I realized I still had everything I needed. "An airplane and a long winter night."

"Valka, what are you—" began Iskra, but then a smile crept across her face.

I jumped to my feet and began pacing. "After the first bombing run is our chance. We can drop our bombs, then send up a red distress flare as if we couldn't get the engine to reengage. They'll think we made an emergency landing. No one will expect to see us for the rest of the night. In the meantime, we keep low and quiet and go on our way."

I headed out of the dugout. I was a few steps onto the freshly shoveled airfield before I realized Iskra was following me.

"Iskra," I said. "This is something I need to do. Not you. You don't need to come."

"Are you planning to drop me off on the way? Bershanskaya will notice if you take off without a navigator."

I hadn't thought of that. But I couldn't ask Iskra to put herself in danger, not even for Pasha's sake. "This will end badly."

"Probably." Iskra didn't move.

"And worse for you. Disobeying orders to rescue a traitor . . . we'll be court-martialed! You know what they'll do to you."

"Shh!" Iskra threw a pointed glance to her left, where Captain Ilyushina was examining a plane's rudder. Ilyushina looked up at the sound of my raised voice, but only shook her head and returned to work. We moved behind the mound of the dugout, out of sight.

Iskra put her hands on my shoulders and fixed her clear eyes on me. "We're part of a system that's done terrible things. And I've helped. I share the responsibility for what happened to my parents. I said everything the NKVD wanted me to say. I share the responsibility for Malakhov's partisans. This once I have a chance to fix an injustice instead of causing one. I'm coming with you."

I knew Iskra well enough to tell when there was no point in arguing.

★ THIRTY-THREE ★

WE WERE GOING TO DISOBEY ORDERS. WE HAD ALREADY
disobeyed orders. This wasn't a matter of nonstandard turnaround
procedures. This was treason by Soviet law.

"Well, eaglets, it's time for us to do our part for Operation
Mars," said Bershanskaya to the assembled aircrews. "We'll be hitting a rail line between Rzhev and Vyazma in hopes of slowing
down the fascist reinforcements."

I hadn't planned what to do once we touched down at the end
of the night. I'd figure that out later.

"We're loading the U-2s with an extra fifty kilos of bombs,
and you'll carry only a single sortie's worth of fuel to compensate.
We'll spend longer on turnaround, so you'll fit in one or two fewer

runs, but the arithmetic works out. Keep your eyes on your fuel gauges, because you won't have the buffer you expect. Otherwise, everything should be by the book. Dismissed."

I couldn't bite my fingers without getting a mouthful of glove, but I balled my fists as I exited the command dugout. I muttered to Iskra, "This is a problem."

"I know," she said, tapping the end of her pencil against her lips. "With a full tank, we could fly there and back twice over. But one sortie's worth will barely get us one way, if we're lucky."

I kicked an oily snowdrift. "The universe is conspiring to keep us apart."

"Baby cousin, you were thousands of kilometers away and now you're close enough to throw a rock at him. The universe isn't conspiring against you. This is just a hiccup in our plans."

"Maybe"—I bit my lip and considered my sparse options— "we don't need to make it all the way to our aerodrome. We just need to find somewhere safe where we can make a forced landing."

"Where? It's German-held territory."

I didn't need Iskra to tell me it was a bad plan. "I don't know. You're the navigator."

It was one day short of the new moon. There were no clouds, only distant plumes of smoke along the western horizon. An endlessly long, dark winter's night, the sort of conditions night bombers loved. I walked around Number 18 one way and then turned and walked around it the other way, running my hands lightly along the wings and across the fuselage with its unadorned coat of translucent white paint. Quietly, too quietly to be overheard by the click-snaps running here and there, I whispered, "Be good to us tonight, girl. We need your best." And I touched the propeller and spat.

When Bershanskaya came alongside us at takeoff, I was sure she had found us out. But she only said, "Keep your mind on the mission, Koroleva," and waved us on. I gunned the little biplane's sewing-machine motor as if I was fleeing.

Something felt different. Or rather, it didn't feel different. I had become intimately familiar with Number 18's ways. The heavier bombs should have affected the little crop duster's balance. I should have noticed the difference as I brought her nose up. But I didn't.

And then a quiet gasp came through the speaking tube. "Valka! Check the fuel gauge!"

I looked. The needle pointed to Full. There was a scrap of paper wedged under the edge of the gauge in my cockpit. I turned on my map light to read the scribbled note.

> *Say hello to Pasha for me.*
> *—Klava*

My heart soared and I said a silent thank-you to Ilyushina. We had a chance after all.

Zhigli and Zhenechka were flying together ahead of us, their plane now visible, looking like a giant white dragonfly, now hidden in the darkness. Below, gunshots, explosions, brief flashes of light. Operation Mars struggled on. Then stripes of light against the black sky. The other biplane was lit up momentarily before it slid off to starboard and out of the beams. The searchlights pivoted and caught it again. It vanished again. In and out, weaving back and forth, the fearless pilot drew the lights away. Zhigli was still taking care of us and I was about to deceive her.

I idled the engine and went into a glide. A thin black stripe cut across the ravaged landscape. A railway. "Target in sight, Iskra."

"Bombs away." A jolt as the bombs fell away from our wings. The U-2, freed of its burden, was lighter, more maneuverable.

I called, "Now, Iskra!"

Hiss. Pop. A brilliant red light flashing across the sky momentarily illuminated every contour of the landscape, buildings and craters and the cover-stitch path of the railroad. The flare faded. I let our aircraft glide away to the west, away from our comrades, into the darkness.

Zhigli must have lost sight of us not long after Iskra fired the flare, but I waited until we were within spitting distance of the ground and well hidden by a patch of trees before I reengaged the engine. It started up obediently at its regular rhythm.

I said, "Zhigli will wonder why we didn't try to glide to Soviet territory. It wasn't far."

"Maybe we had rudder damage."

"They'll worry. The other girls. I wish I could have told them."

"I'm glad of your newfound empathy, but we would only have faced the inevitable court-martial even sooner. Now let's gain some altitude before someone on the ground picks us off with a machine gun."

We ascended into the sky. Away from the bombing site, from the front lines, from the planes of our friends, all was quiet. There were no gunshots, no explosions, no sound of artillery, not even voices, for we had stopped talking, save for Iskra's occasional whispered directions. The only sound was the rhythmic ticking of Number 18's engine.

It was a beautiful night. The thinnest thread of brilliant silver lined the bottom edge of a moon that was otherwise nothing but a blank spot amid a million stars. The brindled white stripe of the Milky Way slashed across the sky. Below, to the north or south, we passed scattered patterns of orange lights in nets or grids. We avoided those, instead finding a path through the dark patches in between. In one of those dark spots, Pasha was hiding.

We'd be arrested for sure when we got back. Shot, most likely. If Bershanskaya had authorized the flight, things might have worked out. Pasha's runaway squad could have been explained away amid the chaos surrounding the offensive. My runaway plane could not.

Part of me was angry at Zoya Kosmodemyanskaya. The whole mess was her fault. But I knew better. Zoya hadn't ordered anyone to do anything. All she had done was die well. No one had come to Zoya's rescue when she was in need, but Pasha's squad had thrown their lives away searching for her after she was dead. Propaganda was worth more to us than actual lives. I wondered what Zoya would have thought of that.

I realized I had no idea what Zoya would think. All I knew about her came from some villagers by way of a reporter, or from her comrade in arms by way of Pasha. Had she really been like they said, proud and defiant? Or was that only the shell she retreated into during her last hours, while inwardly she was curled up, crying and begging for it all to stop?

It didn't make any real difference to me and Pasha. Nor to the authorities who wanted her pictures. Whatever Zoya the pictures showed would become just another facet of the legend they built around her.

The stillness was shattered by the sound of another engine, not a rickety five-cylinder but a roaring V12. Only one type of aircraft had an engine like that. I yelled, "A night fighter!"

"Stay calm, Valka," came my cousin's steady voice. "It's pitch dark. It can't have spotted us."

The engine built up into a scream, then lowered to a Doppler-effect growl as the fighter swept past us. I said, "It's spotted us! Where is it?"

We looked wildly around. Then Iskra called out, "There— above us! Four o'clock!"

Over my right shoulder I spotted a cross-shaped silhouette. I made a sharp turn. A staccato rattle rang out from Iskra's machine gun. The fighter shot past. Milk-white starlight faintly highlighted its canopy and the tops of its wings. I pulled into another sharp turn and dived, in hopes of losing the enemy plane in the night before it came back around.

Iskra asked, "Why didn't he fire on us?"

"I outmaneuvered him," I replied, leveling out a few hundred meters lower.

"Nonsense. He had a clear shot. We should be dead."

The hum of the fighter's engine was building again. "We'll be dead soon enough if I can't shake him."

Sudden excitement filled Iskra's voice. "A lone fighter in the middle of the night. No strategic objectives for kilometers around, who knows how far to the nearest airfield. Valka—he's lost!"

"Good. If he's bad at navigating, it'll be easier to lose him."

"No, don't you see? He thinks we're on a bombing run. He's following our engine noise, hoping we'll lead him to the German lines so that he can get his bearings and find his way back!"

The fighter made another pass. Still it did not fire. I said, "I'll idle the engine and glide, then."

I was reaching to disengage the engine when Iskra's voice in my ear interrupted me. "The Volga. There's a trestle bridge not far from here."

"What does that have to do with anything?" I demanded.

"He's lost. It's dark. He doesn't know where the obstacles are. We do!"

And suddenly I understood. I stopped maneuvering and climbed until the sparse features on the ground became indistinct smudges to even the sharpest eyes. The German fighter continued to circle us, now near, now far, still never firing. Iskra let off a few rounds whenever it came into range, not out of hope of hitting it so much as to keep the enemy pilot informed of our location and, hopefully, enraged. In the meantime she would be focusing on her compass and airspeed indicator and spinning the wheel on her Vetrochet, correlating our location with our invisible destination.

The frozen Volga curved ahead of us, a smooth, winding

white stripe on a white background. In the distance, I could make out the lights of Rzhev. Iskra told me, "Perfect. The bridge is only a kilometer farther—"

She was cut off by a deafening barrage of cannon fire. The fighter dived past us. I screamed, "Iskra! Why is he shooting at us?"

"I miscalculated. He's spotted the city. He can use it to get his bearings. He doesn't need to follow us anymore, so he's shooting us down."

Great. Just great. I couldn't outfly him and I couldn't lose him. I only had one trick left, and it was a dangerous one. "Hang on!"

As the mounting roar warned that the enemy plane was approaching again, I opened the throttle as far as it would go and simultaneously shoved the control stick forward. The acceleration shoved me against my seat. Icy wind lashed my face and howled in my ears. Above it, I could hear the drone of the fighter. Cannon fire ripped the air just beyond the top wing. "Come on," I thought. We were already in his sights. He was close to shooting us down, so close to getting that iron cross. If only I could tempt him into following us into the dive.

The altimeter spun wildly, a thousand meters, six hundred, three hundred. Below, the Volga grew wider at an alarming rate. Flanked by nothing but blackness, I couldn't judge its distance. It might have been a broad river far away or a narrow stream right in front of us.

"Pull up!" Iskra screamed.

I waited one more terrifying second and then pulled up

Number 18's nose with a neck-wrenching jerk. For a moment I thought we would crash into the river. I steeled myself for the crack of the tail skid hitting ice, but it never came. We leveled out. Before us, a stark black shape bisected the river. Now we were climbing, steeper and steeper, then inverting.

I thought doing a loop would feel like hanging upside down off a climbing frame. It did not. The blood didn't rush to my head. Instead, the world rotated around me. Below me spread a sparkling blanket of stars. Above, an orange flower blossomed on a steel vine. The sound of rending metal echoed through the air. By the sullen light of the explosion, the landscape became a landscape again. The broad, frozen Volga. The snowy banks dotted with stands of reeds. The crisscross struts of the truss bridge. And, foundering in a hole in the ice where it had fallen after colliding with the bridge, the crushed corpse of a blunt-winged Messerschmitt.

For an instant I was gripped by the uncanny impression that the broken plane would fall out of the river and into the sky. I felt queasy. Blackness crept into the sides of my vision. Then I finished the loop and the world righted itself. I skimmed the snow-covered ice parallel to the bridge, passing so close to the sinking fighter that I could make out every detail: a bright yellow nose ripped open and streaming hot oil, three shattered propeller blades spinning to a halt, a brown-gloved hand against the cockpit glass, vainly trying to shove open the warped canopy. The plane disappeared into the water.

"That," said I grimly, "is why you never follow a smaller aircraft into a dive."

My cousin's hand grabbed my shoulder. "Valka! You did a loop!"

I laughed. "I did! So it's possible after all. Wait until Lilya hears about this!"

I hit the throttle and steered Number 18 away from Rzhev and deeper into the salient. No fighter was going to keep me away from Pasha.

THIRTY-FOUR

WE TOUCHED DOWN SOFTLY IN A DRIFT OF CLEAN SNOW. Our illumination flare burned on the ground, melting snow where it had fallen, its miniature silk parachute crumpled nearby. It created a pool of blue-white light beyond which all was black. We could have landed on a fascist parade ground for all I knew.

We sat there in our cockpits for a few moments as if frozen, waiting for shouts, gunshots. None came. The winter night was still and quiet. The sound of our breathing seemed very loud. Could this really be the middle of a battlefield?

Iskra broke the silence. "I think it's all clear."

I nodded and unbuckled my harness, letting the straps slide off my shoulders. "Stay here. Shoot anything who isn't me or Pasha. If you get into trouble . . ." Another part of my half-cocked plan I hadn't considered. "If there's trouble, get out of here immediately. Don't wait for me."

"I won't leave without you," said Iskra.

"I'm the commanding officer of this aircraft and those are my orders. If the fascists get their hands on Number 18, it's over for all of us."

Iskra nodded, her mouth tight. As I slipped out of the cockpit and onto the wing, her hand caught my shoulder. "Valka?"

"Yeah?"

"Come back."

I pressed my loyal cousin's hand to my cheek and stepped onto enemy territory.

I had flown over fascist-occupied territory many times, but I had never before set foot on it. Unable to dart back into the sky at the first sign of danger, I felt helpless, like a fly with its wings plucked off.

The first thing I did was to grab the flare by its unlit end and shove it into the ground. It proved surprisingly hard to extinguish. The melted snow only made it hiss and spit sparks. But finally I ground it far enough into the dirt to put it out. Darkness and safety enveloped me.

Raising my goggles, I closed my eyes and pressed the heels of my hands against them to make them adjust faster. When I reopened them, I could make out the faint outlines of my surroundings. A night-bomber pilot quickly learned to make sense of the finest gradations of black and gray. Trees. Bushes. A snow-covered piece of artillery, defunct long before Operation Mars. Number 18. Iskra crouched silent and vigilant in the cockpit, her hands resting on her machine gun.

I felt for the revolver on my hip. I'd never fired it at anything but a paper target, and the thought that I might finally need it intimidated me. It had been a long time since I'd earned my sharp-shooting badge back in Stakhanovo.

I moved as quietly as I could through the knee-high snow, grateful for my soft fur boots. I headed for the trees. I didn't wish to stray too far from the aircraft, but Pasha must not have been close enough to see the flare or he would have come to us. Unless he was unable to. Unless . . . no. I couldn't let my thoughts stray that direction.

I pressed through the woods, mindful of the sound of each footfall and each branch that brushed against me. There were no bodies here. The wide swath of destruction carved by Operation Mars had passed another way. I was grateful for that. I would have felt the need to stop and check every body, even those in Wehrmacht uniforms, rather than run the risk of passing him by.

Crunch. Something brittle shattered under my foot. I knelt to examine it. It was broken into a hundred fragments, but it had once been a glass tube with wires inside. A lightbulb?

While I was on my knee, something else caught my eye. A long, straight wire lay on the ground, running into a thick grove of evergreen trees. Keeping low, I crept toward the grove.

Someone had been living there. A Soviet! A rain cape was

neatly laid out on the soft carpet of pine needles, along with various other bits of gear, a kit bag, a smaller canvas bag, a mess kit. The wire terminated at a pair of steel boxes connected with a cable, one sealed, the other open to reveal a mess of electronics. A bomb? I flinched away from the wire running along the ground. The whole site was a booby trap!

But the boxes had shoulder straps. Why would a bomb need those? I crept closer. The front of the open box was covered with knobs and dials. A second wire snaked up the trunk of a tree. Not a bomb—a radio! The thing I'd stepped on must have been a discarded vacuum tube.

My excitement mounted. I tried to let reason prevail. There were a lot of radio operators in the Red Army. But when I peered inside the radio case, it was as plain as if he'd signed his name on it. In the middle of the tangle of wires was a pencil stub touching a razor blade.

"Pasha," I whispered. I had to stop myself from shouting. He was here! I was touching things he had touched a few scant hours ago.

Then where was he? Why had he left his hiding place if he knew we were coming?

I peered out through the trees. That's when I saw him.

I spotted the soles of his boots first, black against the snow. Not gray felt valenki, but plain high boots.

Pasha had no valenki.

I dashed over, even as the knowledge sank in that there was nothing I could do. I dropped to my knees beside the feet of the snow-dusted body, pressing my face against the worn artificial leather. My shoulders shook. I was too late. He'd trusted me, he'd waited for me, and that had killed him.

I stayed like that, eyes closed, until the snow melted and soaked through my flight suit to bite my knees. My hand clutched one leg of his trousers, spotted where my tears had fallen on them. There was no warmth at all in the flesh underneath. I'd freeze too if I stayed like that, but I couldn't make myself care.

Iskra was waiting. She'd be checking the luminous hands of her watch, her anxiety mounting. Any moment someone might stumble upon our plane. I forced myself to my feet, turning away from Pasha's body. I couldn't bear to see what had happened to him because of me. But I needed to look him in the face. I needed to know.

Hesitantly my eyes wandered up his body to his face. Blond hair and rugged, lined features. The muscles in my chest unclenched and warm relief flooded me. It wasn't Pasha. There was still hope! But I immediately sobered. How could I be happy over this soldier's body? This man surely hadn't deserved to die any more than Pasha did.

The snow around him had been packed down by feet and raked by eager fingers. Someone had been doing a little corpse looting. More than one someone. I followed the tracks, sticking to the darkest path under the trees, my neck prickling with the mounting surety that Pasha had walked into a trap and I was following him.

Voices. Straight ahead, over the next hill. More than two, I guessed, and fewer than ten. I strained to hear what language they were speaking but couldn't make it out. I dropped to the ground and crawled, silently sliding my sidearm out of its holster.

At the top of the hill, I raised my head cautiously. There was a cluster of seven or eight soldiers on the other side of a small clearing. It was difficult to make out any details, but some wore squarish hats with thick ear flaps. Ushankas! They were Russians!

I nearly jumped to my feet and called out to them, but at that moment, all the soldiers tensed and raised their guns. One shouted, "*Halt! Was machst du?*"

I flattened my face into the powdery snow. Not Russians. Germans in Russian gear.

But they weren't aiming at me. They were pointing their guns at one of their own. Now I saw that he wasn't a member of the group at all. He was unarmed. His figure was slight, even bulked up with a padded winter uniform, and the dark hair that hid his face was unkempt and tangled. He had one hand inside his coat, and he now withdrew it and raised it slowly into the air. Anticipation rose within me.

He spoke. "It's only letters and things. Personal stuff."

I knew that voice. I thought it had grown deeper since I'd heard it last, fuller. But I knew it all the same. I'd found him—after all this time, after all the worry and the pain, I'd actually found him! But I couldn't do what I wanted to do, couldn't run over the hill and take him in my arms. I had to think.

One of the fascists stood away from the rest of the group, facing Pasha. He said in thickly accented Russian, "Give me the coat and I will give your letters back to you."

The Russian winter had reduced the unstoppable Wehrmacht to highway robbers. Pasha slid the coat off his shoulders. He handed it to the German soldier, who wrapped himself in it with a grateful sigh. "Your hat and gloves also."

Pasha protested, "You're wearing our uniforms. You could be accidentally shot by your own men."

"What does that matter? Without winter clothes we will freeze before we make it back to them. Give them to me."

Pasha slipped off his gloves and gave them to the Russian speaker, who pulled them on over his red, blistered hands with palpable relief. Pasha's hat followed. The Russian speaker said, "I must apologize for this. I wish you no harm, I promise. We are in a very bad way. We lost three men in the storm."

"My things," said Pasha.

I sized up the situation. The leader of the group, the one who had shouted, was a lanky sergeant who wore glasses and an ushanka torn where the star had been pulled off. Next to him stood a very young soldier, younger than Pasha, with a runny nose and round cheeks crimson from the cold, bundled in stolen Russian clothing. And then there was the Russian speaker. Everything about him was weary, from his sunken, colorless eyes to the creases lining his forehead and the sides of his mouth.

They didn't look like the ruthless invaders I'd taught myself to imagine. After their moment of panic, their weapons once again hung slack at their sides. Were these sad creatures what we'd been fighting all this time?

Darkness was on my side. They didn't know there was only one of me. I couldn't hope to take them all out, but if I could take out the sergeant, Pasha might have a chance to escape while the leaderless squad was confused. Maybe. But I didn't have a clear shot; the others were in the way. I had to be patient.

The Russian speaker reached into the coat's inside pocket and pulled out a book with a green leather cover and a packet of letters bound together with string. His fingers fumbled in unfamiliar gloves. As he handed the things to Pasha, something slid out of his grasp, something small and folded into quarters.

He reached down and picked up the photograph. He unfolded it. His deep-set eyes flicked from the photo to Pasha. "What is this?"

Pasha replied timidly, "It's a photo from my girl. She sent me a picture of her airplane instead of herself."

"My girl." I embraced those words. But Pasha spoke with fading hope. It was all I could do not to shout to him how I felt.

"She is a pilot? A U-2 pilot?"

Pasha nodded.

The German soldier sucked in his breath through his teeth with a hiss. "*Eine Nachthexe!* We know these girl pilots. The Night Witches. Every night we get no sleep because of them."

The runny-nosed young soldier gasped and repeated "*Nachthexe*," followed by a burst of angry German. He raised his rifle and pointed it at Pasha. Pasha shrank away.

I fought to keep my protective instinct in check and focused on aiming the revolver. I wrapped my left hand around my right to steady my grip. Just like at the shooting range. Don't think about what will happen if you miss. And definitely don't think about what will happen if you hit, don't imagine what will happen to that face, don't think about who he is or wonder about his life. He's an enemy. That's all.

I didn't much enjoy being able to see my target.

An argument had broken out between the Russian speaker and the young soldier. The latter was still waving his gun. It was obvious what he wanted. The Night Witches had made him afraid—I had made him afraid—and since he couldn't hurt us, he would retaliate against Pasha instead. The former shook his head and began to lead Pasha away from the others. They were closer now. But the Russian speaker was between Pasha and me. Amid the harsh sounds of his unintelligible language, I heard "*nach Vyazma.*"

I clenched my free hand. I'd begun to think he wasn't as bad as the others. But if he wanted to take Pasha to Vyazma, he was only saying that they should kill Pasha slowly, rather than quickly.

The sergeant had had enough. He told the two soldiers to be silent and drew his own sidearm. He was going to settle the argument by shooting Pasha himself!

There were still people blocking my view of the sergeant. But I had a clear shot at the Russian speaker. With him out of the way, Pasha could run to me. I aimed and pulled the revolver's trigger. It was heavy, as though it was reluctant to be fired, but I squeezed it hard and the gun recoiled into the pad of my thumb with a report that echoed through the open space, multiplying into many gunshots. The Russian speaker crumpled onto the snow-covered ground.

It was so easy.

The German sergeant yelled, "*In Deckung!*" His men dropped onto the earth, looking around frantically for the source of the shot. I fired at them a few more times and shouted, "Pashenka! Over here!"

He turned. His face was chapped by the cold and covered with untidy stubble, but there was a look of dawning recognition. His lips formed the words "Cinnabar red."

I stood up and screamed, "Run!"

Struggling through the snowdrifts, Pasha scrambled up the hill toward me. I was struck by the impression that he was hopelessly far away, that no matter how far he ran he would never be any closer and would never reach me. But he stretched out his arm, and I mine, and then my hand clasped his, bare and cold. We were running hand in hand.

I heard the Germans behind me getting to their feet. They'd figured out that I was only a single person. The sergeant shouted to his men. The sounds of pursuit followed us.

I half led, half dragged Pasha into the trees, through the grove where he had hidden his radio. As we passed it, he grabbed the small canvas bag and slung it onto his shoulder.

Number 18 crouched on the snow ahead, its white body striped by the shadows of the trees. Iskra had heard us coming. She was already firing up the engine. Just a few more steps . . .

Gunshots cracked from behind us. Pasha's body jerked as a spray of dark blood burst from his shoulder. He tried to take another step, but his legs buckled. He fell in the powdery snow.

The bag slithered down his wounded arm. I tried to pull him to his feet, but the strength had gone out of him. No! Not now, not when we were so close.

I went down on one knee in front of him. I lifted his uninjured arm over my shoulder and placed my other shoulder against his chest and lifted him, one hand grasping his forearm and the other, the bag slung over it, around the backs of his knees. I carried him the rest of the way to the airplane, keeping my steps steady because I knew how much pain every jostle must cause him, and mindless of the gunshots that continued to ring out.

A burst of machine-gun fire issued from Iskra's cockpit, so close that it made my ears ring. I set Pasha down on the wing of the plane, allowing him to slump for a moment against the frost-encrusted fuselage, and then reached down and pulled him into the cockpit. He flinched as I strapped the harness over him. I shouted, "Iskra, get us out of here!"

Wind bit my face as the plane began to move, its propeller beating out its familiar rhythmic tick. My arms crisscrossed Pasha's chest as though I was worried he might slip out of my grasp. We lifted off into blackness.

★THIRTY-FIVE★

PASHA LAY HEAVY IN MY LAP. HE STANK OF SWEAT AND urine and salty blood, but at that moment he seemed the most precious thing in existence. I could hardly make myself believe that it was really him. I put my arms around him and whispered with my lips against his cheek, "You're safe now, Pashenka."

He didn't respond. His body sagged in its harness. Something warm seeped through my flight suit where his shoulder pressed against me.

"Pashenka?" I said. Still no response. I told Iskra, "He's out cold."

"Hang in there. We're forty-five minutes out."

I yelled, "We don't *have* forty-five minutes. He's bleeding!

We've got to make an emergency landing!"

"We're over fascist territory. Landing now would not do Pasha any favors."

"If we don't get help, I might lose him!" I had Pasha in my arms after everything we'd been through, only to find him slipping away from me. I couldn't let that happen, not when we were finally together. Not when I could tell him how I felt.

"What do you want me to do?"

The answer hit me. "The partisans! Viktor Malakhov, remember? His camp isn't far from here."

Iskra's voice was hesitant. "Valka . . . we bombed them. If they have a sense of self-preservation, they'll shoot us out of the sky. And they're Trotskyists!"

"Iskra! *This is not the time for politics!*"

Iskra sighed. "All right."

I squeezed a hand that was losing its color and whispered, "Hold on, Pashenka."

Our little plane circled a patch of forest like every other patch of forest. There were no signal fires, only a bit of warm light spilling in long rectangles out of the windows below to highlight rubble, tree trunks, a few patches of open space. I heard a dull pop and hiss as Iskra fired a red flare. I braced myself for the gunfire that would come if Iskra was right. For a long moment, there was only darkness. Then a bright spot of green burst above us and drifted downward.

Iskra came around for the landing. People ran out into the clearing, pointing and shouting. A single shot cracked, making me wince and lower my head, before a figure in the center of the crowd held up his hand and said in a clear, commanding voice, "Hold your fire!"

Iskra clumsily touched down, letting Number 18 bounce across the rutted, crater-filled ground, the plane threatening to nose over at every moment. Pasha's body jostled against me. Iskra steered the U-2 into a snowdrift to bring it to a halt.

Partisans ran up beside us, men and women and teenagers armed with drum-fed submachine guns or black-gripped automatic pistols. The man who had ordered them not to fire carried a snub-nosed PPSh-41 replica with its maker's initials engraved on the stock in intricate letters. Malakhov. He shouldered his way past the others and asked, "What's the trouble?"

I unbuckled my harness. "This man is wounded. He needs immediate attention."

They would refuse me. I was sure of it. The partisans had every right to shoot all three of us on the spot. But Malakhov nodded over his shoulder and a couple of younger partisans, a man and a woman, scrambled up onto the plane's lower wing and helped me lift Pasha out. They carried him to one of the houses, with Iskra in tow.

When I climbed out of my cockpit, I found Malakhov blocking my path. After fighting my way through so many obstacles, my first instinct was to shove him out of the way. I controlled myself. I needed him to save Pasha.

His eyes moved over my plane's worn canvas surface, settling on the tail number. "Number eighteen. Is this your aircraft?"

I nodded, wondering if my guilt was visible on my face. Did a killer look different from an innocent person? Had the war changed me that obviously?

"Brave of you to come back here." His voice was quiet, controlled. "Did you think we wouldn't recognize your plane? It was a memorable night. And you were flying very low."

"We needed help," I managed to say.

"From the Trotskyist traitors you tried to wipe out a week ago? We lost a dozen men in that raid. Soldiers who were fighting to defend you. One aircrew would be fair compensation, don't you think?"

He was right. Being shot would be a fitting fate for someone who had killed her own people despite the twisting pain in her chest telling her that it was wrong, despite Iskra begging her not to. But I had to live for Pasha's sake. I said, "Pasha is innocent. He had nothing to do with the air raid. Don't hurt him to punish us."

"You think I don't consider one life acceptable collateral damage?" To my surprise, he smiled. Crinkles formed around his eyes. "You're right. I don't. I know who my real enemies are. We're all fighting the same people, defending the same Motherland. Remember that."

He stepped aside and let me run after Pasha.

The house had survived many bombs and shells. Its entire second floor was gone, its past existence attested to only by two stone walls intact enough to contain the sills of upstairs windows. A few remnants of the top story's plaster floor supported a makeshift new roof of planks, tarps, and corrugated iron. Some of the windows were boarded up, others covered with oiled newspaper deep amber with indoor light. A blanket hung in place of a door that was absent except for its hinges.

Inside, a stout woman with a deeply lined face and thick, callused hands was tearing a sheet into strips by the light of a tin lantern. Flicking her eyes over the two partisans and their burden, she instantly sized up the situation, picked up the lantern, and ordered, "Bring him to the basement."

I followed the group down a stairwell narrow enough that I could touch both cold brick walls with my elbows. By the looks of it, the cluttered basement served variously as a coal cellar, bomb shelter, command center, munitions dump, and infirmary. The air was warmer than upstairs and close with gunpowder and cigarette smoke.

With one sweep of her arm, the woman cleared maps, compasses, fat grease pencils, cartridge casings, and dirty mugs off a sturdy wooden table. The young man and woman laid Pasha's inert form down on it. When I saw how he looked, my breath caught and I thought momentarily that he was dead already. His face was chalky, his lips light violet, his tunic saturated with dark red. The woman set the lantern down next to him and shooed the rest of us off with one hand. "Go on. You'll only be in the way."

Iskra and the two partisans departed. I remained. I said, "I want to help. He's important to me."

The woman tossed me a cloth. "Keep pressure on the wound."

I laid the cloth on Pasha's shoulder. He flinched when I touched the wound, making me draw back, but the woman gave me a stern look and so I bit my lip and pressed down with the heels of both hands. The cloth was immediately soaked through. Dark blood pooled underneath him, seeping into the wood and getting in his hair. I stubbornly kept the pressure on. The woman put a bottle of vodka on the table and set a kettle on the stove to boil.

A boy descended the stairs silently on portyanki-clad feet with one hand trailing along the wall. He looked about thirteen. It was hard not to look at his face. It was crisscrossed with scars, not bandaged, but red and raw. One of his eyes had been stitched shut. The other, foggy gray, stared indistinctly at the far wall. A pang stabbed through me as I realized that I was looking at my own handiwork.

He asked, "Mama, what's going on?"

"Go back to bed," said the woman.

"Papa says I need to help more if I want to stay," said the boy.

"Not yet," the woman told him. "There are so many things you need to relearn. Get some sleep."

The boy wordlessly retreated up the stairs. The woman tucked a few stray strands of iron-gray hair back under her scarf and turned her full attention to Pasha, brushing me aside. Her short-fingered hands worked with surprising dexterity. She unbuckled his belt, undid his buttons, and slid his arms out of the tunic sleeves. She attempted to pull off his scuffed black boots, the uppers of which were pulling away from the soles, but when she was unable to get them off his swollen feet, she sliced through the leather with a pair of steel scissors. She removed the rest of his clothing the same way, cutting him free of the padded trousers and the grimy, frayed undergarments stiff with sweat and blood, letting the many layers of rags that wrapped his feet in lieu of portyanki fall to the ground in scraps. She ran her blunt fingertips lightly over his body, taking stock of his injuries.

"Is it only the shoulder?" I asked.

"His feet don't look good, either," the woman replied. The compassion in her voice filled me with guilt. I didn't deserve her help. What would she do to me if she knew that I'd tried to kill her? That I'd blinded her son? What would she do to Pasha?

The woman told me, "Get him cleaned up. I'll deal with that gunshot."

I brought the kettle over and set it on the end of the table. I tossed the blood-soaked cloth onto the floor, fetched another, and wiped away the layers of blood and filth that coated Pasha's body. The warm water soothed my hands. Sometime during this process, Pasha began to struggle weakly and his eyelids fluttered. He parted his dry, sticky lips, but I told him, "Shh. Lie still. We'll talk later."

The bullet had torn an ugly, gaping hole in Pasha's right shoulder below his collarbone. The woman uncorked the vodka bottle with her teeth and poured the liquid over the wound. Pasha cried out. The woman said soothingly, "Poor child. You've been through so much. But no one will hurt you now."

She told me, "There isn't much I can do about infection. We've been low on medicine since the supply planes stopped coming. We don't have any penicillin, and we used up the last of the iodine after we were bombed. I can't promise you anything."

She packed the wound with bits of torn-up sheet and wrapped up his shoulder. Then she turned her attention to his feet. They were covered in raw spots and blisters, his toes mottled with black frostbite. She shook her head. "It's too late. He'll lose some of those." She pierced the blisters with a needle and massaged his feet until their normal color started to return.

She shook out a thick flannel blanket and laid it on the floor in front of the stove. "Bring him over here."

I gathered Pasha in my arms as if he were a child who had fallen asleep before bedtime. I laid him on his side on the blanket and folded the rest of it over him, taking care not to touch his injured shoulder.

The woman told me, "I'm sorry I can't give him anything for the pain. For now, the most important thing is to keep him warm. He's lost a lot of blood. He'll get cold very quickly. You need to depart while it's still dark?"

I nodded. "We'd never make it over the front lines in daylight."

"He can still get several hours of rest before dawn. I'll see if I can find some fresh clothes for him, and for you."

"For me?" I looked down at myself. The entire front of my flight suit was soaked in blood. "Oh. I'll be fine." I couldn't think of taking any more from the people I'd hurt.

She shrugged and vanished up the stairs.

I knelt on the floor, letting the dry warmth of the stove roll over me. I looked down at the soldier I had rescued. I would face the camps because of him, but I didn't doubt for an instant that he was worth it. For the first time in a long time, maybe the first time in the entire war, I had done something I was glad of without reservation.

"Valyushka," he rasped, his voice barely audible.

"I'm here, Pashenka." I slipped out of my oversized fur boots, took off my flight helmet and cap comforter, and slid under the blanket next to him. "I'm here."

Pasha's shoulders shivered, then shook. He was crying. I wondered what images were flashing through his mind, what sounds and feelings and colors he was remembering, and I knew that I would not find out. I drew him close so that I could feel the warmth returning to his body. He turned toward me and buried his head in my breasts. Tears joined the other stains on my flight suit. Silent, painful sobs wracked his body for what seemed like ages. Finally they subsided. I felt I shouldn't break the quiet. Pasha would speak when he was ready.

His left hand, the good one, crept forward and his fingertips came to rest on my red star. He whispered, "You wore it."

I replied in the same tone, unsure whether I was whispering to avoid disturbing those upstairs or simply because it made me feel closer to him, "I wouldn't want to disappoint you."

He gave a weak but genuine smile and said, "I finally got to meet your airplane after hearing so much about it. You used to compare planes to horses."

"Not anymore," I said. "Silly thing to do, really."

"I don't think it's silly," said Pasha. "In fairy tales, the hero always rides a white horse."

"I'm no fairy-tale hero," I said, wondering what, amid the pain, had made Pasha think of fairy tales.

"I know," said Pasha, closing his eyes again. And then, "I wish you hadn't killed that soldier."

"I had to. You were surrounded."

"I understand. All the same, I wish someone else could have done it. I don't want you to be . . ." His hoarse voice trailed off.

"Pashenka." It hurt me to say this. After all he'd been through, somehow Pasha was still more innocent than me. I didn't deserve him. I had no right to return to a peaceful civilian life. That had been forfeit when we dropped our first bomb. "He wasn't the first man I've killed. There have been others. Many others. And there will be more. I can't pretend otherwise. If you want to be with me, you have to accept that."

He nodded solemnly. An uneven layer of black stubble speckled his cheeks. I ran a hand over it. "When did you start growing a beard?"

"When I used my razor to fix the radio."

"It suits you. It makes you look more like a man."

"I don't feel like a man," Pasha admitted.

"But you are one."

He was. We were the same height now. He'd grown into his once-awkward facial features. His chest and shoulders were lean and muscled from long marches carrying his radio. He was no longer the boy I had sat beside on the barge from Stakhanovo. And, I realized, I was no longer the girl in pigtails and overalls.

I said, "Why didn't I kiss you on the barge? I've been

thinking about that for more than a year. I've done so many stupid things, but the stupidest of all was not kissing you when I had the chance."

"I wanted you to," said Pasha.

"I thought you were going to kiss me," I said, realizing as I said it how foolish I had been.

"I thought *you* were going to kiss *me*."

"Well, no more of that nonsense." I raised his face with my hand and lowered my own so that our foreheads rested against each other, but I wasn't sure whether I brought my mouth to his or the other way around. My lips were dry and cracked from the winter wind. So were his. The raw patches stung when they came into contact. I wouldn't have stopped for anything.

"This wasn't where I expected to have our first kiss," I murmured.

"Me either," said Pasha.

Then, abruptly, he drew back and curled up protectively. I thought for a moment that I had done something wrong. He said hoarsely, "I'm a cripple, Valyuskha, aren't I?"

"No. You're only hurt."

"My arm. I can't move it at all. I can't wiggle my fingers or make a fist."

"Shh. Don't try. You can't move it because you're in so much pain. You'll heal up like new. That's how it was with me."

Pasha nodded obediently. He asked in a timid voice, "Va-lyushka?"

"Yeah?"

"You were hurt too. You have scars."

"Yes."

"Will you show me?"

And I did.

★ THIRTY-SIX ★

THE SKY WAS A PREDAWN SLATE GRAY WHEN OUR LITTLE biplane departed. For that brief time while we flew, I felt like I was not a part of the war, despite the devastation spread out below us, despite the injured soldier, now fitted out with civilian clothes, in my arms. This was our last moment together, maybe our last moment alive, but it was easy to imagine that it would never end, that it would always be us and the ticking engine.

I wondered what Iskra was thinking back there with her steady hands on the controls. Maybe I could ask her to just fly us away like I'd offered to fly Pasha away the day he left for the front. But we both knew that wasn't an option. We had made our choice and we'd accept the consequences like the soldiers we were. And then we were over our aerodrome, approaching the plowed stretch of runway covered with thick stripes from tires and thin stripes from tail skids. We touched down to meet our fate.

The other women in the regiment were scattered over the trucks and the dugout roofs and the wings of their planes eating breakfast, but when Number 18 came to a stop, there was a general clatter from all across the airfield as everyone dropped her dishes and ran over. Iskra hopped out of the rear cockpit and was instantly mobbed with hugs and kisses from our friends, the girls we'd deceived, the girls who still didn't know about our act of treason. Tanya gave her a light smack on the arm and scolded, "What do you think you're doing, making your flight commander worry?"

Ilyushina, soaked in oil and in the process of dismantling a plane's fuel system, took a moment to give us a thumbs-up.

Zhigli said, "We set out dishes for you. We knew you were coming back. A little engine trouble wouldn't finish off the Korolevas."

"It wasn't exactly engine trouble," Iskra admitted.

I undid my harness and helped Pasha out of the cockpit, saying, "He's wounded. Can someone give him a hand getting down?"

Zhigli's jaw dropped.

It was probably the first time in history that a man had landed at a military airfield and been swarmed by a crowd of curious women. It didn't take them long to divine that this was the mysterious Pasha, and then, of course, he and I were both inundated with questions.

"Give him some space. He's hurt!" I said to no avail. Our aide-de-camp eventually rescued him and whisked him off to the field hospital.

As I slung my leg over the edge of the cockpit, my other foot brushed something. A canvas bag. I had forgotten about it. I pulled the drawstring open. Inside was a handful of photographs. Of course. I took them out and climbed down.

Bershanskaya stood with her chief of staff a little apart from the raucous group, marking down that her lost eaglets had returned. I'd never worked out what to say to her, sometimes wanting to defiantly stand by my actions and sometimes only wanting to beg her not to be disappointed with us. It hardly mattered. Not even Iskra's quick thinking could get us out of this one. So I just saluted and pushed the photos into her hands.

Bershanskaya looked me up and down and said only, "Are you hurt?"

I touched the dark stain that covered most of my flight jacket. "Oh—I'm fine. That's not my blood."

Kazarinova was there in an instant, her arms crossed, the crease between her eyes deepening as she considered me, Iskra, and the photos. I bowed my head, ready to accept what was coming. She told Bershanskaya, "I trust this settles the question of their loyalty."

"Yes," said Bershanskaya.

To me, Kazarinova said, "You two are going to Siberia for this."

No despair settled its black wings on me, only peace. I'd found

Pasha. I'd finished the task that fate had given me. I could handle anything now, even the camps. "Understood, ma'am."

"That won't be necessary," Bershanskaya said brusquely.

"They deliberately disobeyed orders and deserted to rescue a known traitor!"

"They did none of that." Bershanskaya squinted at Kazarinova. She was the taller of the two. I wondered why I'd never noticed that before. "I revised our flight plan a second time last night and reassigned the Korolevas to the rescue mission. Since the first squadron's bombing objective was in the same direction, I had them depart with the rest of the squadron. Isn't that right, Junior Lieutenant?"

The look she gave me was not hard to interpret. Hope flickering in my chest, I said, "Yes, ma'am."

"In fact, I may recommend the three of you for decoration," Bershanskaya mused. "You've all demonstrated great bravery and resourcefulness. I'm thinking, perhaps, the Order of the Red Banner?"

"We also took out an Me 109," I added.

"Technically, the bridge took it out," Iskra corrected me.

"Our regiment's first kill. This *has* been a successful night," said Bershanskaya.

Kazarinova's voice was steely with carefully controlled fury. "Major, I think you don't fully understand the repercussions of what you're doing."

"And I think you're needed back in Moscow," said Bershanskaya steadily. "If you want to get into a discussion with our superiors about why you interfered with a mission to secure strategically important documents, we can. But I would think carefully about whether there's anything in your past that you'd rather not have subjected to further scrutiny." To her chief of staff, she added, "Captain, go warm up Major Kazarinova's car."

Kazarinova threw Bershanskaya one last sullen look and then, walking heavily, favoring her bad leg, she followed the chief of staff. Relief poured over me like warm honey. It was over. No one would go to the camps, no one would be shot, and no one would ever, ever take Pasha from me again. I mouthed the words "Thank you" to my commander. Bershanskaya let her shy half smile creep across her face, but it passed and she told the two of us, "See that your aircraft is fit to fly and then get some sleep. You fly tonight at eighteen hundred hours."

Epilogue

I KNEW I WAS HOME WHEN I SMELLED SULFUR SMOKE. Iskra and I sat side by side on the lead barge's blunt front end as the tow made its lazy way up the canal. We wore not oversized men's uniforms but fitted uniforms with skirts and the shoulder boards of a Guards regiment.

A lump of coal lay on the deck by my foot. I absentmindedly picked it up. It was slick and solid, with an oily rainbow sheen. It would go into the ovens to make coke, which would be used to make steel, which would become machines and bridges and rails. We had destroyed enough. It was time to rebuild our nation, the nation that chose for its symbol the tools of peaceful labor.

Iskra looked at her ripply reflection, her chin resting on one hand. After the delirious joy of victory had worn off, she'd grown quiet and downcast. For her, the war had changed everything and nothing. The Soviet regime was still corrupt and brutal and it still viewed her with a suspicion that even her military service couldn't expunge. She was growing to accept that there might never be a place for her in the Motherland she loved so dearly.

As the familiar dust-gray buildings of Stakhanovo came into view, I found it difficult to believe that a few months ago I had stood on the broken streets of Berlin. There, in the ruins of the fascist capital, I had felt no joy or satisfaction, just weariness. I was tired of endless amphetamine-fueled nights. Tired of watching my friends catch fire in the sky. And most of all, tired of killing.

My memories of the war were already softening, taking on the blunted edges of a dream. Yet the losses were real. The perils of war had claimed one friend after another. Lilya, who had achieved all our dreams by becoming a fighter ace, only to succumb to her own nightmare when she went missing in combat. Zhenechka, brought down by shell fire in Crimea, who would never go back to her beloved observatory in Leningrad. Tanya and Vera, who had been assigned to fly with other girls that night in Poland but had insisted on flying together, as if they knew that flight would be their last.

Even Marina Raskova. She crashed during a blizzard before she ever had a chance to command her dive bombers in combat. When we heard about her death, our sorrow was tinged with the fear that our regiments would be disbanded in her absence. But she had given us what we needed most: the tenacity to keep fighting without her.

And then came the end of the war and, with it, the end of the women's regiments. We cried and kissed each other and promised to reunite in one year. But my heart ached when I thought of the faces that would not be there.

At least there were two friends from the 588th with whom I never needed to part. One human, one machine. I grabbed Iskra's hand.

"There they are!" someone cried. People crowded the loading dock, friends and family who felt like visitors from a previous life. But I only had eyes for one of them. He stood at the front of the crowd, waving to me with his left hand while his right hung slack by his side. His face had filled back out and regained its color. He wore a flat cap and a red work shirt with one sleeve rolled up because he couldn't roll up the other, clothes that suited him far better than a Red Army uniform.

A freckly teen girl stood near Pasha. It took me a second to recognize his kid sister. She pointed at us. "Look at all their medals! There's the Order of the Red Banner, the same one you have . . . the Guards badge . . . Order of the Great Patriotic War . . ."

The barge came to a stop at the end of the canal. Pasha gave me a hand onto the dock and kissed me lightly on each cheek as if we were relatives, because he was Pasha and he would always be shy. I hadn't waited three years for that. I pulled him into a close embrace, receiving a single arm wrapped tightly around me in exchange, and kissed him on his warm, full lips, heedless of all the eyes on us. I could feel his heart beating strongly where his body pressed against mine. It had come so close to fluttering to a halt. I searched his dark eyes. Pain and fear still hid in their depths. War had left its mark on more than our bodies.

"I'm back," I said. "This time it's for good."

He said, "It's been hard waiting."

Together. After four years of letters, I could scarcely comprehend that we would finally be together. Separation had become normal. There was an unfamiliarity to the idea of sharing the mundanities of everyday life with him that somehow felt even more personal than that night in the partisan camp.

I said, "Do you know I haven't heard you sing since before the war?"

He pressed his cheek against mine and sang in his smooth, rich baritone. I was filled with the words of "Katyusha," the song that had gotten us both through the war.

I held Pasha for a long moment before releasing him to hug and kiss my parents and greet everyone who had come to see me and my cousin. It was difficult to remember that these people and this little town had once been my whole life.

"Iosif Grigorevich! Did my shipment arrive?" I called.

"Safe and sound," said Iosif Grigorevich. "Have you thought about my offer? It's about time I handed over the reins to the aero-club."

"I haven't decided." Over the past four years, I'd poured all my energy into just making it to the end of the war. I hadn't put any thought into what I would do now that it was over.

Pasha and I led the way across the rusty bridge, my left hand clasping his right, unmoving but still beautiful. The wound had saved his life. When it became clear that he was damaged beyond repair, he was sent home, minus three toes and the use of his right arm. According to the Soviet Union, he was useless. But I knew they were wrong.

He'd waited out the war in Stakhanovo, listening to his radio and writing to me. I'd hoped that, now that he was safe and loved, his letters would lose the despair they had taken on while he was fighting and sound like his younger self again. Instead they were filled with nightmares and crippling anxiety. Often, he dreamed about Petya. We'd never learned what happened to him. I promised Pasha that we'd go to Rzhev and look for Petya when the war was over, but that didn't stop him from tearing himself up with guilt.

A celebratory bottle rocket went off with a shriek. Pasha ducked automatically as it screamed into the air. I put a protective arm around his shoulders. He laughed it off, but he was shivering. I called, "No more of that! Don't you think enough things have exploded in the past four years?"

Number 18 stood on the Stakhanovo aerodrome's cracked earth beside the aeroclub's old Yakovlev bushplane. On its wings, red stars with thick double borders of red and white. Victory stars. On its tail, the design that I had chosen to decorate my faithful biplane: a prancing white horse. The aircraft no longer carried bomb racks or a machine gun. It was no longer a night bomber, but a simple trainer.

"She's changed since I saw her last," said Pasha.

"Haven't we all?" I said.

The Stakhanovo Aeroclub's fresh crop of young pilots climbed on the wings and sat in the cockpits. Iskra scolded, "Show some respect for the old girl. She's a veteran, you know! See that patch? It's from a flak gun on the Taman Peninsula. And that one? Shrapnel from an air raid near Warsaw."

Pasha's sister hung back by the edge of the canal, a homemade notebook clasped to her chest. Pasha gave her a soft push forward. "Go on. She won't bite."

The girl approached me and looked up shyly. "I was wondering . . ." She drew a circle in the dirt with her toe. Then she held out her notebook. "Would you sign this?"

I let the notebook fall open in my hands. A black-and-white copy of myself looked up at me. The other Valka looked grumpy. She had spent all morning trying to figure out why Number 18's oil pressure kept dropping and wasn't keen to answer questions for a silly piece that would run in *Women's Day*.

I slowly flipped through the notebook. There they were, page after page of stories about the women's air regiments carefully cut out and pasted into the notebook. Page after page of gray raster-dot memories. U-2s flying over the newly liberated Caucasus. Major Bershanskaya profiled as a remarkable military commander. Lilya Litvyak, world's first female ace. Lilya Litvyak, missing, presumed dead.

Seeing the faces of my lost friends preserved by cheap black ink on pulpy newsprint, I felt their deaths anew. Iskra and I would get civilian jobs, we would marry, maybe have families, grow old. We would live. But these girls would remain forever young and smiling in their flight helmets and garrison caps.

"Whenever one of your letters came, Pasha would tell me about your adventures," said the girl. "Do you . . . do you think I could ever do things like that?"

Innocent earnestness shone from her young face. She'd spent the war wanting to be me while I had spent it wanting to be where she was. "How can I explain this to you?" I said. "You don't know what the war did to me. Out there, it didn't feel heroic. It felt like terror and pain and loss. You wouldn't want to have adventures like mine, not if you knew what they were like. And you shouldn't go looking for them."

The girl looked crestfallen. "But you showed everyone! You proved what we can do!"

I looked up into the vast, beautiful, perilous sky. Women would continue to brave it. They'd know the cost and they'd do it anyway. I said, "Yes, you can do what I did. And I can teach you how."

Author's Note

VALKA, ISKRA, PASHA, AND PASHA'S VARIOUS COMRADES-in-arms are fictional. However, Aviation Group 122 really existed, and all the other airwomen in this book are real people. Many of the exploits described here actually happened, beginning with the flight of the *Rodina*.

I did have to make some departures from history for the sake of the story. Dates have been changed, episodes combined, people and sometimes entire regiments included in events they were not actually present for, and so on. For instance, the incident when four aircrews, among them Galina Dokutovich (Galya), are taken out by a night fighter actually took place on July 31, 1943. Zhigli's erstwhile pilot Polina Makogon collided with another aircraft (sources disagree on whether it was a fighter or another U-2) in a separate accident. Nevertheless, I believe that the book presents a fundamentally accurate impression of what it was like to be an airwoman in the 588th.

Zoya Kosmodemyanskaya was a real person, and her execution took place as described. The photos of her execution were later found on the body of a German officer near Smolensk. She was posthumously made a Hero of the Soviet Union, the first woman to receive that award during the war. In one of the photos, a young boy is visible, watching her being marched to the scaffold.

Operation Mars was one of the most costly battles of World War II. Over 100,000 Soviets were killed or wounded in three weeks, and they failed to capture the salient. The Soviet authorities covered up their embarrassing defeat, leaving thousands of soldiers unburied and unidentified. Only after the fall of the Soviet Union did the full magnitude of destruction at the "Rzhev meat grinder" become known. The 588th did not provide air support for Operation Mars because it was still engaged in the battle for the Caucasus, but other U-2 regiments did.

The 588th Night Bomber Regiment continued to excel under the capable leadership of Yevdokiya Bershanskaya, who remained in command until it was disbanded. After the Nazis were pushed back from the Caucasus, the regiment's journey took them to Minsk, Warsaw, and finally Berlin. They flew over 23,000 combat missions. In February 1943, they achieved elite Guards status and were renamed the 46th Tamansky Guards Night Bomber Regiment in honor of their service in the Taman Peninsula. But to the

Germans, they were the *Nachthexen*, or Night Witches, and that is the name by which they are best known.

The reliable Polikarpov U-2, which was renamed the Po-2 in 1944, was one of the most-produced aircraft in history. Some 40,000 were built. U-2s served as trainers, crop dusters, seaplanes, bush planes, reconaissance aircraft, air ambulances, transports, attack aircraft, and of course night bombers.

Tatiana Makarova (Tanya) and Vera Belik were both killed in August 1944 when their plane was attacked by a fighter and caught fire. Both were posthumously made Heroes of the Soviet Union.

Yevgeniya Rudneva (Zhenechka), the regimental navigator, was shot down and killed in April 1944. She was also decorated as a Hero of the Soviet Union. In 1972, an asteroid was named after her.

Yevgeniya Zhigulenko (Zhigli) survived the war to become another Hero of the Soviet Union, flying 968 sorties and rising from navigator to squadron commander. After the war, she put her flair for drama to use as a filmmaker. Her movie *The Night Witches in the Sky* is based on her wartime experiences.

Klavdiya Ilyushina (Klava) also served with the regiment until the end of the war. Afterward, she remained in the military as an engineer.

Lidiya Litvyak (Lilya) went missing over enemy territory on August 1, 1943, pursued by eight German fighters. Her worst nightmare had come true: her plane and body were not found and she was classified as a deserter under Order 270. Determined to clear her name, Litvyak's mechanic embarked on a thirty-six-year search for her crash site, which turned up dozens of other aircraft and finally, in 1979, the body of a female pilot that was identified as Litvyak's. Litvyak was finally made a Hero of the Soviet Union in 1990. She shot down eleven enemy aircraft and an observation balloon during her time as a fighter pilot. She and her best friend, Yekaterina Budanova, who was shot down a few weeks before Litvyak, are the only female fighter aces who have ever lived.

On January 4, 1943, Marina Raskova was killed in a crash while transporting one of the 587th Day Bomber Regiment's aircraft during a snowstorm. She never had a chance to command her regiment in combat. Her death was a severe blow to all the women of Aviation Group 122. The day-bomber regiment, though it received very little publicity, performed well. It was awarded Guards status and renamed in honor of Raskova.

All three pyaterka pilots crashed and died under suspicious circumstances. With the disappearance of Litvyak, all the pilots who had opposed Tamara Kazarinova as commander of the 586th Fighter Regiment were dead or missing. There was never any official investigation into their deaths. Rumors abounded that Kazarinova was using her personal influence to harm the 586th whenever she could and that she even prevented it from achieving Guards status. Although Tamara Kazarinova never commanded again (her appearance at the 588th is fiction), the Kazarinova sisters still got the last laugh. Militsa Kazarinova edited two collections of memoirs by the women of Aviation Group 122, exercising great control to present a positive image of herself and her sister.

For many years, her version of history was the official one.

The bonds that formed between the airwomen of Aviation Group 122 were never broken. They kept their promise and reunited every year as long as they lived.

I hope you found the story of the Night Witches as fascinating as I did. If you are interested in learning more about them, you can read their accounts in their own words in *A Dance with Death: Soviet Airwomen in World War II*, by Anne Noggle (TX: Texas A&M University Press, 1994).

Acknowledgments

WHILE I'M USUALLY INDEPENDENT TO A FAULT, I CAN honestly say that not a single word of *Among the Red Stars* would exist without the support of the many wonderful people in my life.

Emilia, in your hands this book has transformed from a manuscript caterpillar into a beautiful book butterfly. You're a miracle worker. Owen, you made my cover look better than I could have asked for. It blew me away when I first saw it, and still does.

Thao, you took a chance on an unknown writer and you've been a constant source of support and wisdom. I can't wait to see where the publishing journey takes us next.

Fiona, you saw a diamond in the rough when there was a lot of rough and very little diamond, and you patiently explained the necessity of things like "plot" and "feelings." Your lessons will always stay with me.

Jordan, you endured countless conversations that went like this: "Pick a color for this scarf." "Blue." "No, a color other than blue." You have accompanied me through all the most frustrating and tedious parts of this project and yet you manage to remain enthusiastic about it, which must be a superpower.

All my friends and family, you helped me far more than I realized at the time. JR, you told everyone about this book before I had started writing it, thereby obligating me to finish. I should use that strategy more often. Katie, Katt, and Gerard, you all read my writing back when it didn't even pretend to be good and you all refrained from throwing me out a window. Your failure to defenestrate made me the author I am today.

Finally, I owe a great debt to the incredible women of Aviation Group 122. This is their story, and while most of them are no longer around to see it, I'd like to think they would consider it a fitting tribute to their service.